To Kill the
Chosen One

For Bud,

To never giving up

PROLOGUE

In the beginning, there were the Light, the Shadows and the people who served each. The Light gave warmth, hope and tranquility throughout the world. The Shadows sought to destroy everything the Light created, corrupting the soul from within.

The war between them lasted thousands and thousands of years until their magic was only a remnant of the past and both sides were left weak. In desperation, the Knightmares, servants of the Shadows, cursed the world with a poison that would last for centuries, growing worse and worse, slowly and painfully killing all those who didn't serve the Shadows.

Even with the capability of huge technological innovations, such as hover cars and holograms, the citizens of the world could only slow the poison—they could find no way to stop it.

From time to time, a child would be born with special abilities, said to be touched by the Light, born to serve and fight against the Shadows. And though these children lacked the ability to cleanse the poisoned air, that didn't stop people from believing the Light would someday intervene.

As many people turned to faith, the Light sent them the prophecy of the Chosen One. It was said that a hero with strength of heart would emerge with the power to save the world. The prophecy didn't specify when or who — only that the hero would be born in the Kingdom of Oar, in its capital city of Oarlon. Once the hero was chosen, the prophecy would appear as a glowing inscription on their back, showing them the way to break the curse.

But over the next hundred years, the Chosen One never appeared. The air continued to worsen, and the people's only choice was to hope that the Chosen One would appear to save them all… before it was too late.

ONE

THE BOY

A white silk scarf draped over the boy's shoulders as he stared into the purple eyes of the girl in front of him. Her name was Aiva, and the boy had loved her from the very first moment he'd seen her. As some of the only orphan servants in the castle, Aiva and the boy bonded over their shared lack of family.

The boy's parents had been killed long ago, executed as traitors to the Crown, and Aiva's own parents had disowned her due to her unnatural eye color. Three scars ran diagonally across her face where her parents had marked her. But that didn't matter to the boy. The purple eyes didn't matter. The first day they'd met, he'd been whipped for disobeying orders and she sat with him and comforted him. Four years later, at age fourteen, she was still the only person in the castle he liked.

Aiva grinned as she fit the scarf around the boy's neck.

"There. Now you won't get so cold all the time," said Aiva. The boy touched the smooth silk, letting his fingers run down the scarf until he reached the end. There was no musty smell, no speck of dirt on it, unlike the clothes he'd been given — a faded black shirt and ill-fitting pants with holes at the knees.

"Where did you find it?" The boy knew Aiva could never have afforded this. They had no coin, nothing to show for their work. The only payment they received for their service was a roof over their heads, even if that meant sleeping deep in the basement of the castle where daylight never reached. The basement was at least big enough for each of them to have their own room, though they could only fit a small bed and toilet. Their distorted reflections could be seen in the black metallic panels that covered every surface. White luminescent lamps had been placed in opposite corners.

"I just found it lying about," said Aiva with a mischievous glint in her eyes. Next to her was a bag full of items that she'd pulled the scarf from. She stood up and tossed it over her shoulder, peering outside the boy's doorway.

A figure jumped out in front of her. The hair on her arms raised, and she quickly punched the arm of the figure as he came into view.

Thane. A fifteen-year-old who was the son of the one of the King's most prized generals. He was no servant, evident by his gold and black pants and shirt, adorned with the symbol of the kingdom: a circle with stars falling toward the ground. With his prominent jaw and styled blond hair, Thane was considered handsome by the other servants, despite a crooked nose that veered to the left after being broken twice and a fake tooth that looked whiter than the rest.

"Come on! Show me what you got!" Thane grabbed the bag from Aiva and rifled through it. He immediately pulled out a golden orb the size of his hand. "Whoa. This is cool."

"And expensive," said Aiva, snatching it back. "I'm going to sell it tomorrow when I go to the market."

"Well, you better give me half for being your lookout. It was my idea, after all," said Thane, pointing a finger at her and pushing closer to tower over her. The top of her head reached his chin, and his shoulders were double the width of hers, but Aiva didn't wince once at the intimidation.

The boy shifted uncomfortably, unsure if he should say something.

"I did all the work! I'll give you twenty percent. Take it or leave it."

"Fine. But that orb better be worth a lot," said Thane. As Thane and Aiva argued, the boy's gaze moved back and forth between them. He realized that they had both somehow stolen these items from the King and Queen. A twinge of sadness jolted his body. He wasn't concerned that they might be caught—they seemed to have gotten away with it. No, he was upset that Aiva had gone to Thane to be her lookout when he would've happily done it.

"You got that from the King and Queen? How?" asked the boy. He wanted to ask why Aiva hadn't taken him, but any desire to ask was cancelled out by how afraid he was of the answer.

"You going to tell him?" asked Thane, shrugging his shoulders.

Now the boy was interested. Still sitting on his bed, he braced himself against the wall, trying to look relaxed, but inside, every part of him wanted to explode in a rainbow of emotions.

"I snuck into the Princess' room," revealed Aiva.

"How?" asked the boy. Security cameras were everywhere on the upper levels, and there were guards stationed around the castle, especially near any of the rooms of the royal family. The boy had discovered several hidden passageways in the castle but none that went close to the Princess' room.

"She's special," said Thane. "Touched by the Light or whatever. She can turn into anyone she wants to be. A true shapeshifter."

The boy's mouth almost dropped. Having a magical ability was incredibly rare, especially for someone of such low status as Aiva. But the boy couldn't be happier for her and himself. His best friend was special! He must've been grinning because Aiva sighed and rolled her eyes.

"Wipe that grin off your face. I'm still working on it. But yeah, I just turned into the Princess, walked right in and walked right out." The boy touched the scarf around his neck, realizing it was stolen.

"Yeah, better hide that," said Thane. The boy took the scarf and carefully folded it into a small square. Underneath his bed, he searched the floor until he found the only panel with one of the corners chipped. He pulled the panel up to reveal a small storage space of collectibles that he'd found over the years. Some were broken toys or old antique machines that were worthless, but he at least owned something. Now the scarf was his favorite thing, and he would cherish it for as long as he could.

After placing it in its own corner of the hidden cache, the boy snapped the panel back into place and turned to see Aiva and Thane giggling with each other — their bodies close together and their gazes locked on one another.

A long beep sounded as the intercom by the door to the boy's room turned on.

"Floor five — kitchen. Report," said the nearly indiscernible voice of a servant. The boy jumped up and pressed the red button to talk.

"Coming." He looked over to Aiva and Thane, and to his relief, saw that their flirtation was over. Aiva smiled at him.

"I'm sure I'll be seeing you up there," she said.

"Not if I order you to help me with my chores," said Thane with a wink.

The boy scrunched his nose. Reading Aiva's glance, he realized his disgust must've been written all over his own face.

"Don't look so grossed out!" said Aiva, playfully shoving the boy away. As though dismissing him, she turned then and grabbed Thane's hand. "Come on, let me show you some of the other cool stuff I got." With that, they were gone to her room down the hall, and the boy had no choice but to wistfully watch them go. His heart sank and twisted, making each step up from the basement feel heavy.

The kitchen was always bustling with servants preparing different meals for different events. The King and Queen loved to gift cakes as presents, and the Queen herself loved to indulge in them too. The servants made food for everyone, including the boy, not just for the important members of the court. But today, he hadn't eaten anything.

His eyes lingered on a red three-tiered cake with white frosting. The smell of baked flour filled his nostrils and traveled all the way down to his rumbling stomach. He could take a piece, and no one would know it was him. The cameras weren't pointed over here. He knew Thane would do it. Aiva probably would too. But the boy couldn't, no matter how much his body protested.

A swift backhand whacked the back of his head, shaking him from his trance. Gragath, the head servant, marched by him and put his meaty hands on his belly. His eyebrows were so long that they almost overshadowed his black eyes.

"Drooling does nothing. Get to work, boy, or I will report you."

The boy nodded, grabbed the high-powered vacuum and returned to work. The vacuum was so silent that the boy sometimes wondered if it was on. It picked up everything from crumbs to dust and had the unique feature of getting the corners under the counters.

The boy knew that once he cleaned the whole floor, it would get dirty again. The marble floors required constant attention, and no one wanted to maintain it. Gragath moved next to him and talked with two other servants, their voices low but still audible to the boy.

"So it's true—Rejal became a Knightmare," said Gragath in an almost whisper.

"A Knightmare!?"

"Shhh! The King and Queen are trying to keep it quiet. They don't want anyone to know." Gragath then turned his attention to the boy, who'd been vacuuming the same spot for the last thirty seconds. "Hey! What did I just say?" This time, Gragath used the front of his hand to slap the boy on the side of his head. The impact left a stinging sensation, but at least this time he was still standing. A red handprint painted the side of his face. The boy bowed his head meekly to avoid another and darted off.

He didn't know Rejal very well, only that he was a quiet servant. He didn't know much about Knightmares either, only that they were said to be a group of assassins made up of outcasts and that they lived somewhere in the forest. Shadows of the night, the Knightmares always found their mark. But the boy didn't worry. He knew the Knightmares would never come to the castle with all the guards and the shield protecting it. So he continued on with the monotony of his tasks, which put his mind at ease.

"Hey, kid!" Gragath shouted at him, snapping him out of his reverie. The boy winced as he turned, expecting another blow to strike his cheek. This time, Gragath merely pointed to a fully prepared breakfast with curls of steam rising from the eggs. "Deliver this to the Princess in the throne room. Now."

The boy scrunched his eyebrows, but he bowed his head before Gragath could see his confusion and immediately grabbed the dish with both hands. His hands remained steady—his fear of falling and ruining the dish coursed through his veins. He had never delivered food to someone so high up before.

Once out of the kitchen, he walked down the lengthy hallway to the main elevators where two guards were stationed. One pressed the button for the lift to arrive. When the doors opened, one guard followed the boy in.

The entire elevator was made up of glass, and as it rose toward the top of the castle, the boy saw the wonder that was Oarlon spread out before him. The city stretched as far as the eye could see.

Tens of thousands lived down in the five districts that made up the capital city. Just beyond was the forest, at the edge of the horizon, way in the distance.

Aiva and the boy had a secret spot that overlooked the city, a few floors down from the throne room. It was one of the many secret paths he'd found, but despite seeing the view over and over, he never grew tired of it.

The elevator slowed to a halt, and the doors opened to a circular room—the grand throne room. The domed ceiling was made entirely of glass that let the sunlight pour in. Plants lined the circumference, adding warmth and filling up the space. The black metallic floor was the same as the boy's room, and in the middle sat the King and Queen's thrones.

On the Queen's side sat Princess Sera, her daughter. Sera's unusual white hair was presently being combed by another servant. Black tattooed designs of the falling stars crest were visible on Sera's cheeks and forehead, a sign of the royal family. Her ocean blue eyes turned to the boy, and the boy froze a foot outside the elevator.

"Do you need help?" the Princess asked. The boy couldn't tell if she was being sarcastic or genuinely asking. He quickly shook his head, chiding himself for hesitating. He walked toward the throne and bowed, placing the food at her feet and licking his lips. The yellow bundle of scrambled eggs appeared as a small, plain mound. Not even salt sprinkled the top. Even ordinary eggs made the boy's eyes big and his mouth watery. His gaze fixed on the food, his stomach yelling at him to swipe it from the Princess, much to his embarrassment.

"I don't think I've seen you here before," said the Princess. She waved her servant away and picked up the plate. "You're cute." The boy blushed.

The Princess was also fourteen, with a perfectly symmetrical face. Her black and white dress glimmered in the light. Her pose was nothing short of regal, her shoulders back and abdomen locked in. After the servant's careful tending, her hair flowed like waves of water. Despite her compliments, the boy could only think about Aiva.

"You okay…?" the Princess asked him.

He bowed in response, not making eye-contact.

"Thank you for the compliment, Your Highness," he said. He didn't let himself stand up fully until she said something in return. The seconds ticked by like he was watching a tree grow.

"Get some food," said the Princess gently, as she stuffed her face with her breakfast. A bit of egg stuck to her cheek and then fell to her lap.

The boy stood up and walked quickly back to the elevator. His hands were sweaty, and he counted the seconds until the elevator showed up, hoping the Princess wouldn't say anything else. His mouth was dry, his cheeks burned, and he knew they were rosy red.

With another day's grueling work over, the boy put his cleaning supplies away in one of the closets by the kitchen. With a few glances around to be sure he was unobserved, he walked inside the closet and closed the door behind him. The back wall was completely bare, and all the boy had to do was give it a little push. The door slid open, revealing a set of stairs. This was just one of the many secret paths he'd discovered.

As far as he knew, these secret paths ran all throughout the castle. He wasn't sure of the reason they existed or who would've created them. The answer didn't really matter to him though. They were here, and no one else used them, at least no one that the boy knew of.

He traversed the narrow stairs. The wood creaked under his weight. When he reached the top, he looped around a narrow path to a very small opening where he got onto his hands and knees to crawl through. Once he was through the entrance, he found himself in a second narrow stairway that wound back and forth. The boy took a deep breath and braced his legs for the climb, knowing full well that he'd be panting long before he reached the top.

But the view was worth it. It was a tiny room, barely large enough to fit three people, but it had a small window that Aiva and he could see the whole city from. As the boy's muscles ached and his breath quickened, he reached the top to find Aiva already looking out the window.

"You're late," said Aiva, not even glancing over at him. The boy sat down next to her and gazed out at the twinkling lights of the city in the distance. "You ever wonder what it would be like to visit? To see how everyone else lives?"

The boy couldn't help but nod. Despite the beautifulness of the city from here, it was never at the top of his mind.

Aiva caught him staring at her and rolled her purple eyes. "What is it?"

"Nothing." The boy looked away sheepishly. "I saw the Princess today."

Aiva's eyebrows shot up. "Oh, you did? I'm sure she'll grow up to be just like her parents." Aiva sighed. "I can't wait to be away from here. I want to be among the people."

The boy couldn't really say he agreed. All he wanted was to be by Aiva's side. Wherever that was.

"Maybe you can turn into the Princess again and leave? Escape everyone here," he suggested, though it pained him to say it.

"I don't want to hide for the rest of my life," she said before looking at him. Aiva grabbed him by the top of the head and pulled him in next to her.

"Oh, don't worry, I would never leave you." With her arm still around him, the boy leaned against her, putting his head on her shoulder. His heart quickened. Maybe she liked him! That thought blew away quickly as the image of a handsome blond-haired kid popped into his head.

"What about Thane?" He tensed, afraid of the answer.

"Thane cares about me as long as he gets what he wants. I don't think he's ever cared about anyone other than himself."

The boy smiled. Any tension from asking that question melted away. His shoulders dropped, and he took a deep, satisfying breath. The inside air was much better than the poisonous one outside. The castle had many state-of-the-art purifiers throughout that cleared some of the poison, but even then, a little bit of the poison slipped through. According to Aiva, most people didn't have any filter system, unless they lived in the richer districts. Since neither had been outside the castle, they didn't truly know how devastating the air was, only what they heard through the servants' steady rumor mill. It made them both a little thankful to live in the castle, even if they were slaves.

They sat for several more seconds before Aiva continued, "Someday, you and me will ride into the sunset, away from this place. Away from everyone. We'll have our own castle, somewhere where the air is clean." Something in her voice made the boy sit up straight and he caught sight of Aiva's lip quivering. Her gaze fell to the floor.

"What's wrong?" asked the boy.

"Are you mad I didn't tell you about what I can do?"

"No. But I guess I don't love that Thane knew."

Aiva chuckled and ruffled the boy's hair.

"Sorry. I didn't know who to tell. Truth be told, I'm terrified of it.

I don't want to wake up one day and see the inscription on my back. What if I can't live up to being the Chosen One? Will the King and Queen accept me or kill me like the they do to others who've been touched by the Light? How will I clean the air? People keep saying we only have half a century left at most." The King and Queen didn't serve the Shadows, but anyone with special gifts, remnants of the magic of the Light, were killed out of fear that they could overthrow the royal family's rule. The boy grabbed her hand and interlocked their fingers together.

"Even if you aren't, I'll protect you against anything." The boy held Aiva's stare. He'd never meant anything more. Aiva squeezed his hand.

"I'll hold you to it."

The boy and Aiva sat there for a few more hours until it was finally time to sleep. Upon returning, they entered the basement door only to find guards posted all along the hallway at the bottom. The boy and Aiva quickly walked down the stairs to see what all the fuss was about. In the hallway, all the other servants were lined up against the wall. The guards stood across from them with barely repressed hostility.

Princess Sera paced the hallway until the boy and Aiva came into view.

"Finally! Where have you two been?"

"Just cleaning the kitchen, Your Royal Highness," said Aiva before the boy could even think of something to say.

Thane appeared behind the Princess, keeping his head down.

"We have some bad news," said the Princess, her gaze looking at Aiva, then at the boy before turning to the guards and the other servants. The boy wasn't sure where this was going. "Last night, a golden orb was stolen. It was caught on camera." Thunder shook the boy's heart. The Princess' voice shuddered. "We have a changeling here in the castle. Thane claims you both know who it is."

The boy had only heard one curse word in his life—fyrk. He repeated the word over and over again as he looked straight at Thane. His eyes had narrowed, his jaw set in a tight line and his lips pressed together. There was no warmth in his gaze, only the uncompromising anger drilling into Thane's soul. Thane tried to keep his chin high, but his shoulders slightly slumped and he avoided everyone's gaze by staring at the wall like it was the only friend he could find. The Princess approached them. The hands of the guards nearest her hovered around the guns holstered on their hip.

"Please, tell me who it is."

"It was me," said the boy quickly, with no thought for the consequences his confession would bring. Only a few seconds passed before it sunk in that admitting this could be a death sentence for him, but he wasn't going to let anything bad happen to Aiva. She turned to him, her mouth opening to protest, but the boy repeated it. "I'm still learning how to change, but I did it. I stole your orb." His whole back tingled. The hairs on his neck stood up.

"No, he's not a shapeshifter. I am," said Aiva desperately,

looking back and forth from the Princess to the boy. Thane stepped forward before Princess Sera could speak.

"It was him. I've seen him change before."

As the Princess whirled around to face Thane, the boy's eyes were on Aiva. He grabbed her hand just as it began to turn the same pale white of the Princess' skin. The boy almost gasped as the skin changed between his fingers, the bones shifting slightly into a smaller hand.

Before the transformation could finish, the boy mouthed, "Trust me."

Aiva's eyes were wide with uncertainty, and her hands shook. After a nod from the boy, she softened, her hand still trembling before morphing back to normal before anyone else saw.

"I understand," said the Princess softly, like she was in pain. She turned back toward Aiva and the boy. Her hand reached out toward Aiva, who faintly recoiled out of instinct. As the Princess touched her face, Aiva gritted her teeth and forced herself to lean into her hand. The Princess smiled and traced her fingers over Aiva's scars, from her cheek all the way down to her chin.

Then her attention turned toward the boy.

"Guards—" Her voice shook. "Take the boy to the chamber. Keep the girl here, and kill the rest." The words caught the boy off guard. He expected he'd be whisked off somewhere, but killing the servants?

Within seconds, Gragath and all the other servants erupted into screams as the guards opened fire. Bullets flew through the servants, their faces exploding as bullets blew through their brains. Others received multiple shots to the chest, the guards quick and efficient at their work until no one was left alive. The Princess turned toward Thane, who stood frozen in shock, his face pale.

"Go to your father and explain that we had a gifted member among the servants that needed to be eradicated. My parents will require new servants by the morning."

Needing no other excuse to leave, Thane sprinted past the bodies and up the stairs.

The Princess sighed, returning her attention to Aiva and the boy. "I'm sorry for what's to come. Let's go, my parents will want to meet you."

TWO

PRINCESS SERA

The throne room was cold at night, just the way Sera's parents liked it. Rain pattered on the glass dome. Fall was leaving, and winter was here.

The boy struggled as two guards held him in place beside Sera. She could smell his sweat. He hadn't been properly bathed in a while. How sad, she thought. His constant struggle for freedom was futile. The kid was scrawny as a bean pole—there was no way he would escape.

His fate had already been decided.

Sera cleared her throat as two holographic images of her parents, the King and Queen, appeared sitting on their thrones. It was as if they were really there. If they hadn't just appeared, no one would be able to tell the difference.

Sera immediately bowed and stood up. Her father and mother shared her unusual snow-white hair that made them all look older than they were. Tattoos, similar to Sera's, lined their faces. Their eyes were also blue like hers, but she didn't see much resemblance otherwise. Both her parents were built heavy with round features, while she was petite with angular cheekbones. If her white hair wasn't so rare for her age, she'd wonder if she really was their daughter.

"So, this is the shapeshifter. What can he do?" asked the King, stroking his triple chin. He hadn't shaved in a few days. They must've been too busy on their anniversary vacation, Sera thought in disgust.

"He can change into other people," said Sera matter-of-factly, forcing herself to appear polite. She wanted to yell that her father was an idiot.

"How many others know about him?" asked the Queen. Sera knew they would care most about who knew and how many potential people it could spread to. If the citizens of the Kingdom knew that the King and Queen were murdering agents of the Light, the crown might have a revolution on their hands.

"Only Thane. Everyone else is dead," said Sera. Thane, being the son of a highly respected general, couldn't be touched. Sera didn't divulge that the girl was still alive. They didn't need to know that. At least, not yet. She deftly redirected them. "There's the possibility that this boy is the Chosen One. Think how this could inspire the people to believe again."

Predictably, both her parents shook their heads.

"No. That will bring more complications. We can't risk it. Kill him. Tonight," said the King. Sera's heartbeat quickened. She'd known her parents would order him executed but had still hoped otherwise. They didn't want to save the world. Over the years, they had killed several individuals who had special abilities. All her parents cared about was maintaining their own power. That way, they could continue doing whatever they wanted, whenever they wanted. Frolicking up north on vacation was just one way to avoid any responsibility. They didn't think about their only daughter, whose life was being slowly leeched away by the poisoned air. They never thought of the people they could save.

"Of course," said Sera firmly, while the thought of it gnawed at her heart. She bowed to her parents. "Love you both." Her voice was completely flat, but thankfully, her parents didn't seem to notice.

"Put the whipping on our secure channel so we can watch as we travel back. We'll be home in a few hours. Good job, Sera," said her mother. The holograms disappeared.

Sera turned to the boy and saw that he had stopped struggling. Defeat was written across his face. His eyelids drooped, almost closing. His breathing was mellowing. That was why he shouldn't have struggled. Now, he had nothing left.

"Take him to the chamber. I'll be there shortly."

The guards bowed their heads and dragged the boy across the floor to the elevator. Sera joined them in the elevator as the doors opened.

"Please, don't do this," said the boy. His voice could barely reach her ears. The elevator stopped, and the door opened again. As the guards took him away, she watched his head turn back to her, his eyes petrified. She wanted to assure him that she had a plan, but the plan didn't help him.

He would be an unfortunate, painful sacrifice, just like all the servants she had to kill.

The elevator reached the basement, and Sera descended the stairs to the servants' quarters for the second time that day. It was the most she'd ever been down here. The stench of dead bodies assaulted her nose, sending chills down her body. She reminded herself that the guards had already reported the situation to her parents before she'd been told of it. The servants were going to be killed regardless, and she didn't need her parents questioning her about why she'd stopped the guards from doing so. It wouldn't have made any difference.

Still, that didn't make it any easier seeing the guards cleaning the blood from the walls and dragging the bodies onto carts, tossing one onto another. Sera stepped over a few bodies that hadn't yet been picked up. Blood stained the bottom of her shoes, but she put it from her mind. Much more important things were happening.

At the back of the hallway were two guards stationed outside a doorway. A laser grid acted as a barrier, leaving no way of escape. Inside, the girl sat. Her purple eyes were fixed on the ground. The three scars that ran across her face were unforgettable.

"Leave us."

The words hit the girl's ears, and she immediately looked up. The guards nodded and left, standing out of earshot but close enough to come to the Princess' aid.

"Please, Princess, don't hurt him. He's—"

Sera held her hand up to stop the girl from talking.

"I know he's not the shapeshifter. He's a good friend, sacrificing himself for you," said Sera.

Aiva's purple eyes went wide. "But if you know it's not him, why did you take him? Why am I still alive?"

"Because — unlike my parents — I don't believe people who have been gifted by the Light should die. People like you have been sent to protect our world," said Sera.

"Then... why this?" said Aiva, pointing to the carnage outside her cell. "What's going to happen to my friend?"

"Someone needs to take the blame, but I can't let you die. I've bought you time by telling the guards I think you know of more gifted people in the castle. That's the only reason they haven't killed you yet. But to keep you alive, we'll need to act fast. Your friend... I'm sorry. My parents have seen him and ordered his execution." Aiva let out a muffled cry. "But there is something you can do that will keep you alive — and might give him a chance."

At this, the girl got up and came as close as she dared to the laser grid. Her purple eyes reflected the lasers as she locked her gaze on the Princess.

"Anything," she said.

The Princess reached down and pulled her dress up to her knee to reveal a dagger clasped to her leg. Sera pulled the dagger out of the sheath and held it in front of the door.

"Then this is what you'll do."

THREE

THE BOY

The camera in the corner of the chamber clicked to life, a red dot signaling it was broadcasting. Like the throne room, the chamber was circular but smaller and more intimate. A silver, rectangular tank filled with a silvery liquid sat off to the side. It might've been unnoticeable if the liquid didn't reflect the bright, white ceiling light hanging right above the center of the chamber. It was so intense, so bright that the boy could barely keep his eyes open unless looking directly at the ground. The guard had clamped the boy's hands to a chain connected to the ceiling, hanging next to the ceiling light. He had no energy left to fight. He'd been in this room once before and had two grim scars to remember it by.

"We're a go," said one guard to another, an almost blind old man who had served three generations of royals. The old man was so good at his job that he didn't even need to see well to do what he was about to.

The rest of the guards left as the boy looked up at the camera and the blinking red dot. This was why the light was so bright—for the viewing. It needed to be bright enough for the viewers to see what was to come.

A humming sound that he knew all too well filled the room as the electro-whip powered on behind him. The boy closed his eyes and braced himself as it slashed at his back. His mouth let loose a cry, but he had no time to recover as another lash hit right below the first. Were they going to torture him before killing him? There was no one to stop the guard, and nothing the boy could say or do would help. They didn't want anything from him. By the twelfth lash, he was certain that this is how they would kill him—it would be slow.

He tried to concentrate on Aiva, the reason he was enduring this in the first place. It made the pain slightly more bearable. Twenty-two lashes, twenty-two cries later, and the guard finally paused. Beneath them were the original two from his previous punishment, so the boy now had a total of twenty-four lines lacerating his whole back. He was almost numb now. He didn't think he'd even feel it if they gave him another.

The old man pulled a lever to release the restraints, and the boy slumped to the floor onto his back. The pain of contact with the tiles shrieked through him, making his body go rigid.

The old man ignored him, bowing to the camera. Shuffling over, he reached up to fumble for the switch and turned the camera off. He then walked over to the boy, putting two fingers on his neck to check if he was still breathing. The boy's eyes were half closed, but he was still conscious. The old man grabbed him by the chin and moved his head around, squinting at the boy with his poor eyesight. Once satisfied the boy was still alive, the old man clasped him by the collar and dragged him over to the silver tank filled with water. With some effort, he pulled the boy up and threw him in.

"Stay in there for a few minutes. The water will close those wounds."

The old man must've forgotten that the boy had been here before. The silvery liquid wasn't water so much as a complex chemical compound that promoted healing. A bathtub's worth of the healing compound must've cost the King and Queen a fortune, but they deemed this a necessary expense. It would never save someone from dying, but it would close up their wounds enough so that anyone who got whipped could go back to work the next day. It didn't heal the cuts entirely though; the scars remained, just like these ones would.

As chilled liquid swirled around his body, the stinging began. The boy winced, feeling the liquid touch every lash. The old man threw a clean, folded outfit next to the tank. It was nicer than any of the boy's ragged, hand-me-down outfits had ever been. Both pants and shirt were all black—an outfit to bury him in.

The boy pulled himself out of the tub, trying to stay upright, but the stinging pain made his eyes flutter, blurring his vision. He stumbled, grabbing the outfit with his hands and slowly taking off his old, blood-stained clothes. He pulled the new outfit on, going slowly with the shirt, feeling it stick to him from the liquid still wet on his body.

Before the guard could say anything else, a throat cleared and someone beckoned him away. The boy half expected to see the Princess, but instead, it was Thane in the doorway.

"You did the right thing. For Aiva," he said.

The boy turned to him, one last glimmer of hope. "Help me?" he asked, barely able to enunciate through teeth that chattered from the chill and the stinging pain of his ruined back.

The light from one of the white lamps illuminated half of Thane's face. He sighed and shook his head. "I can't. None of us can."

"I... I... don't want to die," said the boy, shaking. Tears were starting to form in his eyes. The idea of dying was settling in. He was on death's door with no choice but to enter.

"Then you shouldn't have saved her. Live with the consequences of your actions. That's what my father has always told me." The boy looked up at Thane as he circled around him. This time, he could see a fresh bruise on Thane's cheek that had been hidden in the shadows. "I used to have this dog. I got him when I was seven. He was the cutest thing. He just wanted to be loved. Three years later, he was stomped to death by some bullies. He didn't do anything to them. He just barked at them as they made fun of me. I used to be good, innocent, like my dog. Until I watched those kids stomp on his head over and over. Now I know, good things don't last."

"Aiva's a good person," said the boy, summoning the courage to talk as tears streamed down his face. Thane was condemning him to death and would do nothing to help him.

"She's a thief. It'll only get worse as she gets older. At least this way, you'll always be a good memory." Thane backed away as the door opened. The boy wanted to scream at him. He wasn't just a memory. He was a person who wanted to live, wanted to live with Aiva, somewhere far away where no one could hurt them.

The Princess' pale skin shone against the light. She noticed Thane and gestured with her head toward the door. "Leave us."

Thane bowed and marched off, always quick to obey her. The Princess observed the boy for several seconds. He knew she could see his desperation, his fear. At this point, he didn't care.

"You did a brave thing," she said.

"What do you mean?" the boy asked hesitantly.

"Every guard thinks you're the shapeshifter. No one suspects the girl down there." The boy tensed. He found himself holding tightly onto the dangling chain from the ceiling. His fear for Aiva overwhelmed the pain from his back. "Yes, I know you lied. She's lucky to have a friend like you. But that is neither here nor there. We have to act quickly, and I need your help."

"Why would I ever help you?" The boy didn't think he could do anything in his condition, even if he wanted to help her. He could barely stand without wobbling.

"Because if you want to live, you'll do as I say," said the Princess bluntly. The boy wasn't sure what she meant or whether she was lying. Why would she tell her parents that she'd kill him if she were just going to let him go? "The guards think you're the shapeshifter. My parents

28

think you're the shapeshifter. So to throw suspicion off the girl, you're going to escape. They will hunt you, but you might just get away with it."

The door opened behind the Princess to a guard waiting outside. Unsure what else to do, the boy followed the Princess out of the chamber and into the hallway where a faceless, helmeted guard waited with a big black bag.

"In. Now." The Princess pointed to the bag and mimed for him to go in. He didn't see what other choice he had, and if she were going to kill him, why not just do it now?

Inside the bag were two little slits for him to see through. The boy lay down on his back but wanted to jump up instantly. The bare ground against his new scars burned.

Then, from behind her back, the Princess pulled out something that caught his attention, distracting him from all the pain: the white scarf. She laid it down on his chest.

"A token of thanks." She smiled. Her blue eyes twinkled with genuine sadness, but there was something else behind those beautiful eyes. Something distant that was as cold and calculating as the order she had given to kill all the servants. The boy clutched the scarf to his chest. At least he had this.

"Are you going to hurt her?" asked the boy before the guard zipped him up. The Princess shook her head.

"She'll be safe here, I swear it. But you best forget about her and never return. Not if you want to live." That answer didn't satisfy the boy, and though he had little to no strength left, he wasn't going to accept that response so easily. He pushed himself up.

"You obviously want to keep this quiet, but I will gladly make a lot of noise as we leave, and then you'll be in even bigger trouble than before."

"That would be a death sentence for you," said the Princess coolly.

"And maybe a whipping for you. As long as Aiva's okay, it's worth it," said the boy firmly. His gaze held hers, and she relented.

"Trust me, I want nothing more than to keep her safe. She's a hero of the Light. I will never harm her." Her expression was inscrutable, and time was ticking away. Finally, the boy nodded. It was the best answer he was going to get. Now, he'd play the game the Princess had for him, and once it was over, he'd find a way to free Aiva.

As the guard zipped the bag up, he heard the Princess say, "Make sure no one sees."

After that, the guard put the boy uncomfortably on his shoulder. Each step hurt. The boy's stomach jabbed right into the guard's shoulder blade. The guard's hand gripped the bag right over his back where the boy's skin still seared. He never thought his dull, meaningless life could get worse. Gripping the scarf in his hands distracted his mind from everything that had just happened. Right now, it was the only comfort he had.

It didn't take long for the guard to carry him outside. The air filtered through the slits in the bag, and the boy could taste the difference from the castle's purified air. His stomach clenched. He almost gagged. Suddenly, the guard tossed the bag into a four-seat hoverer. The boy crashed against the back seat. The cushions were hard, and he had to stifle a cry as his back screamed more than before.

The engines hummed to life, and a little jolt told the boy that they were moving. He sat there, wondering where he was being taken. What was the plan?

Then through the slits came the first morning light. The boy poked his fingers through the slit to nudge the bag open a little further so he could see outside. The sky was still dark blue, but the sun's rays peeked out over the horizon. He couldn't see much more than that, but like the scarf, it gave him some peace.

The hoverer stopped suddenly, doors slammed and the bag was unzipped. The guard appeared above him, but all the boy could see was his helmet, engraved with the royal crest. The guard grabbed him, dragging him out of the hoverer and dropping him right in the mud. The boy coughed and stood up, covered in brown goo and staring wide-eyed at his surroundings. They must be on the outskirts of Oarlon. The silver steel castle was now far in the distance. The boy almost couldn't believe they'd gotten to the outskirts so quickly.

He'd been told the outskirts were where the poorest of the poor lived. They didn't even have the protection of the outposts that surrounded Oarlon. Nearby, a couple of houses sagged as though the roofs wanted to touch the ground. A few doors hung half off their hinges, and other roofs had holes where sunlight poured in.

Further down the unpaved road, the nicer looking shops still had dirt on the exterior. A few people were walking about, their eyes bloodshot and their lungs heaving with every breath. There were no air purifiers out here. The outskirts were a death sentence. Some people passing by gave them curious glances but quickly scurried off. The boy suspected that the royal guard gave them pause.

Every breath was a struggle. The boy could feel the poison fill his lungs, pervading his body, from his chest to the very tips of his fingers. If he wasn't about to be murdered, the poison would take years off his life every day.

The guard took out a white square and set it on the ground. He pressed the center, and the Princess' image appeared, standing above the small square just like she was there.

"Things have changed here since you left. I'm sorry. Run far away from here." The hologram disappeared. The boy looked at the helmet of the guard. He couldn't see his expression, but the guard must've been just as confused as the boy was. What did that mean? What changed?

The guard just turned, climbed back into the hoverer and drove off. In about ten seconds, the hoverer, still in sight, disappeared into a cloud of fire and smoke that must've killed him instantly. The few people wandering about immediately ran inside, cowering away from the commotion.

But not the boy. The boy watched as the helmet with the royal crest flew through the air, landing near the boy's feet. The guard had done nothing to him, but seeing the crest slightly damaged by the fire cooled the lashes on his back for just a moment.

The boy finally turned when he felt a pair of eyes watching him from one of the shops nearby. It was a grown man with a huge mustache. His eyes were locked on the boy. He smiled. His teeth were crooked, and his eyes were black.

"Well done, boy. Well done."

The boy shook his head and turned back toward the crash. "It wasn't me…"

"I'm not talking about that. I'm talking about this." The man pointed inside the shop where a display pad was cycling through the news from the kingdom. The boy had seen the show on occasion whenever he'd been ordered to clean in the castle's bedrooms or sitting rooms. He walked slowly to the shop, wary of the man and his intentions.

The man chuckled to himself and clapped his hands together. "Didn't think anyone could do it," he said. That's when the boy saw the headline: *King and Queen Murdered Upon Their Return.* The boy took a step back. Was this what the Princess meant? Was she responsible for this? Had she killed her own parents? But why? And why spare him?

That's when he saw it: leaked security footage showed the Princess walking toward her parents' room and past the guards to the front entrance. The guards and the Princess seemed to talk inaudibly until the guards opened the door for her. The security camera switched to an inside view of the room by the door. Once the door behind the

Princess closed, the Princess transformed into the boy. The boy took out a knife and went off camera.

Aiva. Aiva must've struck a deal with the Princess to save him, and in doing so, gave the Princess exactly what she wanted.

The King and Queen would be tired from their journey, and despite it being morning, would've gone to bed, giving Aiva the perfect opportunity to sneak in and kill them for the Princess, in exchange for sparing Aiva and the boy's lives. And the Princess must've ordered Aiva to shapeshift into the boy for the cameras so the Princess could frame him and get away with it—that's why she'd wanted him alive.

Now they would hunt him.

Now she would be Queen.

Now he would take her advice and run.

FOUR

PRINCESS SERA

The morning light pierced the glass dome as Sera looked out on the city from above. Her parents were gone and soon, she would be crowned Queen. She wrestled with her plans, determined not to rule as they had. When her parents weren't stuffing their faces with sugar and artificial flavors, they threw parties, went on trips and otherwise ignored the looming issue that people, their people, were dying. But they were still her parents, and while very few, there were moments of love and admiration. She couldn't hate them. She kept telling herself that as the hand of guilt tried to pull her down to the ground.

The purified air in the palace made it easier to forget that most people woke up and went to sleep every night inhaling polluted air that was slowly destroying their insides. Every time Sera gazed out the window, she remembered. If her generation wasn't the last, the next would be. As Queen, she could make decisions. She could wield her power to save Oar. The Chosen One was out there. They had to be.

Adding to the weight of her guilt was the killing of her loyal guard who smuggled the boy out of the castle. She just couldn't leave any traces behind. She'd already sacrificed so much, but she knew it was for the greater good. The boy would be discovered on camera, and she'd ordered troops to search the area where he had been dropped off. They would find him, and they would kill him while the cameras watched everything. The people would rest easy knowing that the killer of their King and Queen was dead. Then she could focus her efforts on finding the Chosen One and saving her people.

A throat cleared behind her. It was her advisor, Mankar. The light reflected off his bald head. Under his eyes were dark circles. He always looked exhausted. Rumor had it that Mankar did some dealings with the underworld of the city during his off time. It was never proven, but Sera would keep an eye on him regardless. Next to him was Aiva, staring at the ground, shaking.

"Thank you, Mankar. Leave us." Mankar bowed his head and returned to the elevator. Sera walked toward Aiva and lifted her chin with her finger to stare into her purple eyes. They used to be so full of life, but now, life had dimmed her spirit.

"Are you going to kill me?" asked Aiva. Her voice trembled. "Tying up loose ends?" Sera placed her hand on Aiva's shoulder to reassure her.

"No. I'm not like my parents. I will never hurt you." Aiva's eyes widened. "In fact, you will move from the basement into the Royal Room."

"But... But that's your parents' room," objected Aiva.

"Yes, but I am remodeling and have no desire to live there. You have already proven yourself a valued member of my council."

"I'm no one."

Sera smiled and put both hands on Aiva's cheeks. "We both know you're so much more than that," said Sera. "We are going to make Oarlon a better place. Together, we'll change the world. Stay with me, and I promise you, I will look after you."

Aiva met her gaze one more time and bowed.

"You are no longer a servant. You are a friend. And I do not make my friends bow to me," said Sera.

Aiva nodded. "Thank you, Your Majesty."

"Sera. You will call me Sera."

"As you wish, Sera."

"Now go. See to your new room. Whatever you want, you shall have."

Aiva nodded and quickly left. The ghosts of Sera's parents were in Aiva's eyes. A knot of guilt tightened in Sera's stomach. She had asked Aiva to do a terrible thing, and now she was asking her to live with it. But Sera had no other choice. Her parents would let the world fall into chaos before giving up their power. They would've murdered Aiva if they knew of her gift.

She closed her eyes, thinking of her parents, the boy, her loyal guard and the servants that were murdered. Tears slid down her cheeks. For Oarlon, for the world, she had to, but that didn't shake the pain radiating deep in her gut. Perhaps her parents' deaths affected her more than she realized.

Her breath trembled as she opened her eyes. No more tears. She had to focus on her next step.

She turned back to the window when it happened: the world before her became blurry, or maybe it was her vision. The colors transformed together, slowly coalescing into a new landscape before her. She was above the city, floating just below the clouds. The air was fresh, filled with the scent of lavender and pine. The world below looked to be greener than ever in the beautiful, clear sunshine. Her body fell toward the ground, but she didn't have any cause to be frightened. Something told her that she was being guided. She stopped just short of the ground, landing on her two feet gracefully in the middle of the Sky District, where most people shopped and convened.

In front of her, people threw their hands to the sky in celebration. Others took a deep inhale followed by a satisfied exhale. Tears slid down their cheeks as they embraced their neighbor next to them. Their prayers had been answered.

The vision stopped suddenly, and the Princess found herself back in the dome. She rubbed her forehead. The vision was so clear, it couldn't have just been a daydream. There was more to this, and as Queen, she would figure out what.

FIVE

THE BOY

Rain pattered the stone streets in the night. The boy tried to hide as best as he could throughout the day, but despite his best efforts, the royal guards were closing in on him. The only thing he could do was run to the middle of town in the Sky District. Thankfully, the rain kept most people inside, so there was less of a chance people would see him.

He hid in a trash can for a few hours, and when he didn't hear hoverers nearby, he continued, moving away from where he assumed the search party would be. The rain soaked his clothes, leaving him shivering while his stomach cried out for anything to eat. He'd found some uneaten takeout food in the trash can hours ago, but it didn't satisfy the growling of his stomach. He was thirsty enough to open his mouth wide and let the raindrops fall in.

He would have to find a solution soon. He considered breaking into a house to steal some food, but then he thought of the people he'd be stealing from, and his heart sank. He could find a rich family that wouldn't feel the loss so much, but even then, the sight of an intruder could terrify them. Who knows what they might do. They might have guns or weapons. He was just a malnourished kid, accused of killing the King and Queen. Maybe he could find someone who hated the King and Queen? Maybe they would shelter him? No, even if they hated the royal family, hiding a shapeshifting murderer would make anyone uneasy.

His hand touched the scarf around his neck. Aiva had stolen this. It's what got them into this mess. Stealing more might just make things worse, yet the world hadn't been fair to him. Maybe he should. What was right?

His dilemma was quickly forgotten as he crept out of an alleyway. He had to cross a wide street, so he looked both ways to make sure no one was around. He took one step out, ready to book it across, when a hoverer appeared over the roofs and flew down to the street. It shone a spotlight directly on him. The light blinded him long enough for another hoverer to fly down into the alleyway behind him, making going back the way he came impossible.

"That's him!" shouted one of the officers. The boy knew that if he surrendered, he would be executed. But if he ran, they would shoot, killing him just the same. Each vehicle had cameras that recorded every interaction. The footage of his death would be well documented. The Princess planned well, and he had no idea how to save himself.

That's when two shots rang out, hitting the spotlight of the hoverer in front of him. Another two bullets shot from the darkness, killing both guards in the vehicle. Blood splattered the wind screen as their bodies fell from the hoverer. The boy was transfixed, staring wide eyed at the blood as a shadow whooshed by him.

The guards from the second hoverer shouted, their surprise turning into two quick death rattles. The second hoverer powered off, and so did the spotlight. The rain and the darkness were the only things left. The street light flickered as the boy backed away from the alleyway. What was happening?

Out of the darkness, the answer came in a long, dark green jacket, with a green undershirt and tie. A person encased in shadow emerged from the alley. This was a Knightmare. The shadow covered the Knightmare's skin and seemed to be subtly swirling. A gun was holstered to their hip. The Knightmare was slender and tall and walked toward the boy, cocking their head back and forth as if examining him.

The boy turned to run, but as he turned, the Knightmare reappeared from the darkness in front of him. The boy fell backwards onto the wet stones. The Knightmare kneeled down and grabbed him by the scarf.

"Come with me." It wasn't a question. The Knightmare picked the boy up and tossed him over their shoulder. He could see two daggers sheathed at the small of the Knightmare's back A small hoverer was nearby. The Knightmare threw him onto the bike and jumped on behind him.

The boy was confused and overwhelmed. After his near death experience, his legs were shaky and his arms were like noodles. Outrunning the guards was one thing, but a Knightmare? He didn't know much about them, but after seeing what happened to those guards, all he could do was sit and wait for whatever happened next.

The Knightmare zoomed out of the city, expertly avoiding the city patrols. Once they were past the outskirts, all the buildings disappeared, giving way to fields of grass as they headed toward the forest.

The boy took one more glance back at Oarlon and everything he was leaving behind. Never in his wildest dreams had he imagined himself going anywhere outside the castle. That was Aiva's dream. He just wanted to be beside her.

The bike hoverer flew around the trees at high speeds with only the light of the moon to guide their way. The boy gasped, jostling in his seat every time they sped close to a tree, but the Knightmare never flinched. After a while, the boy's breathing eased, and he put his full faith in the driver.

The bike pulled to a stop in the middle of a foggy clearing. The boy couldn't see anything in the pitch black. The moon overhead was gradually dimming as the clouds moved in, joining them in their escape from the city. The Knightmare grabbed the boy's hand and led him through the darkness while the boy clutched his damp scarf.

The boy heard a stone rolling and a latch release. He squinted as the dark circle of the door rolled open to reveal a huge stone hallway lit with white fire. The Knightmare dragged the boy in, and the dark circle rolled closed behind them. Two more Knightmares appeared before them in the hallway.

"Congratulations, Rus," said one. Rus said nothing and continued pulling the boy into a huge open room at the end of the hallway. White fire lights were posted all around the wall of the room, and at the very end of the room sat a Knightmare on an elevated throne with a crown made of black thorns atop their head. A symbol of the sun broken into pieces marked the floor between the boy and the throne. Rus stationed the boy in the center of the symbol and bowed to the Knightmare.

"Seer, I bring you the boy who slayed the King and Queen," sounded Rus' gravelly voice. Judging solely on his voice, the boy guessed Rus was already an adult, and an older one at that. The Knightmare Seer stayed quiet, tilting their head as they studied the pair. The boy wanted to correct Rus, to tell this Seer that they had the wrong person, but no sound came from his lips.

"You're a shapeshifter? An agent of the Light?" said the Seer. Their voice was low and even more threatening than Rus'. The boy cleared his throat. His hands were shaking. Part of him wanted to lie, but these were the Knightmares. They might kill him if he was an agent of the Light. The other part of him shook to the core, wondering if they would kill him upon discovering he wasn't the person who murdered the King and Queen. At least with the truth, he could be honest with someone.

"No. The Princess framed me to cover up that she killed her parents to assume the throne." The Seer put their hands together, their long fingers touching one another in a mockery of prayer.

"Do you know who we are?" the Seer inquired.

"The Knightmares," said the boy, his shoulders still tensed.

"Yes. We are the outcasts. We are the forgotten. We are the ones that haunt people's dreams. We are assassins." Shivers ran down the boy's spine. He couldn't tell if he should be thankful or afraid. Or both. "Our cause has prevailed for thousands of years, when the Shadows made the first Knightmare. The Shadows have protected us and given us a greater purpose."

"What do you want with me?" the boy asked.

"To recruit you," said the Seer.

The boy didn't know what to say or do. He didn't want to be an assassin, but he had nowhere else to go. He didn't want to die, but how could he refuse?

Rus struck him on the back of the head. "Be thankful."

The boy rubbed his head. "Th-thank you," he said.

"Rus, take him to the chamber and complete the ritual. You will be his mentor. You will train him," said the Seer. Rus bowed.

"He will be the best Knightmare we've ever seen. I swear it." Without any more hesitation, Rus grabbed the boy and dragged him from the room. He pulled the boy into a smaller circular chamber — similar to the chamber he'd been tortured in hours earlier. The white fire illuminated Rus more clearly here. The shadow the clung to his skin hid his face in complete darkness. There was no way to see it — to know what he was thinking or feeling. The shadow just stared at him as Rus positioned the boy in the middle of the room.

"Would you like to see your face one more time?" The boy instinctually took a step back from Rus and crossed his arms, shuddering.

"You mean, forever?"

"Yes."

"No. No, I can't do this…" He wanted to leave. He didn't care now what happened to him. He didn't want to be a shadow monster. He didn't want to kill. Why did he always have to sacrifice everything? Tears welled in his eyes, ready to fall down his cheeks.

"Look, boy, you're dead if you go out there. Here, you'll have a purpose. Now, stop fyrking crying and stand in the middle of the room." Defeated, the boy did as he was told. Out there, he had no shot. But here, despite what this meant for his life, he might have a chance at finding Aiva and saving her. He took the scarf off and folded it into a small square. He placed it near the edge of the room. If he could see Aiva one more time…

"One last chance to say your name and see your face," said Rus. The boy shook his head. He didn't need to. What difference would it really make? Rus nodded and started chanting. "Shadows, let the darkness shine in the light. Bring this boy into your arms. Give him strength, and he will be your blade. Take his past and his desire. Give him your love, and he will return it." As he chanted, darkness rose from the cracks in the ground, circling around the boy. "From now on, your name is Koe—a shadow of the night."

The darkness completely shrouded the boy, but he could still see everything around him perfectly. He watched the darkness pierce his skin and settled beneath his clothes. The shadows swirled around his hands slowly until his palms could be seen no more. He looked up to Rus who watched him and bowed.

"Welcome, Koe."

The boy slowly bowed back. Tears once again formed around his eyes. This time, Rus couldn't see it. His true name was gone. The life that he knew was gone and his dreams with it.

The nightmare was here. Koe was its name.

He looked to the folded-up scarf. There was still hope.

SIX

KOE

Fifteen Years Later

The first snowflakes of winter fell on the frigid roof. Koe walked along the roof beam. The bottom of his long black coat drifted as a gust of wind blew past him, almost pushing him off the roof. But Koe did not waver. The cold was one of the last things that reminded him of his youth, before his time as a Knightmare. One of the last threads tying him to the person he was.

The shadows had done more than take away his former life. He knew the poison in the air had gotten worse in the last fifteen years, but the shadows that covered his body protected him. He was never sick, not from the poisoned air. Not from anything.

He jumped to the next roof, landing on the slanted tiles. He'd been thinking about what Rus said during his briefing: *This is highly important. Don't miss.* Koe hadn't missed since completing his training.

He never failed a mission. Rus had kept his promise and made him the best Knightmare ever. His kill count was over a hundred, yet Rus expected more. He always did.

Koe watched from the rooftop as hoverers passed one another down below. Their headlights and the street lamps were the only source of light at this hour. Koe was nearly invisible in the darkness. The shadow that swirled over his face was matched by his black shirt and pants. He wore a black fedora and heavy boots. His jacket wasn't for warmth, but it was comfortable. So was the white scarf he wore around his neck. The other Knightmares used to make fun of him for it, but as it became increasingly clear that his lethality and efficiency exceeded their own, their words became whispers. Eventually, they started looking over their shoulder to see if he was there.

Rus was the only one to still criticize his scarf to him. When Koe first began training, Rus used the scarf to motivate him — threatening to tear it up if he failed a given task. Every night, Koe would look at the scarf, think of Aiva and wonder where she was. Did she think of him too?

The scarf gave him hope that maybe they could escape from Oarlon and the Knightmares and go somewhere far away together. But every night, he would lay down and feel the scars from the lashes on his back. They didn't hurt anymore, but like the scarf, they reminded him of the past, reminded him he could never escape this life.

He slid down the roof and jumped off, landing in an alley next to a small warehouse.

The door was already broken, kicked in. Koe knew his target was inside.

He silently made his way to the main room where the only light source was. He watched four men as they circled around a man with a bag over his head, tied to a chair. These were the henchmen of Wystan — the kingpin of the underworld. The men were anxiously pacing. Their catch was valuable — too valuable for them.

"The royal guards are on our tail! What're we going to do?" said one, followed by a loud mucus-filled coughing fit. No doubt, from the air.

"Relax! Wystan will be here soon. Let's just calm down and let him figure this out. Okay?" said another. Koe sized up the henchmen. Two of them were portly and round, another was muscular and the nervous one was skinny and short. They had guns, but that wouldn't make much difference.

Koe crept in the darkness. He knew how to move quickly, without a sound. Four common thugs were no match for one Knightmare. Let alone, him.

Koe kept his gun holstered — he didn't want gunshots attracting attention. Since these henchmen worked for Wystan, it was a good bet that they all were murderers. Wystan dealt with drugs, sex trafficking and pulling off hits for anyone who'd pay. Koe had wanted to go after him before, but the Knightmares adhered to a strict code that only the Seer, the chosen Knightmare who saw the will of the Shadows in visions, ordered it.

Koe reached for his belt and into one of his small pockets. There were mini smoke grenades the size of grapes in there. As he pulled one out, one of the portly henchmen discharged his gun accidentally, firing directly into the ground. The other three quickly chastised him. Koe put the smoke grenade back. These were fools. How they stayed alive this long was a mystery.

Koe reached behind his coat to his lower back, grabbing the daggers sheathed there. He took a few steps into the light. The henchmen noticed him immediately. They stared in shock. Their faces betrayed their terror, and their bodies were frozen in time. Anguish crept across their features. The nervous one cried out, and that's when they all went for their guns. But it was too late.

A Knightmare could vanish, melting away entirely into the shadows. It could only be done outside of direct sunlight. Joining the shadow made Koe invisible and moving was quicker while inside it.

Like flipping on a switch, the shadow stretched over Koe's clothes, and he vanished. He was already gone by the time the henchmen fired. Koe took advantage of those few precious seconds of confusion, running behind one of the henchmen, reappearing momentarily just to slice his throat. The blood sprayed everywhere. Koe disappeared back into shadow as the gun shots missed him completely. Staying light on his feet helped him to remain undetected. Not even the artificial light could reveal where he was.

He targeted the muscular one next, slashing his leg to bring him down to his knee and then using his second dagger to stab his throat.

Without even a pause to aim, one of Koe's dagger's flew through the air, stabbing the third henchmen in the eye. The last one left was the skinny, small man who immediately threw his gun away and got onto his knees. Koe drew his dagger out of the muscular henchmen's neck and walked toward the groveling man.

Koe outstretched his arm, calling the other dagger to his hand. The daggers had been bathed in Shadow magic and were connected to their Knightmare. The dagger extracted itself from the henchmen's eye and flew into Koe's grasp. Koe knelt down before the last terrified thug.

"You beg for forgiveness?"

"Yes. I'm sorry," squealed the henchman. He was younger than the others—had to be in his late teens. Koe almost felt bad for him. The smell of urine found its way to Koe's nose as a pool of yellow grew below the henchman, but Koe didn't flinch or shy away in disgust.

"Where's the drop off point?" asked Koe. The henchman, still shivering, tried to look where he thought Koe's eyes were, but he could barely keep his head up.

"The Iron District. House 74." The young man had given the answer quickly, despite knowing that he was about to die. Maybe there was some part of him that wanted to do the right thing in the end.

He knew no other Knightmare would have given this cowering fool a second thought and ended his life there and then. But he wasn't Koe's target, and despite serving the underworld, he was young and could live a life away from all of this. Best guess, this teenager ended up working for Wystan against his will.

Koe recognized the look in his eyes. It wasn't his choice, just like it wasn't Koe's choice. His mind made up, Koe stood.

"Run and forget this life. If you ever hold a gun again, I will not be so kind." The teenager nodded, quickly getting up and running out of the warehouse.

Koe's attention shifted to the man tied up.

He approached the man and pulled the bag off his head to reveal Mankar—the Queen's personal advisor. Mankar's eyes had dark circles under them. His old age accentuated the lines on his face. Tape had been put over his mouth to keep him from making a sound. At first, Mankar saw the dead henchman and looked relieved, but when his eyes fell on Koe, despair filled every wrinkle.

"Hello, Mankar," said Koe. He'd never really known Mankar in his previous life at the castle. All he knew were recent developments, and now he was here to settle them. He cheerfully ripped the tape off Mankar's mouth, taking a few facial hairs with it.

"Why... Why are you after me?" he asked, his voice quivering.

"The Shadows have named you. But I know all about your life," said Koe. "You've been trafficking girls for decades. Some as young as fourteen. You've been spotted taking some of them to bed yourself. I know about your deal with Wystan. I know that you've been skimping out on paying Wystan, and that's why his goons took you. Why the Shadows have chosen you, I do not know. They must think you have some part to play for the Light. What I see is a monster, a monster I'll gladly put down."

"You don't know what you're doing! I am the Queen's advisor! You can't touch me!"

"You overestimate your position and value. The Queen can't find us, can't stop us. No one has, and no one will. In reality, she will use your death as an opportunity to target the underworld. I wouldn't be surprised if she thanked us."

Koe watched Mankar squirm in his seat. There wasn't anything he could say or do. Nothing would buy his freedom, and Mankar knew it.

"Will you make it quick?" asked Mankar. Koe leaned down in front of him.

"No." Koe thrusted his dagger into Mankar's liver. A piercing cry shook the warehouse. Koe removed the blade slowly and slashed Mankar several times across the face and body. The blow to the liver would kill him in time. There was nothing anyone could do to save him now. The markings were torture, to make him feel as much pain as possible.

Koe took a few steps back and watched Mankar bleed to death. No matter how many people Koe killed, every kill felt like the first: oddly satisfying, yet his insides wanted to claw out of him, wanted to escape.

Koe left the warehouse and found his bike hoverer where he left it a few blocks away. He climbed on and took off down the side streets. The Ocean District was rather empty at night. Tonight however, guards patrolled the streets, looking for any sign of Mankar or the kidnappers. If they hadn't heard the gunshots, they'd find Mankar's body in the next few hours.

On the other side of the river, the Iron District was a stark contrast to the Ocean District. While the Ocean District was quiet after all of the workers had clocked out and returned home, the Iron District came alive at night. Its bars and brothels littered every corner. The Queen had tried to crack down on the brothels, ordering them illegal, but that didn't dissuade people like Wystan from financing underground establishments. If the Queen raided one, they'd just find a new place to set up shop.

No one seemed to mind anyway. Everyone, from people on the outskirts to royal advisors, frequented what the Iron District had to offer for entertainment. Koe parked his bike in a dark alleyway and climbed to the rooftop of a bar. He didn't want to be spotted in the Iron District. He wasn't even supposed to be here. His job — his mission was over. But he couldn't help himself.

Koe easily passed over a stretch of bars unnoticed while people drunkenly groped each other outside and then proceeding to throw up on one another. The upside to the Iron District was that it was largely self-policing. Since Wystan had such a huge presence here, very few guards ever came.

Koe jumped to the ground near house 74. The house was worn, and based on the old rotten sign still hung up over the door, used to be a store of some kind. Koe took out his gun as he put his ear to the door. He could hear loud music and some triumphant celebrating inside.

A swift kick tore the door off its hinges. Koe entered and quickly identified three men and one woman as patrons. Everyone else had collars around their necks and were completely naked. Their eyes were rolling back in their sockets from the heavy drugs running through their veins, and their skin had turned a subtle green from air sickness. They were frail, just skin and bones. The four patrons were all engaging in sexual acts with them, clearly forcing the men and women around them. Koe recognized one patron as a sergeant of the royal guard and another as a messenger for the Queen.

Pop, pop, pop, pop. One, two, three, four shots. The patrons had no chance to react. Their bodies fell limp. The slaves around them didn't even react to the blood. Most of them were too drugged, but even the ones who weren't still didn't seem too fazed to see so much death. They didn't even care that they had been saved. Koe locked eyes with one of them— her ghostly stare barely registered his presence. No matter what Koe did, they were already gone.

Koe left without a word. He was just glad none of those slaves had been Aiva. Wherever she was, he hoped she was living a better life than he imagined the Queen had given her.

SEVEN

QUEEN SERA

Queen Sera stood in a grassy field filled with flowers in full bloom.
She took a deep breath. She was beyond Oarlon, far south, and had
traveled through the forest where the Knightmares kept their secret
temple. People had long since stopped entering the forest since
Knightmares made their home there long ago. But they weren't there
now, Sera had seen to that. She finally found their hiding place and
eradicated them all.

As the fresh air made its way to her lungs, the feeling was better
than any of the castle's purified air. The sun bathed her in golden light,
and she let it touch every inch of her exposed pale skin. She turned to see
a few kids jumping in a small creek nearby, their laughing and jumping
made her smile.

It was what she'd always wanted — this peace for Oarlon. The
peace that her parents never sought for. The peace that she had been
searching for ever since becoming Queen.

Then slowly, the grass withered away. The musty smell of the poison air displaced the fresh flower aroma. The kids laughter died, and the creek dried up. Everything around her blurred. She blinked, trying to hold on to the image, only to find herself in her room, lying in bed—the morning light penetrating through her shades. The light in the room told her what time it was without her checking the clock.

A muscular hand reached from the other side of the bed and gently pulled her face toward his. The captain of her guard and her lover, Thane. Handsome, despite just having woken up. While the black and white strands of her hair tumbled every which way, Thane's short blond hair was stuck in the same style it always was: up and combed to the side. His muscular body took up most of the bed. He pulled himself up to kiss her. It was how he greeted her every morning.

"Did you have another vision?" he asked, edging closer to her so their bodies were pressed together. Sera turned to face him, skimming her hand down his arm, feeling the hairs on his arm stick up.

"It's the same one I've been seeing for so long," she said, gazing into his eyes. "I still don't know how to get there. What's the cure?"

Thane took her hand and brought it up to his lips.

"Don't fret. You're carrying the weight of the world on your shoulders. You'll figure it out." He kissed her hand and then rolled on top of her.

"Thane—" she started to say, but he kissed her neck and she wrapped her arms around the smooth muscles of his back.

"You're my savior," said Thane.

Sera felt his hands move toward her waist, but she grabbed them before they could get there. That last line was cheesy, and normally she'd tease him for it but not today.

"Don't play with me right now," said Sera.

Thane sighed and rolled off her.

"Your mood worsens with every passing day. You've read book after book, met with every foreign dignitary for advice. You're doing everything you can. I just want to see your cute smile again."

She looked deeply into his eyes. He was right, she had read thousands of books and exhausted the deepest archives for any clue that could point her in the direction of finding the Chosen One. She'd tried to access her visions to find answers, but nothing came. The only spark of light giving her hope was that her visions had been increasing. When she was a new Queen, her visions were short and rare. But in the last year, they came frequently — some leading to successful raids on the underworld. Thane brought up the idea that she might be the Chosen One herself, but Thane stoked her ego too much. It's why she loved him, but also why she never fully trusted him.

Three quick knocks at the door meant they were late to the meeting. Sera threw on her royal robes of gold and black. They ran all the way down her arms and to the tips of her shoes. Her crown resided by her bedside. It was a combination of her father and mother's. She had them forged together as a last reminder of their rule.

Thane quickly donned his gold and black armor, his sword hilt attached to the armor at this back.

His gun rested in his holster. On his gold breastplate was the insignia of the royal family — the falling stars.

The doors opened to servants ready to carry the train of her robes. Thane followed behind her as two guards flanked behind him. Everyone in the kingdom knew that they were sleeping together. Most of the court expected them to be married soon. Much to Thane's chagrin, Sera continually delayed the wedding. It wasn't time yet. That was always her excuse. She didn't want to give the people any reason to think that saving Oarlon and the kingdom wasn't her top priority.

The guards guided her through the glass hallways to the elevator. After a short ride, she stepped out to the throne room. There, her council waited for her patiently as she approached the throne.

She quickly did a headcount and noticed Mankar was missing. Maybe he'd finally gotten some much needed sleep.

Her throne was positioned in the middle of the room, and before she could sit a pale child with tattoos of falling stars on his forehead ran up to her. If it was anyone else, the guards would have stepped in, but no one could or dared control her son, Gaven. Now nine years old, he still retained the whimsical spirit that so many lose with age. He always involved himself in royal affairs, despite not knowing what was going on around him. His birth only strengthened Sera's resolve to save Oarlon.

Gaven plowed into her side and wrapped his tiny arms around her.

"Mommy! Guess what?"

"You didn't have another nightmare?" asked Sera, pulling him into her arms.

"No, I made you something," he said. Sera's gaze flashed toward her advisors patiently waiting, some murmuring to one another.

"Show me after we're done," she said, stroking his cheek. Thane grabbed Gaven off her and pulled him to the side. Thane was his father. It was an open secret in court, but Sera never confirmed it to the people. Some might look down on her for having a child out of wedlock.

Sera turned her attention toward business and sat on her throne, facing her council members. The five of them looked grave, imploring each other with their eyes to speak first.

"What's wrong?" said Sera. Hanna, her youngest council member, just a little younger than Sera herself, took a step forward.

"Your Highness, we have some bad news. Mankar was found early this morning. Murdered." Terrible as it was, Sera breathed a sigh of relief that this was the news that made them look like death warmed over. Sera hated the man. She would have thrown him off the council sooner if his ties with the underworld weren't so strong. He was instrumental in ensuring Wystan stayed in line. As Queen, she wanted to break down the underworld once and for all, but Mankar cautioned against it. The situation in the Iron District was delicate, and Mankar believed that an all out assault on the underworld would lead to chaos. He didn't believe it would be possible to smoke them all out. Wystan was always on the move, and his top enforcers rarely poked their heads above ground. Staying hidden kept them alive.

"How?" asked Sera. She wasn't going to pretend that there was any sadness to be had.

"We found him with some underworld thugs. They were also dead with wounds consistent with what we know of Knightmare methods of assassination."

A Knightmare? Attacking a high noble such as Mankar? Now, that was interesting. Sera edged forward in her chair. She realized she could use his death for tougher restrictions against the underworld. The people would be scared that a high-ranking official was murdered. They would rally behind her. Her heart stung at using someone's death in such a political move.

"And what about the raids I ordered in the Iron District?"

"We've seized several crates of drugs and money. Exactly where you said they would be. You can bet Wystan is feeling the effects," said Hanna.

"Good," said Sera. Her eyes flickered over to Thane, next to her throne. Gaven followed his father's example and did his best to appear stoic. "Send word out at once. Let's get out ahead of it. Is that all?"

Hanna shook her head. And Sera's heart stopped.

"Our scientists have revised their current assessment. They believe we have only a few years left before the air becomes so deadly that it will be unlivable. Even the purified air of the castle won't be enough."

"Try to increase the filters and start installing them on the outskirts. Order the teams to continue working on ways to increase the filter efficiency," ordered Sera. "I will return to the royal library. Did any of the archivists find anything last night?"

None of the council members reacted. Clearly, the answer was no. Sera rubbed her forehead.

"We must get on with the day then. Send the next batch of books to my study."

All the council members bowed and scampered off. Once they were gone, Gaven leapt onto his mother's throne and beamed at her.

"Want to see what it is now?"

Sera pulled him close with one arm, kissing the white strands in his otherwise black hair. "Yes, absolutely."

Gaven reached into his pocket and pulled out a folded piece of paper. He unfolded it to reveal a stick figure drawing of Sera, Thane and him all holding hands. It was the worst drawing Sera had ever seen. There was nothing to distinguish them other than the crown on Sera's head. It was nothing like how a nine-year-old should draw. Sera took the piece of paper and quickly folded it up without commenting on it. Gaven's excitement was still written all over his face.

"Thane, is our friend still in the chamber below?"

Thane quickly confirmed they were. Sera turned her attention back to Gaven and lifted one eyebrow like she knew something he didn't. "I think it's time I taught you an important lesson about wearing this crown. Are you brave enough for it?" Gaven nodded, his blue eyes bright. "Let's go downstairs," she said. Thane led the way toward the elevator as Sera grabbed Gaven's hand and followed behind.

"Are you going to hang up my drawing?" he asked. Sera still clutched the childish drawing in her hand.

"I will find the perfect place for it," said Sera. Before walking into the elevator, Sera handed the drawing to one of the on-duty guards, out of Gaven's view.

Once inside the elevator, Gaven tugged on his father's belt.

"Did you see it too, Daddy?" Now that they were alone, Thane broke his indifferent posture and smiled, kneeling down right in front of Gaven.

"I loved it! I want you to make another one."

Gaven giggled, and Sera smiled. She hated how Thane lied. Gaven was too naive, and as a prince, no one ever challenged him. It was the same sort of childhood her parents had, growing up too comfortable. They needed to start showing Gaven what he'd be dealing with when he grew up, especially if something happened to Sera. He would be king.

The elevator stopped, and the doors opened to one of the floors she could never forget. It was on this floor that she had so many memories.

The most prominent one was of torturing the boy who she'd framed for the murder of her parents so long ago. Every time she came here, Sera thought of that boy. Somehow, he'd escaped capture. She liked to think he made it to another kingdom across the ocean or hid himself so well that no one recognized him. Hopefully, he was happy—and safe—living life to the fullest. It would help heal some of the guilt pressing down on her heart.

Sera led her son to the interrogation chamber door, but before she could open it, Thane touched her hand.

"You sure about this?" he said.

"Not everything can be sunshine and rainbows," said Sera. Her father and mother also believed in children needing to grow up quickly. It was one of the few lessons she would pass down. Ironically, it's also what killed them.

"Gaven, this might be scary, but just know we're here with you," said Sera. Nervously, Gaven grabbed her hand. Any trace of a smile had disappeared.

Sera pressed the button, and the door slid into the wall, Behind it was a man tied to a chain tethered above his head, slumped over on his knees. His shirt lay on the floor out of reach. In the reflection of the black metallic panels of the wall, the man's blood-soaked back caught Gaven's eye. He couldn't stop staring.

Sera pushed Gaven toward the man. The man's hair covered his eyes, but Sera caught them looking at Gaven. He chuckled and returned to staring at the ground.

"Too bad your son got your genes."

Thane grabbed an electro-rod off the wall of the chamber, touching the tip to the man's back and sending a shock of electricity arching through him. The man stiffened and groaned, and Thane drew back. A small burn mark was now visible between the lashes of his earlier whipping. Some still bled.

Gaven immediately took a step back and grabbed his mother's

arm, trying to hide behind it. Sera pushed him forward rather forcefully, almost causing him to fall face-first. Gaven caught himself in time.

"Who is he?" asked Gaven, regaining his footing.

Sera waved Thane over, taking the electro-rod from him. She presented it to Gaven like a gift.

"He's a very bad man who's done bad things to our city. We're trying to get answers from him to prevent more people from being hurt."

The man chuckled again. He was only a henchman of Wystan, a lowlife who didn't matter, but the authorities had picked him up and brought him here to be questioned.

"You really going to make your son hurt me?" he asked. "I thought you were kind."

"Silence," said Sera.

"You have no power over me," said the man.

Sera pushed Gaven forward again. Gaven looked at the rod and then at the man.

"Sometimes, as rulers, we have to do things we hate doing for the greater good. As king, you will have to do them as well."

Gaven shook his head back and forth so fast he began to look ill.

"Gaven, do it," ordered Thane.

"You're better than this, kid. Don't listen to them," said the man.

Gaven looked into the prisoner's eyes, and ultimately, he turned toward Sera with his head hung in shame. Sera looked down on him, heaving a heavy sigh. But she could still turn this around. She leaned down and put a hand on Gaven's shoulder.

"This man killed several people because they wouldn't pay him. Several innocent people that didn't deserve it. If he could, he would hurt your father. He would hurt you. He would hurt me. He doesn't deserve a second chance. He doesn't deserve mercy. If you want to be king someday, you must be firm."

Gaven just stood there, his gaze flashing back and forth between the man and Sera.

"Go on, ask him what he's done."

Gaven turned back to the man and asked, "Did you hurt people?"

The man sighed and shook his head. "What does it matter?"

Gaven took the rod from Thane's hand, pressed the button to activate it and pushed the tip against the man's chest. He cried out again, louder than before, and Gaven quickly released.

"Do you want to hurt my mom?"

"Go fyrk yourself, kid."

Gaven hit the same spot again, right in the middle of his chest. This time, he held it a few seconds longer.

"Answer me!"

The man spat at Gaven in response, the spittle hitting Gaven's eye. Gaven wiped it off and electrocuted him for the third time, this time hitting closer to the neck and holding it steady.

Finally, he stopped, and the man looked to be unconscious.

"Good, that's enough," said Sera. With her permission, Gaven dropped the rod and ran out the chamber. She was sure she saw tears forming. Following after him, Sera found Gaven curling into himself against the wall. She sat next to him, putting her arm around him.

"It's going to be okay. You're okay. You did so well—"

Gaven threw her arm off him and bolted to his feet. He sped down the hallway and out of sight just as Thane left the chamber to join them.

Sera sighed and ran her hand through her white hair. She gestured with her head toward the direction Gaven ran in.

"I don't think he wants to talk to me right now," said Sera, wondering if she'd made a mistake.

"On it," Thane said.

She'd known it would be tough to witness, that it would take time to build Gaven's resilience to this life. She hoped he wouldn't have to deal with everything she had to, but no matter when the Chosen One saved the world, there would always be new problems for him to learn to deal with as king. She just wanted him to be prepared.

The hallway around her blurred, the image before her dissolving like liquid into a new image—a room with floor-to-ceiling bookcases full of volumes of books. It was the library downstairs, where thousands and thousands of books gathered dust.

The hall was so huge, with so many aisles, that it would take several lifetimes of continuous reading to get through only half of the books there.

Then the image shifted as if she were walking between the shelves, all the way to the aisle against the back wall. A ratty old book stuck out from the bottom shelf where all the other books were perfectly aligned.

Sera wanted to touch it, open it, but before she could reach it, the book pulled itself from the shelf, falling to the ground and opening up to the middle section. A searing pain shot through her head, and Sera fell out of the vision, realizing she'd been screaming.

Back in the hallway outside the punishment chamber, there weren't any guards, so no one had seen or heard her. Sweat dripped off her brow, sliding through the falling star tattoos on the sides of her face.

The elevator door swished open, and heavy boots pounded the black metallic floor. The Queen's assassin, nicknamed 'Assassin of the Shadows' by some of the court, walked toward her. Two guns were tied to the woman's waist next to a belt full of pouches. Her hair was tied back in a ponytail. The jacket she wore stopped just short of her wrists. Her hat kept her eyes in shadow until she looked up.

Today, Aiva didn't hide the three scars on her face or her mesmerizing purple eyes that landed on Sera sitting in the hallway. Aiva stood straight, not hurrying to bow before the queen like others would. That had taken a few years and a couple of kills and missions to instill, but Aiva slowly ceased, and Sera appreciated her all the more for it.

"Why are you on the ground?" Aiva said, raising one eyebrow.

Sera stood up, dusting off her dress. She hadn't even noticed Aiva was dragging another of Wystan's barely conscious henchman behind her. A blood trail stained the floor from Aiva's feet to the elevator.

"I had a vision, but unlike the other ones, it was… painful," said Sera. "But it could… be something. A breakthrough."

"Get some sleep. You're been working too hard."

"I have to keep working. It seems like I'm not the only one who's not resting," Sera said, pointing to the drooping henchman.

"He doesn't know anything about Wystan," said Aiva. "But he got a father of three addicted to a few drugs. When the father couldn't pay, this man here killed his whole family. So tonight, me and him are going to talk before I dispose of him." Aiva used her head to gesture to the chamber. "Is it in use?"

"Yes, but I doubt the man inside knows anything about where Wystan is hiding," said Sera, unable to focus on anything other than the book from her vision.

"Then I'll get rid of him first," said Aiva, taking out one of her guns. "If that's okay with you, of course." Aiva paused her dragging the henchman toward the chamber. Setting aside the vision for a moment, Sera snapped back to her friend waiting on her.

"Stop asking me for permission. You know better," said Sera.

Aiva smiled and inclined her head.

"And you know better than to bow," added Sera.

"Yes, my Queen," said Aiva, dragging the body.

Sera shook her head, knowing Aiva was purposefully trying to get under her skin.

"Be careful, Sera. If the vision is painful, it might be best to stay away." Aiva continued on without looking back, opening the chamber door. Sera heard a gunshot ring out along with the echo of Aiva's warning. She didn't know why this vision had hurt, but she needed to know the book's importance.

Sera hurried downstairs to the library with its walls and walls of books. Her guards, rejoining her, sped after her, huffing and puffing underneath their armor. Sera paid no attention to them, finding the last aisle and the shelf exactly as the vision had show her, only this time the black-bound book was sitting neatly pushed in with the others.

She snapped the book out, and it immediately sprung open to the middle, where traces of old ink smudged the paper. At the top was written *Prophecy of the Chosen One*.

Sera's heart quickened. Her guards had caught up with her finally, standing at the end of the aisle with their hands on their knees, their exhales reverberating throughout the silent library. She thumbed through the other pages, but they were all blank, leaving Sera wondering why this old book was kept here at all. But her vision had led her to this, so she flipped back to the middle, to the only page with text on it.

The Light will shine on the answers you seek
Chant the words and the prophecy will be yours

Swear your will
Use your power
Take your soul to the edge
To rid this world of evil

Sera repeated the words out loud, almost tripping over some of them, trying to make sense of why this was such an easy find now — when they'd been seeking the words of the prophecy for years. She'd been touched by the Light like Aiva.

Perhaps the Light was finally ready to fight back.

"Uh, Your Majesty?" said one of the guards. All the guards' eyes were wide, their lips trembling. One pointed at her.

"What is it?" Sera did a quick scan of the aisle to make sure nothing else was out of the ordinary.

"Your back," the guard said unhelpfully.

Sera did her best to look over her shoulder, seeing just a small strip of exposed skin above the top of her dress. A white glow pierced her eye.

"Get Thane. Now," said Sera urgently. "And a mirror."

The guards scattered. One returned with a mirror only a few minutes later, positioning it against the end of the aisle. She sent him outside to wait for the others, and once alone, Sera pulled the strings loose on the back of her dress. The dress shuffled down her shoulders toward her abdomen, but she caught it there so it wouldn't slip further.

She once again twisted her neck, resting her chin on her shoulder. Her gaze found her reflection in the mirror, seeing cursive writing spread all across and down her back. Each letter of each line glowed white.

Sera took a heavy breath. She understood it now. The Light wanted someone who would choose to take on the task, the duty to be the Chosen One. She never imagined it would be her, but a part of her had already accepted it. She smiled, her heart lifted, and the tension in her muscles were gone. The search was over. Now, it was time for the real work—saving the world.

The guards shifted away as a figure pushed past them, stopping short of Sera.

"Sera…?" asked Thane incredulously, taking a beat. "I knew it."

EIGHT

KOE

Moving through the familiar bushes and trees of the forest toward the Knightmare's temple was the most routine thing Koe had in life. The tree with a bump on the trunk that resembled a nose, the rock shaped like an egg with a crack at the top, and the dead branch sagging from a tree that attempted to give him a concussion every time he hovered through. The first few times Rus made him find his way back, Koe thought he'd never learn the route, but knowing now where the temple was, it was easy to pick up the almost invisible trail. The light on the hover bike illuminated three feet in front of him, but he didn't need it.

His mind drifted as it always did on the ride back.

Flashes of Aiva's purple eyes appeared before his, only for him to feel the remnant sting from Rus' backhand. Koe instinctively reached toward the back of his head with one hand while the other steered. He paused, knowing there was no wound.

Just the memory.

Fifteen Years Ago

Rus always wore a vest and tie—he was the only Knightmare to do so. He always looked professional—like a gentleman. It was only a month since Koe had become part of the Shadows, and once again, Rus and him were downstairs in the basement of the temple in a huge open room with bowls of white fire hanging from the ceiling. Large columns supported the temple. Koe sat down on the sidelines, watching Rus swerve around another Knightmare, duck under another, and trip both off their feet with a swift kick. The other two were bigger, and judging from their footwork, faster, but Rus knew how to stay just a few steps ahead.

"Enough demonstrations," said Rus. "Resume training," he declared to the other Knightmares and their pupils. Rus grabbed Koe off the bench by his shirt and threw him into a dueling circle across from him.

"Combination three," commanded Rus without giving Koe any time to adjust.

Rus loved combinations, and Koe tried to keep track of Rus' moves, but remembering all the steps was tough, especially when all he wanted was to run away.

Koe began with a few swipes of his fist, adding in a kick and then retreating. Rus parried each blow easily and advanced.

"Good, faster."

Koe repeated the steps, trying to go faster, but Rus switched up a move, slamming his foot into Koe's face. Koe backpedaled, falling onto his butt and feeling his nose swell up.

"Ow!"

"A battle is not a pattern. Every battle is like a tiger stripe—no two are ever the same."

Koe stomped his foot, his frustration making him angry.

"I don't even want to hurt people," said Koe, still touching his nose that he was sure was broken.

Rus looked pointedly to the other students, training with their teachers with evidently no problem doing so.

"Long ago, magic existed in this world, but as our technology advanced, it left us. The Shadows are the last part of that magic. We serve them because the Shadows accept us, give us a second chance. To do that, we must use the power we wield to make those that the Shadows name to us answer for their crimes. You might not be able to see the scars on your back, but I do. That is what humans are capable of. And they will answer for what they did to you. Won't they?"

Koe wanted to say yes. He wanted to hurt the new Queen so much for what she did, not just to him, but to Aiva and all the other servants that she'd murdered. When it came to it, though, he couldn't imagine going through with it.

Rus saw his hesitation and spoke. "Fine," he said, his voice low and raw. A quick backhand to the face sent Koe staggering off balance and onto the ground once again. Pain coursed through his jaw and cheek. He could feel how hot his face was but had no idea how bad the damage was without being able to see himself. The shadows obscuring a

Knightmare's face would hide his wounds as well.

Koe struggled to his feet, and before he could say anything, Rus hit him again, this time harder. One of the other students chuckled from across the room. Koe could feel blood drip from his lip. It fell from beneath the shadows that covered him to land on the floor, a red splotch that slowly spread into a wider circle. Koe picked himself up, this time ducking before Rus could hit him. He still refused to strike in return. Rus maneuvered, sending his foot directly into Koe's chest. The cycle repeated. Blow after blow.

It didn't matter how much Koe tried to dodge or anticipate Rus' moves, he only ended up on the floor each time, in more pain than before.

It took a few hours without food or water and to be hurt so much that Koe finally cried out, tightening his fists. Then, finally, Koe stepped out of the way as Rus kicked. He swerved around Rus, thrusting his fist toward his waist. Rus disappeared into shadow before his blow could hit. A proud clap reached Koe's ears. He turned to see Rus at the other end of the arena, walking toward him. The other teachers had no visible reaction, but Koe was certain that they were judging how long it had taken him to break. Snickering, the other students were more obvious in their judgement. Rus stood directly in front of Koe, looking down on him.

"You hear those laughs?"

"Yeah." Koe spat blood onto the floor and drew his dagger, keeping a wary eye on Rus.

"If you could see their smiles, wouldn't you want to wipe them off?"

"Yeah," said Koe, gripping the blade in his hand a little tighter.

"Then draw blood." Rus pointed to one student, Hil, who had been the loudest. Koe recalled meeting him once outside the basement before a training session. He'd barely met any of the other students, by choice. Koe hadn't really wanted to. He didn't want to accept that this was his life, whether he liked it or not.

"Should I challenge him?"

"Knightmares have no honor. We do whatever it takes."

"But I don't want to kill him."

"Did I say anything about killing him? Knightmares do not kill other Knightmares. But we aren't a family either. You want to hug it out with him? I didn't think so. Your heart has to be iron. You can draw blood without killing him."

Koe dropped his dagger and marched over. Hil had turned his attention away and was practicing with his teacher. His teacher saw Koe coming and quickly backed off, but it was too late. Koe jumped and tackled Hil from behind. He fell flat on his stomach, and Koe was there to pin him, preventing Hil from turning over.

He slammed his fists into the side of Hil's face as he tried to turn his cheek to see what was going on. Koe wrapped his arm around Hil's neck and yanked his head back. His arm became a blade, tight against Hil's windpipe. Koe could hear the little gasps from Hil as the boy struggled to get free. Koe rested his knee on Hil's back, preventing him from turning. He must be going blue now. Koe released his hold, and Hil wheezed, his lungs working overtime.

As Hil gasped, Koe turned and saw Rus looking his way. He didn't know what Rus was thinking, but for good measure, Koe turned back to Hil and shoved his head into the ground. He heard a loud crack, and a lot of blood followed. A deafening cry came from Hil's mouth. Koe stood up and walked away. Not even Hil's teacher helped him up.

It was only the beginning of Rus' true teachings.

Present Day

Hil didn't last long. He was always approaching Koe, sitting next to him and laughing without saying anything. As Koe's skill improved exponentially over the next few years, the Seer kept a keen eye on him.

Hil thought himself ready to go out in the field and did so without the Seer's permission. Rain pattered the roof he where he stood. When he jumped, his foot slipped on the slick tiles, and the bones in his knees crunched against the ground three stories below. Two bullet holes found their way into his heart from a patrol. He never had a chance.

Now that it was winter, the snow was falling heavily, blanketing the forest floor with powder. Koe arrived at the temple and parked his hoverer in his usual spot. His feet hit the snow and sank a little. Each step toward the temple was accompanied by the crunch of snow beneath his boots. The revolving door opened, and Koe walked into the familiar entryway with white fires glowing from the ceiling hangings.

A commotion in the big throne room reached his ears, and he instantly knew that something important had happened. It couldn't be his success in killing Mankar. That was expected, nothing to celebrate. No, this was something different.

Koe entered the hall to see every Knightmare gathered in small groups or lines, waiting for the Seer to appear. Seeing everyone standing in one room was rare, and it made their whole group feel smaller. There were only about twenty Knightmares left. A fraction of what there used to be.

Koe knew them all, but he couldn't say that any of them were his friends. All of them hated him to some degree. Why should he care for them? All these people were here because they were banished from society. They were outlaws. Some were criminals. They'd be exactly the kinds of people Koe wanted to hunt. But according to the Knightmare philosophy, once the Shadows took your face, everything from the past went with it. Rus never questioned if Koe lied about not killing the King and Queen. He didn't care what had truly happened. What mattered was that he was here, ready to do as commanded.

Based on his suit and tie and his polished manners, Koe believed Rus had been some sort of high royal. It was never confirmed, but a few of Rus' peers believed him to be the criminal known as the 'Boatman Killer'.

The Boatman Killer was said to be a nobleman who would prey on women down on their luck. He'd strike every few months, kidnap a relatively unknown woman, someone who wouldn't be missed, then rape her and leave her dead body in a boat with a gold coin over each of her eyes. Other Knightmares disputed it, claiming the Boatman Killer had been killed by a Knightmare, yet no body was ever found.

Koe knew that most of his peers had similar rumors and stories attached to them. At first it mattered, but as time passed, Koe realized that he couldn't do anything about it. So he kept his distance, and they kept theirs.

A footfall thudded to Koe's right. A dagger moving through the air. It was quiet, but Koe was listening for it. He leaned back as a dagger shot into view from the right. If he hadn't moved, the dagger would now be embedded in his skull. Koe grabbed the wrist holding the dagger and pulled the Knightmare from the shadows and onto the ground. He twisted the Knightmare's hand and seized the dagger as he pinned him on his back.

Koe placed the tip to the Knightmare's neck. Fye. He knew it before he saw him. Fye consistently bathed himself in a pine-scented soap that could be smelled from across the room.

"Almost got you that time, eh, Koe?" Fye laughed. His laugh was shrill and high pitched. Koe sometimes wondered if Fye killed people by laughing so shrilly that their brains suddenly exploded.

Koe slammed the dagger into the ground next to Fye. He was a muscular Knightmare with a bit of a belly. He copied Koe's outfit, but instead of wearing all black with a white scarf, Fye decided to be more colorful, opting for a purple coat, a gold shirt with purple pants and a yellow bandana around his neck. His hat was also a fedora, like Koe's, but it was smaller and deep, dark purple like his jacket.

"You're noisy, and you smell. You might think you were close, but trust me, you weren't." Koe straightened up and purposefully stepped on Fye's face as he walked toward the center of the room. Their scuffle attracted everyone's attention.

In one corner, a few of the older Knightmares who'd been passed over for the role of Seer huddled together. They were old-timers and rarely went on jobs anymore. No one could exactly kick them out, but no one wanted them here either.

Then there was the younger crowd. In a dull brown shirt, wearing an oversized jacket, was Jec. He was a new Knightmare, a recent graduate. He shook in place seeing Koe, quickly bowing.

"Hi, Koe. Hope you're well," he stuttered to say. Koe gave a silent nod of acknowledgement. While kind, his anxiety either made him too brash or too hesitant, both problematic. Yet he had passed his tests. Barely. If Rus had been his teacher, he wouldn't have survived.

Then there was Zos. If she could see Koe's face, she would see his nose scrunch every time he saw her. Koe couldn't recall a pleasant interaction he'd had with her in the decade they'd known each other. She wore a dark maroon coat and hat, with a light tan undershirt. At six feet, she was almost as tall as Koe, and her arms were long, giving her a reach that almost no other Knightmare had. She'd be the best—if it weren't for Koe. She stepped out in front of Koe as he neared. Everyone's attention remained on them. Koe knew what she was going to say before she said it.

"Yes, I got Mankar," Koe said, answering Zos' unspoken question. A few cheers from the other Knightmares sounded through the room. "And it was easy. Even you could've done it."

Only Fye laughed.

"Took you long enough," said Zos. Her smooth voice was like silk, but her tone was haunting. "I'm glad to see you're still in one piece, brother." She gave him a small bow and returned to her group. With all eyes on them, she'd done what she always did—challenged him indirectly.

Koe found a spot far away from the others, near one of the exits. He leaned against the wall, waiting for the Seer to appear. Arms crossed and staring straight ahead, he hoped no other Knightmares would attempt to talk with him. He looked forward to getting the news of the day and then retreating to his room to rest until another job was assigned to him.

The door from the opposite side of the room opened, and in came Rus, wearing the crown of the Seer, his newly appointed position. His tie was perfect, and his vest was clearly ironed. The other Knightmares gave nods of respect. Like Koe, Rus didn't socialize much, preferring to hold himself apart from the others.

Rus approached Koe in the corner before going to the throne.

"You were supposed to get in earlier," he said.

"I was hungry," said Koe. He didn't understand why everyone was questioning him about his delay in getting back.

"Don't treat me like a fool. I know you went to the Iron District.

The Shadows whisper of your movements," hissed Rus.

"No cameras caught whoever did. You sure it was me?" Koe played coy on purpose, seeing Rus' hand twitch. Koe knew he wanted to resort back to his teachings and leave a mark on his cheek.

"Do not doubt the Shadows," warned Rus. "Ever since becoming Seer, I hear them whisper about you a great deal."

"Am I supposed to be honored?"

"You will be Seer one day. It is a blessing that the Shadows have already got their eye on you."

"And everyone here hates me for it," said Koe. The Seer was the one chosen by the Shadows to be their voice. The Shadows showed the Seer the people it marked for death, sent whispers with orders and instructions. It was the Seer's job to lead the rest of the Knightmares. Rus had become the Seer in the last year, and while he still growled at them, he hadn't laid a hand on any of the Knightmares. To some, like Zos, he had become soft.

"Because you're the best," said Rus. "I trained you. Many Knightmares here are old. Too many young ones go out prematurely and die in seconds. The Queen's assassin killed Pyf two days ago while you were gone."

"Pyf was hardly anything special," said Koe.

"But he was a Knightmare. There was a time when that name sent fear through the people's veins. With the latest string of deaths, we're becoming laughable."

Koe shrugged it off, glancing around the room to see most of the others still in conversation but subtly watching them ever since Rus had entered.

"I'm going to need you to fall in line… for what's about to come," said Rus, his tone hushed and his voice gravelly and deep.

"What do you mean?" asked Koe, but Rus strode away from Koe, toward the throne. He sat down, and the others all bowed, except Koe.

"Welcome, brothers and sisters," started Rus. His voice shook the walls of the temple. "The Queen has been declared as the Chosen One."

Koe instantly pushed off wall and stood attentive. A fire burned in his heart. "It is time for us to protect what we have built. This job will not be easy. It will take the best of us to accomplish. For our survival, we must kill the Chosen One."

NINE

QUEEN SERA

"The people of Oarlon are celebrating in the streets, Your Majesty," rang Hanna's voice among the council members. Sera watched the snowflakes lazily land on the glass dome above, instantly melting. The glass was heated just a little for the winter. No one wanted the view obstructed. "They're chanting your name."

A monitor was set up for the Queen showing the local news display with Sera's back and the glowing inscriptions on it. Sera could just see it as she watched the snow. The image switched to a crowd in the Sky District hollering, jumping up and down and dancing in the streets.

"Every news outlet across the land has seen this," added Hanna.

"What's the bad news, Hanna?" asked Sera, returning her gaze to the council. She knew they were holding something back from her. Hanna's voice quieted, her smile dimmed.

"Well, the Leaf, Crown and Sky Districts are celebrating. Ocean and Iron, on the other hand, are… mixed." That meant Wystan and the rest of the underworld were scrambling, wondering how this would affect them. Sera expected this. The Crown would always have enemies, but now that she was the Chosen One, the status quo was upended.

Hanna kept talking, trying to reassure Sera that the news was positive, when a paralyzing headache struck Sera. The pain was localized, but it burned with a fire of unimaginable agony. Sera gripped the armchairs of her throne, digging her nails into the gold fabric. Her head was going to burst. These headaches were going to be the end of her.

Her vision blurred. She could see Thane and others rushing toward her as she fell forward into darkness.

Sera awoke on her knees, but now it was night. Everyone was gone, and she was alone. The dim white lights by the elevator drew her attention. She rubbed her head in relief. The ache vanished. Then the elevator doors opened, and four Knightmares entered the throne room, fanning out into a line. Sera remained kneeling. One stepped forward. His only distinguishing feature was a white scarf tied around his neck. He drew his gun, and before she could say a word, he fired.

The blast jolted her out of her vision and back to reality. Thane was kneeling over her. She lay on her back on the cold ground, a pillow under her head.

"She's back!" announced Thane. The other council members came into view. "Where's the doctor?" Thane asked.

"On her way now," said Hanna.

"No doctor," said Sera."

"But—" started Thane.

"I'm fine." Sera got to her knees, clawing at the armchair of the throne. "Everyone leave. Not you, Thane." All the council members and guards shuffled into the elevator, leaving just the two of them.

"Are you okay?" he asked.

"I said I was fine," she snapped. She wanted to add 'don't worry, you still might be king' to it, but she refrained. "Get Aiva here. Now."

Thane pressed the transmitter in his ear—a small circular device. He muttered a few words while Sera stayed on her knees, staring at her reflection in the black metallic floor.

"She's coming," he said.

"Good, now leave me," said Sera, her breathing uneasy.

"Are you sure? I can—"

"Thane, please don't make me repeat it."

Thane bowed. "Yes, Your Majesty."

He quickly departed, leaving Sera on her knees, holding onto the throne. It only took a few minutes of waiting alone before the elevator door opened again. Her breathing mellowed. The same heavy boots she was so accustomed to hearing marched on the black marble.

With her back toward the elevator, the hairs on the back of her head stood on end as she remembered the Knightmares. But she refused to be afraid. Aiva's purple eyes came into view on her right.

"Another vision?"

Sera bit her lip when Aiva lifted her up onto the throne without asking Sera if she needed help.

Now seated, Sera shook her head, her hand trembling.

"It was so real. Four Knightmares were in this room. Sometimes I know my visions are grand, but this... This one was so real," said Sera.

"You're safe here," said Aiva. "Thane, me, the shield. There's no way they get in here."

Sera waved her off. "No, I'm not afraid of death. What if I don't succeed? What if I die before I find the cure?"

"You're the Chosen One, the Light won't let that happen," said Aiva simply. Sera stood, taking a deep breath and turning her back, pulling her hair over her shoulders.

"The picture we released has most of the prophecy in it—except for the last three lines," said Sera. Aiva casually unzipped Sera's dress, pulling the back down to read the inscription.

> *Child of the Light, you have been chosen*
> *To lead us to our salvation*
> *To break the curse, the Light will need your strength*
> *To cut the ties that bind*
> *To save us from the Darkness*
> *Cleanse the sky of the clouds*
> *Only then*
> *Will you see the secret*

Aiva pulled the fabric of the dress down further to see what was hidden from the picture.

Time runs short
The Light fades
Only a spark remains

"This doesn't mean you won't succeed," said Aiva, zipping the Queen up again and waving her worry away with a flick of her hand.

"I just… didn't think it would be me, you know? I always thought I would find the person, save them and that would be it…" Sera trailed off, seeing a world where someone else had the inscription on their back, and instead of being front and center, she could be behind them as they spoke to the kingdom.

"No, you've always wanted to be a savior. Don't kid yourself," said Aiva.

Sera snapped her head toward Aiva, almost shouting an order to apologize, but she held her tongue. She'd always appreciated Aiva's bluntness. No one else would challenge her. "It's why you called me here, isn't it? For the truth."

"That," began Sera, "and I need you to be on call. No more adventures for now. When I have a lead on the Knightmares—"

"I'll kill them," said Aiva.

"The Knightmares may not be as strong as they once were, but the ones that are coming… You're the only one who can stop them." Sera pulled her hair back off her face and tucked it behind her ear.

In the past, the guards had managed to kill a Knightmare, but Knightmare retribution was swift. Killing one of their own marked the killer for life. Even if the killer displayed superior skill, there was always a more lethal Knightmare to take revenge. The Knightmares couldn't kill Aiva, though. Not only did her shapeshifting help hide her from the Knightmares, but even when a Knightmare did track her down, they'd just lose in open combat. She knew how to think like a Knightmare.

If Sera hadn't blamed her parents' murder on that boy she'd claimed could shapeshift, she would put Aiva on a pedestal to give people hope that even murderers like the Knightmares could be stopped. However, doing so would make the people of Oarlon question how the Queen could employ a shapeshifter like the one who killed her parents, like the one who was never caught. It raised too many questions, so Aiva and her talent would remain their little secret.

"As you wish, Sera," Aiva turned without a bow and left. Her voice was hardened, but Sera paid no attention to it. It'd been that way for years now. After Aiva killed her parents, day by day, her voice grew colder, her eyes more distant, and her sword sharper than ever.

TEN

KOE

The roar of the Knightmares battered Koe's ears, but he paid no attention to it. He'd been waiting, wanting and praying for the Shadows to pick the Queen as the next target. But knowing it would be their hardest kill ever, he assumed it would never happen. He didn't know if it would even be possible. There was no doubt that it would create chaos, dwarfing the unrest from over a decade ago when Aiva killed the King and Queen. With time, that unrest settled. He supposed it would again, Chosen One or not.

"Everyone quiet down," shouted Rus over the tumult. His voice echoed off the corners of the great room, and everyone quieted down. "The Shadows have also whispered to me who is to go. Jec, the Shadows believe that your ascension at such a young age will give this team the vitality it needs to succeed."

Rus shifted his head toward Fye and Zos.

"Fye, your strength, and Zos, your speed are unparalleled. The

Queen and her guard will not stand a chance against you." Koe tapped his foot while the Knightmares around Zos and Fye congratulated them. Zos briefly looked over at Koe, and he could only imagine the evil grin plastered on her face.

He needed to get on this team, Shadows willing or not.

"Silence," hissed Rus. "While he has never led a team before, this mission can't be done without Koe. Take your place as the leader, and execute the Shadows' will." Koe stepped forward. The room remained silent as he stood in front of Rus and the throne. He didn't care that Rus was making him the leader of the team. He could only see the Queen — her white hair, the black tattoos that inked her skin. Those deceitful blue eyes that appeared kind but held a deep evil.

"To kill the Chosen One would destroy any hope for the Light. The Light would fade into nothing and only we would remain," continued Rus. "You leave before dawn." Standing, Rus vacated the throne room and the other Knightmares dispersed. Koe followed Rus out into the dimly lit hallway.

"You knew this was coming before the Shadows told you," Koe accused Rus' back.

"Oh, did my face give it away?" Rus didn't lose a step. Koe simply eyed him as he paced down the hallway.

"You're too calm. Even for you," said Koe. Finally, Rus stopped and turned around. "You taught me to read body language. How to anticipate a lie — or a dagger strike. Even you would be afraid of going after the Queen."

"What matters is the mission. Focus on it." Rus swerved back, throwing his finger in Koe's face. Koe no longer flinched at Rus' quick movements. "Put your personal feelings aside. She's another target. Nothing more."

"She's much more than that," said Koe. He'd been waiting for this, waiting for any opportunity to go after her. Rus moved closer. He wasn't as tall as Koe now, having lost much of the power he once had over him.

"At times, I've lost faith in you, but then I'm reminded of how much you belong here. Out there, they don't care about you. Many don't care about you in here either. Maybe you don't believe I've ever cared about you, but the Shadows always have." Koe instinctively touched his scarf as the echo of Rus' boots grew further and further away.

Koe turned swiftly back around, the end of his coat swirling with the motion, slapping his boots as he walked toward his lodging. Down the spiral staircase were a row of rooms, the familiar white fire torches burned on the walls, guiding him as they always did. Koe's room was at the very end of the hall. His only neighbor was Zos, and in the last fifteen years, he'd never heard a sound from her room.

Inside his room was a wall of shelves full of books. When Koe wasn't training, he would read everything from poetry to history and fiction. During his training, Rus prevented him from participating in anything that could be considered fun. He'd made Koe read, but as Koe got older, he realized he wanted no part in socializing with the other Knightmares anyway.

He took off his hat and hung on a hook near the door. The torch on the wall ignited on its own when he entered, illuminating the small room before him with a soft white glow. His bed was nestled in the corner on the opposite wall of his bookcase. A desk sat against the back wall. He tugged his scarf off and gently folded it, placing it on the edge of the desk.

He kicked his boots off, and his jacket soon followed. He set his weapons down beside his scarf. The more layers he took off, the more of the shadow he could see. Even now he'd still forget he was a shadow. It was only at his most vulnerable that he was forced to remember.

His fingers ran over the silk white scarf. There was still a chance that Aiva was alive. She might still be a servant in the castle. No, if anything, he hoped that she'd escaped from the castle and Oarlon. Imagining her living her dream somewhere beyond the horizon was better than the thought of finding her in the castle still. Would she remember him? He could still picture the scars running down her face and her purple eyes smiling brightly at him. He imagined the soft embrace of their arms wrapping around one another again. The tears they would both shed.

The fantasy played on a loop in his mind for hours. He still felt the same euphoric rush every time he imagined meeting Aiva again.

A soft knock broke him out of his trance. He walked toward the door and opened it. There before him was Jec, who quickly bowed.

"Don't, Jec."

Jec immediately stood straight up. "Sorry, sir. Old habit."

Koe sighed. "Don't call me that."

Jec had a habit of idolizing different Knightmares. It came off innocently enough, but everyone knew he was a self-serving bootlicker.

"Sorry, Koe," he said.

Koe stared at Jec. He wasn't sure why Jec was here, and it took a few moments of them staring at one another for Jec to speak.

"I was wondering if I could talk to you?"

Koe sighed and let him in. Jec grabbed the desk chair before Koe offered it to him, sitting down across from Koe, who took a seat on his bed.

"If you're here for lessons, I won't teach you," said Koe. Jec had asked for lessons with Koe several times, but Koe was never interested in training anyone, so he always refused.

"No, it's about this mission," Jec said. His voice was young—Koe could still hear the cracks. His voice was beginning to catch up with his tall, slender frame however.

"What about it?"

"I know I only have a few kills, but I'm ready for anything."

Koe was glad Jec couldn't see his face. He grinded his teeth and furrowed his eyebrows.

"The Shadows wouldn't have picked you if you weren't," said Koe, monotone and disinterested. He could barely bring himself to enunciate his words.

"You don't believe that," said Jec, a bit of venom slipping into his voice.

Another silence grew between them, moments where Koe wished he could see Jec's face. When Jec's hand twitched, Koe smiled.

"What are you saying, Jec?" said Koe.

"Some of the others say you don't believe in the Shadows. Not entirely."

"What do you think of that?"

Jec shifted in his seat.

Another voice answered. "He thinks the same thing everyone else does. You don't belong here. You don't deserve the attention the Shadows give you," said Zos, leaning against the door frame. Jec almost jumped out of his seat. Koe remained still.

"You're almost as loud as Fye," said Koe. In reality, Zos was an expert at sneaking up on people, but he couldn't give her that satisfaction.

"If I wanted to sneak up on you, you'd never know. And who's to say how many times I might have already?" said Zos, strolling into Koe's room and examining his bookshelf. "You've added a lot." She ran her fingers across the books and turned her attention back to Jec. She placed her hands on Jec's shoulders. "Get out of here, rookie."

Jec bolted from the room without another word as Zos took a seat in the now vacant desk chair. She drew one of her daggers, holding it up to her eyes.

"You look comfy," Zos said.

Koe smiled. His heartbeat was steady. "You sent Jec in here to question me? Are you really that desperate?"

"Oh, I didn't need to. Everyone already talks about it," said Zos smugly. "Why do the Shadows care so much about the one Knightmare who doesn't care about them? And why is this Knightmare going to be the next Seer? It can't be just about skill."

"Rus will be Seer for a long time," he replied.

"Long enough for favorites to change," said Zos. Her head turned to Koe's weapons on the desk and back at him. "Is it really this easy?"

Koe chuckled. "You're a good Knightmare, Zos. If something happens to Rus and the Shadows declare me the Seer, I'll decline and recommend you. Now, stop eyeing my weapons before I show you why you're not the favorite."

Zos chuckled and leaned forward. "You would decline the blessing of the Shadows? Why?"

"The Chosen One is all I care about," said Koe. "Nothing else matters." He would never reveal the true reason. Other than Rus, no one else alive here knew his backstory. He wanted to keep it that way.

"Well, unlike you, I have faith in the Shadows. If they chose you, I believe we'll succeed. But I won't pretend. I'm hoping this is your last mission."

Koe snatched his gun off the desk and pointed it at her before she could react. "With any luck, it will be. Now get out."

ELEVEN

KOE

That night, Koe cleaned his gun and sharpened his daggers twice. He kept seeing images of the Queen, her body laid out on the ground of the throne room and him standing over her. Blood ran from her stomach as she crawled helplessly away. She threw up a hand toward him as he pointed his gun at her. The recoil of the bullet leaving the chamber sent shudders up his arm and all through his body. Then as he stared at the Queen's body, there was nothing but silence.

He replayed the kill over and over as he marched across the hallway, up a flight of stairs to a small chamber just off the Knightmare temple's main throne room. Fye was already swirling around on a stump of a chair with no back while Zos leaned against the wall across. Jec was right next to Zos, whispering in her ear. Once Koe walked in, Jec immediately backed away and sat down next to Fye.

"There he is! Team leader!" said Fye. "You ready for this, captain?"

"Don't call me that, Fye," said Koe.

"Someone's a little cranky."

Koe ignored the comment and stood patiently, waiting for the door to the Seer's personal conference room to open. Thankfully, he only had to wait a few minutes. Within, white fire burned brightly. The conference room was a perfect square with a rectangular table in the center. Rus sat at the head of the table, and the light from one of the torches reflected off his crown.

"Be seated," said Rus.

Koe took the chair at the other end of the table. Jec took his place close to Zos, while Fye had a side of the table all to himself.

"The Shadows know how difficult this mission will be, and I don't need to remind you of the importance. If we do not succeed, not only will the Queen break the curse, she will find us. If she does, even we won't be a match for her army."

"We will not fail," said Jec.

Zos quickly slapped him on the back of the head. "Don't speak over the Seer," she said.

Rus' chair scraped as he pushed it back. His lanky build slid over to Jec, and he leaned down, inches away.

"I hope you're right. Even the Shadows can't see the future. There's a very good chance none of you will return." Rus patted Jec on the back, and Koe was certain their newest Knightmare was trembling. "The Queen's power is growing. She's desperate. Power and desperation are a formidable, unpredictable combination. The faster you move, the better chance you'll have." Rus moved to a crate in the corner of the room, returning moments later. He threw the head of a man with maggots crawling out of his eyes onto the table. Fye's high-pitched shrill overpowered the audible groan coming from Jec.

"This is Pyf," said Rus. "The Queen's assassin took his life, and you can be sure the Queen will send them after you as well. When you do find them, do not hesitate." One maggot crawled out of Pyf's nose and fell splat on the table.

"You will go to Wystan," said Rus. Koe leaned forward off his chair. Wystan? The underworld crime lord? "There's no way around the castle's shield, but Wystan has a contact that can smuggle you in. Once inside, there should be nothing to stop you. May the Shadows protect you." Standing, all the others bowed, leaving one by one. But Koe remained, placing his hands on the top of the chair and leaning on them.

"What's on your mind, Koe?"

"Wystan? That's our plan? He's no more our ally than the Queen is," said Koe. After all, Koe himself had killed so many of Wystan's people and destroyed several of their operations, costing them money and power.

"He hates the Queen as much as we do," replied Rus with a growl in his voice.

Koe took a deep breath. He hated the idea of begging the likes of Wystan for help. He was a murderer, rapist, drug trafficker and more. Scum like that deserved to die as much as the Queen did.

"Right," said Koe.

"You're not prepared to lead this mission, are you?" said Rus.

Koe quickly faced Rus and took two steps toward him, standing straight.

"What are you saying?" asked Koe.

Rus chuckled with a mighty exhale. Koe could smell the garlic lingering on Rus' breath from his morning meal.

"Even Jec's face is hidden from me, but I still see your face, plain as day."

Koe's grit his teeth together like rocks rubbing together. "Do you doubt the Shadows and what they've shown you about me? Even worse, do you doubt yourself?" asked Koe, referencing the brutal lessons that Rus put him through the last fifteen years.

Rus stayed silent.

To admit any type of failure, even small, was unheard of from the older Knightmare.

When he spoke, his voice was low and sinister.

"Kill the Chosen One and become part of the Shadows once and for all."

Rus left without another word.

The Knightmares holstered their guns and sheathed their daggers, keeping their weight light. It was a risk to not bring supplies like food and water since this wouldn't be a quick trip, but each of them had starved before. Each had stolen before. They were ready to do whatever it took.

The night sky was still dark as they used their hoverers to travel through the woods. They were going the long way, all the way around the perimeter of the forest to the other side of the city. They were going to enter through the Iron District. The winter snowfall piled mounds of white powder taller than Koe himself.

The hoverers puttered to a stop. Koe could see the Iron District's entrance not too far away, but the sun was rising, so any chance of sneaking in now wouldn't work. Knightmares couldn't disappear in the sunlight, plus they'd been travelling through night. They would need their rest before potentially fighting a war with Wystan and his organization.

They found a patch where the overhanging trees blocked out the sky. Each one chose a tree to lay against, though they were still fairly close to one another. Koe took off his scarf and folded it gently on the ground next to him.

"Where'd you get that?" asked Jec, who was directly across from him.

"Oh, the scarf! Don't ask, mate. That's just a bad idea," said Fye. "He loves that scarf. Won't let *anyone* touch it."

"He's clearly desperate, clinging to what was," said Zos. "The real question we should be asking is if he's truly dedicated to being a Knightmare."

Fye laughed his shrill, high-pitched laugh that rang in Koe's ears for several seconds after he was done.

Koe paid no attention to them, but everything in his body

groaned. He couldn't believe that he had to do this with a team, especially this one. Fye was just annoying and unpredictable. Zos was untrustworthy and wanted him dead. Jec was naïve and susceptible to the whims of others. Koe kept silent though. There was no point in engaging.

"Did the scarf belong to someone you love?" asked Jec. Once again, Koe was glad no one could see his face. He knew his eyes would've moved though, giving some indication that they were onto something.

"Don't bother, Jec. No one knows Koe's story. Just the rumors," said Fye.

"Rumors?" asked Jec. He kept turning his head back and forth between Koe and Fye like he was scared that Koe was going to attack him. He had some confidence, Koe would give him that much. Not many would ask a Knightmare questions so personal.

"Just a few," said Fye.

"Why do you care?" said Koe. Jec's foot softly tapped against the ground over and over.

"What if your feelings get in the way of the mission? Our lives are on the line, and if we fail, the Shadows are at risk."

Koe let Jec's confession sit in the open for a few minutes without moving a muscle. There was no answer needed, nothing he cared to say. Over the course of the silence, Jec's foot tapped faster and faster.

"Why are you here, Jec?" asked Koe, wanting to turn the conversation away from him and onto someone else.

"We're not supposed to—" started Zos.

"Ah, come on, Zos! No one follows that rule. We're all a bit curious about what lies beneath the shadows," Fye said. "Think I might be handsome, do you?" Fye shuffled over closer to Zos and was greeted by a quick jab to the throat, sending Fye reeling back. Zos cracked her knuckles as she massaged the hand that hit him.

"I'm good," said Fye, gasping between breaths and waving his hand for Jec to speak.

"Why should I?" asked Jec, crossing his arms. "I'm not leading this mission."

Koe drew his dagger and threw it in a straight line directly at Jec's head. Jec moved in time as the dagger stabbed into the tree. Koe called it back to his hand, and splinters of bark fell onto Jec's shoulder. Fye erupted into broken laughter, his voice still recovering, while Zos stayed silent.

"You... You almost killed me!" yelled Jec. His voice rose a few octaves. He couldn't believe what Koe had done.

"I wouldn't miss."

"It would have hit my head if I didn't duck!" exclaimed Jec.

"Then it's a good thing you did," said Koe. Jec looked to Zos, but she just looked away.

"Talk," said Koe. "That's an order."

Jec dusted away the splinters of wood and cleared his throat.

"I had a brother. He was older than me. He worked for a couple of merchants in the Iron District. He made pretty good money and it helped keep us afloat, but then he started gambling. Got deep with some of Wystan's thugs. He stole from the merchants to repay his debts, and when the merchants found out, they just killed him right then and there. He had no trial, nothing. The merchants paid people off, so they didn't care about the law. There were no consequences. It never even made the news. So after a few years of starving, I tracked down the merchants, and I delivered the justice that no one had given me.

"It was a clumsy kill. I only managed to stab one of them before the other one attacked. He was stronger. He disarmed me, but I kept a second knife hidden. He didn't see that one coming. But so many people saw what I'd done, there was no way I would get away with it, so I ran into the forest and was found by the Knightmares. That city out there... The way I see it, it can all burn," Jec finished.

Koe wanted to sympathize, saying he too knew the craving for revenge Jec felt deep in his heart. One that remained inside him for so long. Unlike Jec, he didn't have the satisfaction of the kill.

"After you killed them, did you find peace?" asked Koe.

"Yeah. Becoming a Knightmare was the best thing I ever did, besides killing them. I found my calling."

A bit of envy crept into Koe's chest. He longed for that peace, for that moment when his dreams turned into reality and he didn't have to dream anymore.

"Oh, how heroic!" mocked Fye. "Oh, my brother died, and I killed the people who did it? Who the fyrk cares?" Jec immediately drew his legs to his chest, making himself smaller. "I'm tired of all these sob stories. Where are all the good ol' fashioned stories?"

"Not all of our stories can be yours," said Zos dryly.

"What did you do?" Jec asked Fye. His voice was now more hesitant.

"I was the Butcher of the Bells, kid. Not the fyrking copycat. The original."

"Who?" asked Jec.

Fye immediately gasped and yelled out, "I was all over the news!"

"Yeah, like fifteen years ago," said Zos. "There was a week when Fye over here kidnapped kids and killed them at midnight to the sound of the bells in the Leaf District. He killed three of them and then was swiftly caught. The end."

"You make it sound so dull! No, these kids were outsiders at school. I was doing them a favor. They had no friends, they weren't smart. These kids never should've been born, okay? They were just one more person sucking up whatever air was left," he continued, "and I escaped before they could lock me up. Then a few years later, a kid is killed at the sound of the bells, and everyone think it's me again, but no, it's just some dumb copycat who was caught after just one day."

"I'm surprised you influenced anyone," said Zos wryly.

Jec ignored her, absorbed in the story in a way that made him seem suddenly very young. "What happened to the copycat?" he asked.

"Went to prison or something…" said Fye, trailing off.

"And?" said Zos.

"I slit his throat, okay? Is that what you wanted me to say?" Fye threw his hands up.

"He wasn't your target," said Zos, before turning to Koe. "But he's far from the only one to go after a target he wasn't supposed to, isn't he?" Koe felt all their faces turn toward him. He drew one of his daggers and twirled it in his hand.

"Oh, we know all about it. How many times have you been disciplined by the Seer?" asked Fye with a small, high-pitched chuckle.

"Probably higher than you can count, Fye," said Zos.

"Brutal! That's why I love you, Zos," said Fye. "Come on, Koe. Share your story. We know the rumors. Let the kid in. We're all going to die anyway."

Koe balanced the bottom of the hilt on his index finger, and with his other hand, spun the dagger. He didn't need to concentrate — the dagger kept spinning without any risk of toppling over.

"I grew up in the Leaf District. I was a privileged child," began Koe. "My parents were rarely home. They were often working and had no time for my sister and I." Koe watched Zos as he continued, keeping his dagger perfectly balanced. "My sister was older and would often receive the brunt of my parents' hand when things weren't perfect — a trait that she learned and used on me when they were gone. One day, she broke my hand, a hand that hasn't truly healed. I bashed her head in with the first thing I grabbed. I realized I liked how it felt. My parents tried to have me arrested, but I ran. I'm sure I came back and visited them when I was a Knightmare. That I'm not certain of, though."

Zos said nothing. Jec and Fye looked over to her.

"That true, Zos?"

"How did you know?" asked Zos, her hand resting on the hilt of her dagger. Since a decade earlier, when Zos joined the Knightmares, Koe never heard Zos' voice falter, never revealed a weakness—until now. Koe stopped his dagger from spinning.

"Just stories."

"No one knew that. Not even the Knightmare who found me."

"Always be paying attention, Zos." Koe sheathed his dagger.

He remembered he was sent out on a mission, one of his first, when Zos arrived at the Knightmare temple. Usually there were some rumors, but there were none about her. No one knew anything, so after Koe had finished killing his target, he did some investigating in the news archives. Her story never broke in the news throughout the city, only the Leaf District, where crime was almost unheard of unless some underworld henchman was dumb enough to attack the quiet residential sector.

Zos' parents had tried to cover it up as much as possible. They couldn't let people know that their own daughter had killed their other daughter. It would ruin their reputation, so they staged it as if their daughters were both killed. Yet, there was only one body. Koe hadn't known much about crime scenes at that point, but upon examining the blood pattern, he could tell that based on the splatter, Zos' older sister had been hit with a blunt object held by a very small person.

Before long, Zos' parents started turning on each other, hurting one another as they only had each other left to control. Once Zos began treating Koe like an enemy a few years later, Koe went back to the house and discovered the parents were long gone. No one knew what happened to them, but when he interrogated a few of the neighbors, he learned they'd disappeared around the same time Zos went out on her first couple of missions.

Koe had done the same type of investigating for several other Knightmares that didn't have well-known backstories. Some of the older members were harder and at times nearly impossible to investigate, but these newcomers were the Knightmares he might work with in the future, and any knowledge he had available to use might be needed — especially with the way they all hungered to kill him.

Maybe it wasn't because he was the favorite. Maybe it was because they knew, deep down, he wasn't like them. Like Zos had pointed out, he didn't follow the Knightmare code often. At the very least, he bent the rules.

"Well, Jec, meet the shapeshifting murderer who killed the old King and Queen," said Zos. Koe was sure Zos was smiling. Her tone had turned to gleeful. She thought she had him. How very wrong she was.

Fye gasped audibly. "Now you're back to finish the job, eh?" he said.

Koe took his hat off and put it over his eyes. Let them think what they wanted to. The rumor at least reinforced why he was here. If they knew the truth, that he was set up, a runaway, it might draw more attention to his tenuous commitment to the Shadows than he wanted.

Koe closed his eyes, the distant talking of the others slowly faded as he let his mind run to the fantasies he'd always wished were true.

His dream took him to a field of grass, with the castle of Oarlon barely visible in the distance.

Aiva sat across from him. She was an adult now. Her features were blurry, but he could still make out the purple eyes and the scars on her face. They were sitting, just gazing at each other as the sun went down.

She smiled at him and grabbed his hand. He realized he could see the skin on his hand. He quickly withdrew his hand and touched his face. His fingers ran through his facial hair.

Aiva smiled again and placed her hand on his cheek too. He could hear light footsteps crunching a few feet away from them. He looked around but could see no one.

"Look at me," she said, redirecting his face back to her. "Just stay with me." Her voice repeated over and over. He couldn't take his eyes off her.

A faint whistling pierced the air, but it wasn't coming from his fantasy. Koe knew the sound all too well—the sound of a Knightmare dagger traveling towards a target.

Twelve Years Ago

Three years into his training, Koe laid his head on his pillow, his eyes shut, drifting into the darkness when the door burst opened. He found

Rus with a dagger out. His suit was wrinkled, a rarity. His tie was loose. His clothes reeked of rum, and upon further inspection, parts of his vest looked damp.

Rus swung the dagger toward his bed. Koe swerved in time and pushed himself up. With a swift kick, Rus retreated a step outside the door. Koe grabbed his daggers from his bedside and entered his battle stance at the doorway. White light poured in from torches in the hall, but the shadows covering Koe's face shielded his vision.

Rus sheathed his dagger, tightened his tie and cleared his throat. All a trick.

"I thought you were—"

"Going to kill you? Good," said Rus. "That was easy. Soldiers are loud. People who kill Knightmares are not." Rus left the hallway, with the white flame of the torches vanishing as he disappeared.

Three nights later, the sound of a door unlocking took Koe out of his deep slumber, dreaming of trees and fields of grass and running with Aiva. He opened one eye to see not just the door unlocked but already open. The next sound was a gun loading, pointing right at Koe. A second later, the bullet would've been lodged in his head. Instead, it found his mattress. Koe couldn't dodge the second bullet—it skimmed his shoulder.

"Next time, that goes into your arm," said Rus.

For the next month, Koe did not sleep. Rus came into his room almost every night, attempting to shoot Koe, and when Koe pushed him out of the room, Rus retreated. Those nights were better than the ones when Rus didn't come by. The empty nights were the sleepless ones, the ones where Koe could only hold his arms, keeping his ears perked up, hoping to hear the sound of Rus silently walking in so he could shove him out and fall into a deep sleep.

Then the dagger training began. The click of the loaded gun was replaced by the soft whistling they made as they sliced Koe's leg the first night. He hadn't even heard Rus walk in. After a few failed attempts to wake up, Koe stayed up all night fending Rus off, but Rus was not impressed.

"So you'll stay up every night forever?" he yelled, unleashing a huge slap across Koe's face before leaving. Koe took what small energy he had left from staying up for nights on end and charged at Rus as he walked down the hallway back to his own room. Koe kept his feet light, dagger in hand. Rus swiftly countered, throwing him onto the ground.

"Even if you killed me to end your suffering, there is another me waiting to kill you tomorrow. You must sleep, but you will never rest."

For four straight months, Koe listened for the dagger whistling through the air. Rus came to his room less and less as he got better, more vigilant. The cuts from the times he'd failed healed, and Koe hadn't slept deeply since.

Present Day

That familiar sound was here now. His eyes flew open, and he threw himself away from the tree as a dagger sped into the bark where his head had been laying. Koe turned invisible under the shadows of the tree, recovering immediately to his feet. His footprints in the snow gave his position away, but it didn't matter. The sun was out, and it was daytime, meaning they couldn't disappear as easily. Jec was the only one standing. His hand was outreached, calling his dagger back to him.

Koe reappeared and tackled him into a sunny spot, giving them a small arena. The snow stuck to their clothes. Jec scrambled to his feet and frantically looked toward Zos, who had just woken up along with Fye. They both stood up but did nothing.

"What the fyrk is going on?" said Fye.

"This little rat just tried to kill me," said Koe, pointing to the tree where the mark of a dagger had split the bark.

"Oh, he's fyrked," said Fye, shrugging his shoulders and taking a step back. Smart, thought Koe. Fye loved to try to get the jump on Koe, but even he wouldn't gamble if he didn't have to. He certainly wouldn't partner with the rookie.

"Zos!" yelled Jec. Zos did nothing but watch. Koe chuckled.

"A mouse might help the lion, thinking it's won an ally, but the lion has just won a free meal. She set you up. You kill me, you get blamed—and the Knightmares kill you."

With his free hand, Jec went for his gun, but Koe was quicker. Koe drew one of his daggers and sliced Jec's hand as he pulled the gun out.

"You were smart to use your dagger. Guns are easier. I could hear them being drawn and the noise of the bullet. Daggers are quieter, not many would hear them. But you never trained with Rus," said Koe. Jec yelled out, attacking Koe with basic form and only average speed. Koe swerved out of the way easily, applying two quick cuts to Jec's back. Jec fell to his knees, and Koe placed the tip of his dagger to Jec's throat.

"You do not deserve the love of the Shadows," said Jec against the blade. "You do not deserve to lead this mission for them. You do not deserve the glory!" His voice shook, but he held still. "I won't die for you."

There it was. The truth. Jec was afraid to die. Koe sheathed both his daggers and brushed the snow off his jacket.

"With me, you have a chance. Without me, you'll surely die," said Koe. "There's truth in the whispers you've heard, but all you need to know for certain is that I will kill the Queen. Put your doubts aside, because if you question me again, I don't care that the Shadows put you on this mission—I will gladly take you off it."

Jec scurried away.

"The sun will be setting soon. Get ready." Koe walked past Zos. "Good try."

TWELVE

QUEEN SERA

The fog swirled around Sera. Dirt and mud clung to her white cloth shoes. The hem of her white dress dragged against the ground, ruining it. The cold air scraped against her cheeks. She walked forward, but every step was the same. The scenery was the same. A whiff of blood filled her nose. It was the same rotten odor of death she'd smelled when looking upon her parents.

A nearby clanging caught her attention, and she moved toward it, edging closer as the sounds of grunts and cries grew in the impenetrable fog.

A man in the black and gold armor of the kingdom, with white streaks in his black hair, swung his sword at another soldier, similarly clad. Their swords clashed, the soldier slicing the man with the white streaks across the cheek. His face was still young but more angular. However, it was the hair that gave him away. This was Gaven, but at least a decade older.

Gaven swung wildly, missing completely. Sera saw the sword of the other man rise in the air. She tried to move forward, but her feet were now submerged beneath the dirt. She tried to yell, but her voice was soundless. She tried to crawl forward, yet her nails dug into the dirt. The clanging of swords disappeared, replaced only by the sound of her beating heart, thumping faster and faster.

The soldier swung, impaling Gaven in the gut. Gaven cried out, slowly falling to the ground as the fog crept over him. Sera closed her eyes, only to open them and find herself standing in front of the sink of her bathroom. Water ran over her hands, but for a moment, all she could see was blood. The door swung open, sending a jolt through Sera's heart as Thane entered, sword drawn.

"What are you doing?" said Sera, even though she was fully clothed. She switched the faucet off and dried her hands on the towel next to the door. She stood tall, despite the ache that plagued her heart.

"I heard screaming. Another vision?" Thane sheathed his sword and put his arms around Sera.

"One that doesn't show me any real meaning," started Sera, knowing she was deflecting. She couldn't think about it too hard. She needed to look at it objectively instead. "It was Gaven, but older, dying in battle. Is that his fate? Why show me this now?"

"You were worrying about him last night, about what would happen if you weren't here," reminded Thane.

Sera waved him off, putting a large diamond necklace on, fitting it to her neck and letting it rest against her collar. "I just... I just need my

116

visions to not be so metaphorical. Then I could act on them. The people are already wondering why I haven't done anything."

"It's only been a day!" exclaimed Thane. "This can't be solved overnight, but you will do it, I know you will." He brought her in closer, squeezing her softly while kissing her neck. "You're the Chosen One. You can do anything. Now, let's stay up here and recreate last night."

Sera pulled his hands off her and shook her head, marching out of the bathroom.

"Gaven's swim test is happening now, and I don't want to miss it."

On an upper floor of the castle was a magnificent indoor pool, big enough to fit hundreds of people comfortably. Bringing the water in was a feat in engineering itself, a mark of the Royal family's power. Black reflective tiles ran along the pool edges. A skylight from above, almost as large as the roof itself, let the light from the sun glimmer against the pool water. Tall windows like the one in the throne room paneled the side walls.

Royals often had extravagant parties here. There was a full bar in the connecting room, where all the adults could drown themselves in alcohol. Sera never participated. She never liked swimming but believed it to be an important skill—one that she wanted her son to learn. To advance to the next stage, Gaven would have to swim back and forth across the pool multiple times, each time with a different stroke.

Sera sat in a golden throne, smaller than the official one but still ornate, placed a few feet away from the pool. She didn't mind being splashed, but some of the kids loved to cannonball, and she was in no mood to change again. She watched the many kids playing in the shallow end. Gaven worked hard with his instructor, swimming into the deep end. He showed no fear or any kind of hesitation.

Thane stood to her left. Sera knew he was also watching Gaven. Gaven looked up to Thane and his bravery. He thought the world of being a soldier, but Sera knew that Gaven had to be more. He would be king, and Sera would need to do everything she could to prepare him for it. She wouldn't let her vision become a reality.

Thane leaned down and whispered in her ear. "His instructor says she's really impressed with Gaven. He's improving significantly."

"Yes, he is," said Sera quietly, still looking at Gaven practicing his breast stroke.

"You're still thinking about your vision?" asked Thane. He knelt down next to her. Sera didn't mind. As long as he didn't try touching her. They had to keep up appearances. But then his hand touched her shoulder, and she shrugged him off in irritation.

"Thane," she said sternly. Thane cleared his throat and stood up again. Gaven climbed the few steps out of the pool. A guard waited there to throw a towel over him.

As he dried himself off, Gaven's eyes met his mother's and he instantly recoiled. Clearly, he was still upset about the excursion to the interrogation chamber and what followed. He'd get over it. Just like she'd get over this fear from her vision. Gaven walked slowly over to her.

"Give me a hug," said Sera. Gaven did so, but it was soft and nothing like the hugs he used to give. "Did you pass?"

Gaven pulled back and shrugged. "I did," he said half-heartedly.

"What's wrong?" said Sera.

"I can't figure out how to do the butterfly right... and the other kids were making fun of me."

Sera searched the pool. There were several kids playing about. Gaven interacted with most of them regularly, as they were all kids belonging to upper-class families, either living in the castle or right outside of it.

"Who?" demanded Sera.

"Iaz," said Gaven. "It's okay though. I think he was just teasing." Gaven dipped his head.

Sera could tell that their teasing had really bothered him. She placed one finger below his chin and guided his head back up so he was looking at her.

"You are a prince. If it bothers you, we can talk to the parents and let them know." Thane cleared his throat. Sera side-eyed him, silencing him. She didn't want to hear whatever he was going to say, but he spoke anyway.

"Iaz has a habit of this, doesn't he, Gaven?

Gaven nodded. Sera smiled at him.

"You sure that's the only thing that's bothering you?"

"He... also said you might be the Chosen One. What does that mean?" Sera pulled Gaven in closer.

"Well, you know how the air is making everyone sick? Let me tell you a little secret." Sera leaned forward and whispered in his ear. "I'm going make it all better." She pulled back and grinned. Gaven gave her an answering smile, almost as if things were back to normal between them.

"Whoa," he said. "How are you going to do that?"

"Well... I'm still figuring that out," she admitted.

"Maybe you just need to talk to someone, like a friend or something, who can tell you what to do."

Sera pulled Gaven in closer again and hugged him. She kissed his head.

"I will be talking to so many people. And remember, when you need something, you can always come to me. You can always ask me anything, Gaven. I'm here for you." Sera wanted to make sure her son knew that. That was the mistake her parents made — they'd kept their distance from her. It made it all the easier to kill them and feel nothing doing it. She especially wanted to reinforce that after the interrogation incident.

"Okay. I do have a question," said Gaven.

"Go for it," said Sera with a smile, pleased with his change in demeanor.

"Why can't I call Daddy my father in public?"

Sera bit her tongue. Thane was right there, and she knew he would hear whatever answer she gave.

"It's complicated. Just formality."

"Formality?"

"A rule that we have to follow as Queen and captain of the guard. Maybe soon though, once this is all over, I will be able to make your dad king, and then you can call him whatever you like."

Gaven smiled, his head spun toward Thane. "Did you hear that?"

Thane just winked without turning his head. He knew how important it was to keep up appearances, not just for the people around them but for Sera in particular.

"All right, now go shower."

Gaven nodded and rushed off. Sera told him what she needed to. She honestly didn't know what to do with Thane, but this bought them time until after she cleaned the air and saved the people. Maybe then she'd feel differently about allowing him to become king. She looked over at Thane. How could she live with her desire for the coarse touch of his palm on her back, his smile when his gaze met hers, his voice singing encouragements, all while needing to keep him a foot away at all times?

"Thane, tell Hanna and the others — schedule some civilians to come meet with me. Make it televised. It'll buy us some time. Meanwhile, search for gurus of the Light. Not the regular advisors," said Sera, quickly clarifying. "I want counselors who are off the beaten path."

"Should I ask why?" said Thane.

"No," said Sera quickly, before taking a breath. "I just need a new perspective, someone who cares more about the Light than about pleasing their queen."

THIRTEEN

KOE

With the sun behind the horizon, the Knightmares moved swiftly toward the city's entrance and into the Iron District, near-invisible shadows in the growing darkness. Koe paid no attention to his comrades as he led them. He knew they would keep up as they were trained to and stay out of sight. Outposts with searchlights were stationed along the outskirts. Each had two to three guards they would need to avoid.

Almost every year, a young Knightmare would make a comment, saying they were *thinking* of taking out an outpost for fun. To do so would be easy, but it ignored the Knightmare code. Their marks were handed down from the Shadows to the Seer, then assigned to them — going rogue was against the rules and garnered a swift punishment.

All that was required now was to avoid the searchlights. The guards knew that if a Knightmare was spotted, they'd act in self-defense. Rus believed the guards purposefully did a bad job of using the searchlights so that they wouldn't spot a Knightmare.

The lights were still tonight, shining on one patch of snowy grass. Koe ran in a straight line past the outposts and into the Iron District. Immediately, the world went from dead quiet to deafeningly loud. The stench of alcohol and vomit filled every corner. Among all the buildings, not one was a place of residence. Every one was either a bar, club or restaurant that was accustomed to the drooling late-night customers.

Koe slowed to a halt before entering the lit street where people sang out of tune and stumbled over their own feet, trying to dance. Lines of people waited to get into specific clubs and bars. The snow and the cold didn't seem to bother the majority of them. Some wore coats, others wore very little. A body lay motionless, face down in the snow. Anywhere else, it might be assumed that the air had killed them, but here in the Iron District, dead and too drunk to move were interchangeable.

Despite the heavy coughs, the bloody noses, and being unable to stand — and not from drinking — the crowds remained. The poisoned air might be killing them, but nothing would stop these people from having the time of their lives. And thanks to Wystan, every patron could live out their deepest, often darkest desires. Koe had seen it just days ago. For the right price, Wystan would let patrons hack limbs off servants, rape them, murder them. As long as they paid up, nothing was off limits.

Wystan himself was a mystery to everyone. Only a few knew his face, making it that much harder to find him. But he did have several prominent, popular establishments that he would likely want to monitor in person.

"Zos, Fye, check out the Chatty Cat Club. Ask around for Wystan. You won't find him, but it'll get word out that we're looking for him. Jec, you're with me. We're going to the Mosquito Bite."

Koe wanted Jec close to him now, allowing him less time for scheming with Zos. While he didn't think Jec would try again, Koe wouldn't take any chances. Zos and Fye climbed up the pipe on the building next to them to the rooftop, disappearing into the cover of darkness. Jec was about to follow when Koe grabbed him by the collar and pulled him back. "We're not going that way." Jec brushed Koe's grip off him and straightened his jacket, saying nothing.

Koe took a step into the light, and Jec followed. It was rare for a Knightmare to walk among the people. Usually it didn't take long for guards to be called. The guards would act if they had enough numbers. Not in the Iron District though. Many people were too belligerent to notice, and the few who did would never call guards here. No—they'd call Wystan.

The Mosquito Bite had one of the longest lines and a huge bouncer letting a few people in at a time. Whispers traveled through the crowd as Jec and Koe walked alongside them toward the front. A few people ditched at the sight of the two Knightmares approaching, but most stayed. Knightmares were often treated like a bear. No one wanted to see one up close and coming after them, but as long as they weren't the target, it would be rare for bystanders to be hurt.

The bouncer puffed up his chest and rested a hand on the gun holstered at his hip. If he was afraid, he didn't show it.

"We're here to talk to Wystan," said Koe.

"He's not here," said the bouncer. The bouncer guessed where Koe's eyes were perfectly. They locked eyes, each staring at the other to the exclusion of everything else. Big mistake.

"Then we'll get a drink."

"You're not allowed here."

"You're brave, I'll give you that. But you've already lost." Jec appeared behind him, having been invisible for the last few seconds. One of his daggers was pointed directly at the bouncer. The tip was a millimeter from his neck. "You can let us in or we can paint the rocks a new color. Your choice."

Koe tapped his foot in warning. The bouncer nodded hurriedly and took a step away from the door. Koe walked past him with Jec behind. "Good work." Jec still didn't say anything. Whether Jec appreciated the compliment or just hated Koe even more, Koe wasn't sure. He also didn't care.

The long red hallway opened up to a huge bar with a dance club far at the back. Red lights dangled from the ceiling, reflecting off the black metallic walls and floor. Music blared throughout the club. All the patrons in the club area were dancing their hearts out. Most danced alone, but there were a few with partners. One such pair were facing each other, swaying their hips against the other to the rhythm. They leaned in and kissed passionately—their love being the only thing in existence. Koe found himself staring too long, thinking about a life he never had.

"What is it?" asked Jec over the loud music.

"Nothing," said Koe almost under his breath, too quiet for Jec to hear. Koe moved on, pushing past anyone in his way. The patrons at the bar began to notice the Knightmares among them, some looking around nervously and others brazenly disinterested. Koe clocked a few as Wystan's people. They were less drunk than most. Their eyes were constantly scanning the crowd, and most importantly, their guns rested on their hips.

Koe pushed past everyone to the bar where a sole bartender took orders, tall and lanky like a light pole and with teeth like crooked piano keys. The bartender's hair was neat and tidy, a contrast to the disheveled look of the partiers around them.

With no beard blanketing the bottom half of his face, he almost looked younger than he actually was. His eyes gave his age away. Koe had seen those eyes before—the eyes of someone whose innocence had been stripped away from him. No doubt, he was part of Wystan's group and probably one of the only ones that wouldn't immediately draw on them.

The bartender's eyes flickered over to Koe and Jec. The other patrons at the bar moved to nearby tables, just in case, except for one middle-aged man with a symmetrical face, his jaw angular and covered with a meticulously groomed beard. He remained, swirling his drink with a straw and paying no attention to the two Knightmares. The music kept playing, but Koe noted they'd lowered the volume.

"Well, gentlemen. Or ladies? Or neither? Any are welcome here."

The bartender smiled. His crooked teeth and steely eyes made even Koe a little nervous. "What can I get for ya?"

"A meeting with Wystan," said Koe.

The bartender laughed.

"I'm still trying to meet with Wystan," he said. "I can tell you he's not here." The bartender flipped two tin cups in his hands, landing them perfectly on the mat behind the bar. He pulled out a bottle and poured liquid into the bigger tin cup.

"Then talk to whoever you need to. We're not leaving here until we see Wystan," said Koe.

"So you can kill him?"

Koe wished. "We need his help. This benefits him as much as it does us," he said.

"I wish I could believe that," said the bartender, adding different juices to the drink. He then slapped the second tin cup into the larger one at an angle and shook it with one hand, all while staring at Koe.

"You don't want us making trouble, do you?" said Jec, stepping forward. He drew his gun and slammed it onto the bar top. The bartender didn't sway, but the man at the end of the bar flinched.

"Kyer, Delvin!" shouted the bartender. The music shut off, and after the crowd quieted down, wondering what had happened, two big pairs of feet marched toward Koe and Jec.

None of the patrons moved, but when Koe turned around to face his two opponents, he could see many of their faces, terrified.

In front of Koe was a petite woman, thin with an angular face, whose jaw was just as sharp as Koe's daggers. Beside her was a muscular man, each of his arms the size of an average torso. His arms bulged even bigger as he crossed them in front of him. Koe could see the veins protruding beneath his skin.

"This is Kyer," said the bartender, pointing to the woman. "And this is Delvin. They're a cute couple, are they not?"

Jec chuckled, which turned into full-blown laughter. "This is what you got?"

More of Wystan's people stood while the uninvolved patrons remained sitting or moved toward the back. Koe looked at Kyer, then to Delvin. Their gazes were unwavering. They were too confident to be mere hired guns.

Koe shifted a step back toward the bar, glancing down to check out both Kyer and Delvin's hips. Delvin had a dagger but no gun. Kyer didn't have anything.

"We just want to speak to Wystan. We don't want any trouble," said Koe.

"We're the managers of this bar," said Kyer in a gruff voice. "We don't appreciate you harassing our staff. Either leave or be removed."

Jec looked over at the man at the end of the bar and nudged Koe. "That guy."

Koe took another look. The man's hardened stare showed no signs of fear like the other patrons did. He wasn't one of Wystan's men. He was too calm overall, except for that moment when he'd flinched earlier.

"I bet he's Wystan," said Jec, almost whispering. "He's the right age. He's not moving. He's in control."

"What's it going to be?" asked Delvin. His voice was surprisingly soft, but his stare was not. Koe drew his gun and pointed it at the bartender behind him. In an instant, all of Wystan's people drew theirs. The man at the counter even stood, albeit with no weapon. The bartender held his hands up.

"Wystan's here. Right now. You two are his bodyguards," said Koe, looking at Kyer and Delvin.

"These two?" asked Jec incredulously.

"They're touched by the Light."

Jec, immediately regretting his assumption, hastily grabbed his gun off the bar and pointed it at the bodyguards. "How do you know?"

"Their confidence. Lack of weaponry. No one's foolish enough to try to bluff a Knightmare. Am I right?"

Kyer smiled, but neither one said anything. Even Koe was unsettled by her cocky smirk. Although he'd figured out they had powers, he still had no idea what kind of powers they were. He could only hope that he was right about his other assumption.

Jec pointed his gun towards the man at the end of the bar. "Then, this is Wystan," he said.

"No, this is," said Koe, gesturing to the bartender with his gun.

The bartender shook his head, confused. "Sorry, I wish I could say I was. Honestly."

"Then you won't be missed," said Koe, ready to pull the trigger.

"Wait!" said the man at the end of the counter. The bartender threw up a hand toward the man and a hand toward Kyer and Delvin.

"Silence, Borq!" said the bartender. Genuine fear flashed across his face. Borq returned to his seat.

"Pleasure to meet you, Wystan," said Koe.

Wystan smiled and then shrugged, dropping his hands. "No one's ever figured it out before," he said, taking a sip of a drink.

"Your friend gave you up," said Koe, motioning over to Borq.

"That can't be it," said Wystan.

Koe said nothing.

"Well, don't keep me in suspense. How did you know?"

"These two are your bodyguards. Them having powers means they could only have one job: protecting you. I, like my friend here, thought it was the guy at the bar. The real Wystan wouldn't cower away from a fight—you wouldn't be a successful boss if you did. So that meant it could be any of your people here." Koe motioned toward Wystan's people surrounding them with guns, waiting to act. "But all of them are too eager. So that just leaves you and Borq. We know Wystan is a man of information, and what better way to trade in information than by posing as a lowly bartender?"

Wystan clapped and chuckled. "Well done, Knightmare, or should I say Koe?" Now it was Koe's turn to flinch. "Should I continue?"

Koe shook his head and then touched his scarf. His scarf is what gave him away, but it didn't matter.

"Yes. The famous white scarf. You're a legend. I don't think I've ever said your name aloud and not seen someone shudder." Wystan looked over to Jec. "Who's the pup?"

Jec predictably turned his gun toward Wystan. "My name's Jec. Remember it well."

"I don't think I will," said Wystan.

Koe dropped his gun and motioned for Jec to follow, but Jec didn't. Part of him hoped the rookie would simply shoot Wystan. Another part of him wished he could do it himself.

"Despite what you may think, we're not here to cause any trouble," said Koe.

"That's uncharacteristic of you lot. I thought it was finally my time," said Wystan.

The fire that told Koe to use his gun burned brighter. Wystan's power had killed many, more than any Knightmare had, and many of those were innocent people. The despondent eyes of the slaves Koe had freed just days earlier still pulled at his heart. Wystan's influence and power would ruin countless more lives. Koe could see himself shooting Wystan in a second and feeling satisfied, no matter whether he made it out of here alive or not.

However, there was a bigger objective.

One that the Shadows wanted, and one that Koe wanted even more.

"We need your help," said Koe, biting his tongue.

"I'm not really in the mindset to help an enemy."

"This is about the Crown. The enemy of my enemy is my friend, correct?" said Koe.

"Ah, yes. I assume it has to do with the Queen announcing she's the Chosen One. See, I don't believe it. I think the whole back glowing thing is a trick, just like I think you'll kill me after I've helped you, seeing that you now know my face. I can't take that chance." Wystan threw up his hand and signaled to his cohort. Everyone cocked their guns, tension thickening in the air.

Kyer cracked her knuckles and smiled again.

"Let's all calm down. There's a lot of innocent people here," said Koe. "We just want the name of a contact of yours."

Wystan puffed up his lips and tapped his chin, pretending to consider it.

"Uhh, no," he said.

"We'll kill you before they get a shot off," warned Jec as the henchmen took a step closer. A mysterious grin crossed Wystan's face. His eyes lit up. Koe took another glance at the terrified civilians, knowing there was no reasoning with Wystan.

"I don't think so," said Wystan. Before Jec or even Koe could react, Delvin slammed into Jec at an inhuman speed. The cracking of ribs reverberated throughout the bar. Jec's gun dropped from his hand, falling over the counter. Wystan snatched it out of the air as it fell, twisting it around and aiming at Jec.

Koe threw one of his daggers into Jec's gun before Wystan could fire, destroying the gun. Out of the corner of Koe's eye, he saw Kyer charging at him. He pushed back, turning invisible and narrowly avoiding Kyer breaking through the counter as it if were cardboard. As she did, she shielded her eyes, deflecting the pieces of wood that splintered off into fragments. She was strong. Her skin had no visible scratches. It was clear why she didn't need a weapon.

Jec scrambled to find his footing as Delvin toyed with him, punching and zooming away before Jec could land a blow. Wystan's men fired at Jec, who jumped over the counter, landing behind it as the bullets hit the bar and the wall behind, shattering glasses and bottles.

Wystan quickly moved away from the fight, closer to Borq. He put a hand on Borq's back and muttered something to him, trying to lead him away. Borq nodded and turned to follow, eyes scanning the room for the hidden Knightmare.

Koe drew his second dagger and unveiled himself. He threw the dagger in a straight line, right into the back of Borq's calf. A low scream echoed, but Koe summoned both his daggers to him and switched his attention from Wystan and Borq. He just needed to slow Wystan down. With a quick turn and two throws, the daggers found their way into the necks of Wystan's henchmen. Gunshots from the others raced toward Koe at the same time and speed as the massive figure of Delvin. Koe jumped onto a table and turned invisible in time to avoid it all.

Delvin crashed into the wall, unable to stop himself in time. For a moment, he appeared dazed, and it was just enough time for Koe to draw his gun and fire.

Delvin tried zooming out of the way, but the bullet hit his

shoulder, throwing him off balance and onto several civilians in the corner.

Jec, having turned invisible, revealed himself in the midst of a cluster of henchmen with his daggers out. If he was wounded, he hid it well. He twisted, aiming perfectly as he slit the throats of many. His dagger then found the throat of Kyer, but instead of a river of red flowing like the others, the dagger broke in half as it touched her skin.

Jec stopped. He must've been surprised, and that was all the opportunity Kyer needed to grab Jec and slam him into the ground. She held onto him, her knee crushing his abdomen. She wasn't going to let him disappear. Koe knew it was a death sentence for Jec if he couldn't get out of her grip and away from her. Koe fired at Kyer, but the shots bounced off her, and that's when he felt a huge shove from behind.

Koe toppled off the table, landing flat on his face. He knew from the force of the impact it must've been Delvin. He rolled over just in time as Delvin punched the ground with his incredible speed, cracking the wood plank where Koe's head had been. A huge crunching sound, followed by a harrowing cry, came from Jec, somewhere behind Koe.

Koe jumped to his feet and drew his gun, firing several times at Delvin, but Delvin dodged every bullet, snickering every time Koe missed. The light from above highlighted half his face. A shadow passed over it, and when the light returned, Delvin's gaze was still held on Koe.

Koe stopped firing, returning his gun to his belt. Delvin's eyebrow shot up inquisitively, but he didn't have long to react as a dagger pierced his back and protruded through his chest. Zos stood behind him. He cried out, bolting toward Koe, blood spilling out behind him as his knees buckled and he stumbled. Delvin couldn't stop, careening straight into Kyer as she held Jec, about to finish him. The force was just enough to push Kyer off, and Delvin smacked into the wall just as Fye burst through the window next to him.

"Oh yeah! This is a party!" shrieked Fye happily, slitting a henchman's throat and grabbing Kyer off her knees as she tried to get up. He hurled her across the room, breaking the bar once again.

Zos drew her gun, and three bullets left the chamber. The bullets hit Delvin in the back of the head, splattering the floor with brain matter.

Kyer regained her footing, turning her attention to Koe. The last few remaining henchmen aimed their guns at the Knightmares. Koe jumped out of the way but realized that he'd been standing with his back toward a small group of civilians huddled in the corner. Their gasps and cries reached his ears. He turned back and saw blood. Several of the civilians had been hit, wounded in different areas. One, a man Koe had seen dancing just minutes earlier, had been hit directly in the forehead. His partner cradled the man in her arms, her tears falling onto his cheek.

Koe took no mercy on the henchmen, throwing his daggers faster and shooting indiscriminately. His rage built. It didn't have to be this way, and now innocents had died. They weren't expecting their lives to end or be irreparably damaged at the whim of one man. If only Wystan had listened!

Koe stole a quick glance over to Wystan and Borq. Borq was up against the wall, sitting down. Wystan had ripped his own shirt to wrap

Borq's wound. Koe's dagger had hit him perfectly. Borq wouldn't be able to escape, and judging by the way they gently touched one another, Wystan wouldn't leave him. It gave Koe time to deal with the only obstacle left: Kyer.

One of Jec's arms was clearly broken—it twisted backwards at the elbow, dangling loosely. Using his free arm, Jec crawled toward Fye, who half picked him up with one hand and dragged him to one of the corners. Kyer stood a few feet away near the entrance. She cracked her neck.

"Should I finish him? Or will you? He's worthless now, isn't he?"

"He's not dead yet!" yelled Fye, circling Kyer from behind. Zos silently disappeared, reappearing to dispatch two henchmen coming through the door. Koe hated to admit it, but with Jec's arm messed up, cracked ribs and whatever else Kyer broke, he'd be in no condition to try and kill the Queen now. Maybe it would be merciful.

But Knightmares weren't about mercy. Jec's gun was destroyed. One of his daggers was in pieces, yet Jec could still fight. He might still have a use, a purpose Koe didn't know of.

Despite Jec trying to kill Koe earlier, in Koe's gut rested a twinge of pity for him. When he was a cocky, wannabe top dog, Koe could stab him a million times without a second thought. Now, he was a fly without wings, crawling back to safety with a whimper, desperate not to be stepped on.

"You feel bad for him, don't you?" asked Kyer. "Don't worry, I'll be merciful. Right after I deal with you three."

One shot was all it took. Straight through the eye. Koe's aim was perfect, drawing his gun faster than Delvin could run. The bullet penetrated her eye but stayed lodged in her skull. Kyer wavered, trying to remain standing. She didn't cry out. She didn't say anything. She just toppled over.

Using his good arm, Jec braced himself against a table as he limped over. "How did you know?" he asked through labored breathing.

"She covered her face as she slammed into the counter." Koe then turned to the civilians. "Get out. Now." The ones who were still alive and unwounded immediately ran, pushing past each other in an effort to save their own skin. Koe left Jec with Fye and walked toward the back of the bar where Wystan crouched over Borq, applying pressure to his leg. The bleeding hadn't stopped. Wystan, with his back to Koe, stilled as he heard Koe's footsteps.

"This didn't have to happen," said Koe, gritting his teeth. "You chose this."

Wystan chuckled and then stood up to face Koe. "Then you'd best kill me now. The rest of my people are on their way here. None of you will make it out alive."

"So this is Wystan," said Zos sinisterly. She then looked over at Borq, whose face was paler now. "Who's that?"

"Stay away from him," said Wystan coldly. "He's not a part of this."

"They weren't either," said Koe, motioning to the dead civilians who'd been collateral damage in the senseless violence.

137

Wystan took a long pause and then threw his hands up with a hefty sigh.

"Fine. I'll help you bastards, just don't hurt him."

"We know you have a contact, someone who can get us past the shield and into the castle," prompted Koe.

"Yes, the Fox. She can get you in. She owns a bakery on third street. Sky District."

"Let's move," said Koe.

Zos grabbed Koe's arm before he could leave. "Wait, that's it? You're just going to let him go?"

"He's not the target. As much as I wish he was," said Koe.

A dagger flew out of Zos' hand. Koe turned swiftly, expecting to see Wystan with a dagger in his stomach, but no. The dagger found itself back in Zos' hand, blood running from the tip. A gash on Borq's neck drained what little blood he had left. His body slumped to the ground. Wystan didn't look. He just stared at them.

"I said he wasn't a part of this!" yelled Wystan, even louder than before. Koe had made sure when wounding Borq that the wound, while severe, wouldn't be fatal. Zos' move was pure sport.

"That's for hurting Jec," said Zos.

Wystan's eyes raged, yet tears filled them to the brim. The Knightmares left. Jec walked alone, weeping between every breath. Fye just cursed, annoyed that he'd missed much of the action. Zos stayed silent. So did Koe. Deep down, he knew this was only the beginning.

FOURTEEN

QUEEN SERA

A laborer from the Ocean District lay prostrate before Queen Sera in the throne room. She hadn't gotten up for two minutes, saying her prayers in an endless cycle. Several cameras were trained on the Queen sitting on the throne and the civilians lining up to meet her, broadcasting the procession of worshippers to the whole city. Nothing escaped their view. Sera hoped the devotion and belief of their peers would inspire her subjects and buy her some time to figure out how to move forward.

Aiva had advised against it. An assassin could masquerade as a peasant and attempt to kill Sera, so she shapeshifted into a burly guard with a huge beard and watched over Sera by standing close to the throne. Sera didn't let thoughts of an assassin linger in her mind or cause her heart to quicken. She was only concerned about the Knightmares, and they couldn't hide themselves as others might. Not in the middle of the day.

The vision of them in the throne room, standing over her, still sent shockwaves through her core. She refused to speak about it again. She couldn't let anyone know how much it affected her.

"May the heavens bless you, Chosen One. You will save our world. We will forever be in your debt," said the praying woman. Her face was long and narrow and her nose straight. Dirt smudges outlined her face and clothes. Dried blood filled the creases around her nose. Sera put a smile on her face and bowed her head.

"You and everyone out there listening are the reason why I'm here. The reason why I will save this world. My visions come to me daily. My power is growing, and I will not be afraid of it like my parents were." She still couldn't give a true reassurance so, after her lie, she bit her tongue. Lying wouldn't clean the air. "I will save us all."

The woman smiled and clapped. She bowed again.

"I have no doubt about that," she said. The woman left, and Queen Sera signaled her guards to bring the next person forward. He was a small man, a little chubby, with hair sticking up in every direction and bloodshot eyes. He coughed a few times as he was led to a spot a few feet from the throne. He didn't bow, and Queen Sera's stomach clinched. Something was off. Her hands gripped the arms of her throne. Her eyes remained fixed on him. Aiva put a hand on her sword hilt.

"Hello, Queenie. My name's Goreth." The shabby man coughed a few more times, not bothering to cover his mouth. "If you really are the Chosen One, why did it take so long to find out?"

Sera stole a quick glance over at Thane near the elevator. She was sure he could see the fire in her eyes. Everyone should have been screened beforehand. Thane took a step forward toward Goreth, but Queen Sera lifted a finger to stop him. It was too late now. She couldn't just remove him. What kind of leader would she be if she couldn't handle adversity?

"Hello, Goreth," said Sera softly. "That is an excellent question. I'm not sure why it took so long. I wished it hadn't. I wished that I could've been born hundreds of years ago so I could have solved the air problem then. I'm not sure why the Light has chosen it this way." Sera's voice hardened, the warmth vanished. "I do not question the Light. The Light is what will save us. I am honored to be a part of its plan."

Goreth shrugged and swayed back and forth in place.

"That's good and all. The Light. So the Light is what took my daughter away from me? She was born with undeveloped lungs. She couldn't handle the air. Even me, someone who's been healthy all my life, is sick now. Not all of us have the luxury of a purified palace."

"I wish I could turn back time to save your daughter. I really do." Sera really meant it. Her teeth grinded together as he questioned her, but she reminded herself that this man was in pain. The curse that she had been dreaming of fixing all her life was within her grasp, and yet still, so many had died and were sick, never to get better. It wasn't fair. "It's not fair what happened. I am angry too—"

"Don't you dare compare yourself to me and what I've lost!" shouted Goreth. His voice was weak, but his resolve was strong.

"I'm sorry, Goreth. What was your daughter's name?"

"Liliana."

"I don't understand what you've been through, but I promise you, I will save us. I will make sure what happened to Liliana does not happen again."

Goreth chuckled and threw his arms up. "The doctors said that too. They still failed! What actual actions will you take?"

Sera's heartbeat quickened. No one talked back to her. She didn't have a concrete answer for him. The silence between them stretched to eternity and back. Her mouth opened to speak, but no words came out.

"See! How can you call yourself the Chosen One when you can't even answer me? That inscription on your back is a fake. You're just doing this for your image! You're a fraud!"

The guards moved in to grab Goreth, but Sera raised her hand to stop them.

"I won't just clean the air. I'll clean the streets too. I'll rid this city of the crime that has plagued us for decades. The mob will cease to exist. I'll find and destroy the Knightmares in the forest. I will not rest until their temple is found and every single Knightmare is killed. I will clean the air. I'll admit, the Light has not told me yet what I must do. But the Light has shown me my victory. I've seen this city safe. You want results, Goreth? I will give you them. And once I do, you will bow." She shouldn't have told him he'd bow to her, but it slipped.

The subtle threat reached Goreth's ears and sent visible fear throughout his body — his legs trembled, his eyes went wide and he almost stumbled in place.

"I'll believe it when I see it." Goreth swiftly turned and left.

Thane quickly cut off the rest of the civilians waiting to get their turn to see the Queen. They didn't need another one of the commoners questioning them—no matter how it looked to send them away early.

As soon as the cameras cut, Sera stood up and left her throne, charging right toward Hanna. Hanna winced as Sera stood only inches away from her. Sera could smell Hanna's mint breath and see the terror in her eyes.

"I'm sorry, my Queen. We thought we had screened them well—"

Sera held up her hand to stop Hanna. She didn't need to hear excuses anymore. She needed results.

"Where are we on the guru? I need someone now."

Hanna looked over to the other council members who all shrugged. "This is unfamiliar territory, Your Majesty. We're still looking—"

"I found someone," said Thane, stepping up. He stood at ease, unlike the others, his voice confident. "There's a woman claiming she's a spiritual guide from the outskirts. She's odd but may be what you need."

"Bring her here immediately," ordered Sera. She turned back to Hanna. "If this doesn't work, I expect you to have a list of backups a mile long. Do you understand?" Hanna nodded and rushed off with the other council members. Thane barked orders to the guards to retrieve this self-proclaimed spiritual guide. The room emptied as the guards rushed to collect the woman. Sera was turned away, lost in thought when Thane wandered over and placed his hands on her shoulders.

"You okay?" Sera shrugged his hands off and turned to face him.

"What if he's right? How many more people will die before I can save them?" said Sera. Thane drew in closer and gently placing his hands on her shoulders again.

"It's like you said, the Light is on our side. You will save Oarlon. You will save the world."

"What if I can't do it in time? Everyone is counting on me. If I don't produce results, more people will follow in Goreth's footsteps. They'll lose faith," said Sera.

"I will always have faith in you," said Thane.

Sera pushed Thane back. "Stop making it about you! This is serious, Thane."

"Okay, okay. Look, even if some lose faith, they'll just be proven wrong. Everyone who keeps their faith will be rewarded. The Light has a plan. We need to have faith too. As long as there is hope, the Light lives," said Thane.

Sera rubbed her forehead. She knew Thane had a point but right now, she didn't want to leave it to Fate. She needed to act.

"Just leave. Bring the guide to my personal chambers when she's here."

"Sera, I—"

"That's an order, captain."

Thane bowed and left. Sera stayed in the throne room alone, frustrated that her visions hadn't been clearer—that they weren't happening at all now.

She left and returned to her quarters, dismissing the guards posted there. She lit the fire herself, warming the room, and moved her chairs to the couch in the corner. The warmth provided some comfort, even if it wasn't enough to calm her frustration.

An hour later, she heard a knock at the door, and Thane entered with an elderly woman walking with a cane. Her cheeks sagged, the wrinkles etched deep into her face, and her gray hair was thin and falling out. Sera almost gagged at the sight. This is who Thane thought would be her guide? She reminded herself that her frustration wasn't with this woman. She had to keep an open mind.

"Hello," greeted Sera. The woman smiled and bowed.

"Hello, my Queen." The woman's voice was strong and low. She took a seat by the couch, and before Sera could command Thane to leave, the woman did it for her. "Leave us." Thane bowed and left. The woman sighed and gestured with her hand for Sera to sit on the couch. Sera did so, but hesitantly. She didn't love how authoritative this woman was. "My name is Quila."

"Thane says you are a spiritual guide?" asked Sera.

"Yes. His mother used to come to my cabin before she passed. She found peace near the end." Sera didn't care, she just wanted to know if Quila could help her or not.

"He thinks you can help me. To unlock my power."

"Well, I think I would have to know more about your situation," said Quila.

"You will be provided with just the necessary info," said Sera.

"I cannot help you unless you are open with me," said Quila. "You must tell me everything."

Sera gritted her teeth. "Fine, then this is over." She stood up and gestured for Quila to leave. Quila stayed put.

"Your visions are blocked. The ones that get through are often unclear. You need someone to help you figure it out. Am I right?"

Sera remained quiet and still. Her face gave nothing away.

"I believe I can help you."

Sera slowly sat back down. She remained skeptical, but Quila appeared to be confident.

"How?" Sera asked.

"To cut the ties that bind. The prophecy says you must free yourself. Let go of all your attachments. You can only truly be the Chosen One if you follow this lesson. Together, we can make a start here, right now."

"Proceed," said Sera.

Quila reached inside her coat and pulled out a bag, placing it on the table.

"The Light has chosen you. Now you must put your faith in the Light," said Quila. "Inside this bag are twelve stones. You will reach your hand into the bag and pull out one stone. You will see something in that stone, something that no one else, not even I can see. We will begin the first lesson when you tell me what you've seen."

Sera eyed the bag, unsure whether she should blindly stick her hand in. Quila would've been screened, but there were ways to hide weapons or tricks. However, Sera couldn't accept that the Light would let the Chosen One die by the hand of this elderly woman.

Sera reached in and felt several smooth oval stones. All of them were identical to the touch, so she just grabbed one and pulled it out. The gem was white and shiny. While it was beautiful, Sera could see nothing other than a pretty rock.

"Well?" she asked, annoyed.

She turned the rock over and over, finding nothing. Quila raised her hand.

"Let it rest in your palm. Clear your mind. There are no expectations here. Only the truth."

Sera placed the stone in the center of her palm and focused on it, emptying her mind of any doubt or frustration she had. As ridiculous as she felt, she was desperate. The white on the stone began swirling around like it was coming to life.

"Can you see this?" asked Sera, her gaze fixed on the swirling.

Quila didn't answer. The room went dark. She was gone.

A mist of shadow seeped out of the stone, filling the room. Sera's hands shook anxiously. The stone rattled around, never falling out of her palm. Pockets of light appeared on the stone. A beam of light shout of the stone. Sera turned her head and watched the light penetrate the darkness.

As the beam cut away the darkness she could see Gaven sitting next to her on the throne. She hugged him tightly. Aiva and Thane flanked the two of them like statues, hands resting on the hilt of their swords. Then two figures appeared, standing at the edge of the light. Their shadowy outlines were immediately recognizable, sending shivers down Sera's spine. Her parents. She'd thought she would never have to see them again. They turned their heads toward Gaven, beckoning him. Gaven slid from the throne room and walked to them. She immediately reached and grabbed Gaven's arm, pulling him back toward her. She made him face her, but his eyes were lifeless.

"Gaven! Do not go near them." But no matter how hard she held onto him, he slipped through her fingers. She watched him go. Was this what she was meant to see? She watched Gaven vanish into the darkness with her parents. Sera turned to Aiva, shouting at her in panic. She grabbed Thane's arm and shook him. Slowly, like machines, they too walked into the darkness. Thane fell to his knees, becoming one with the mist. Aiva gave one last look to Sera, her purple eyes getting darker and darker until she too was gone.

Sera, suddenly jumped to her feet. Light flooded out of her eyes. The light radiated out of the throne room and through the entire city of Oarlon.

The sensation was so overwhelming that Sera closed her eyes. When she opened them again, she was back in her bedroom. The stone was still in her palm, just a rock once more. Quila smiled and took the stone from her, placing it back in the bag.

"Tell me, what did you see?"

Sera quickly recounted everything she saw with a mixture of dismay and puzzlement.

"What did it mean?" Sera wasn't used to this—feeling like a child, asking someone for help—but after what she just saw, she was convinced Quila could help her.

Quila took a deep breath and smiled. "Only you can figure that out. Let's start with your parents. I imagine their deaths must have been a surprise for you?"

No, was the answer, but Sera couldn't tell Quila the truth. Still, she didn't want to lie either.

"I didn't have the best relationship with them. They didn't have the best relationship with the people. I'm not all that surprised."

Quila clicked her tongue and shook a finger. "This will not work if you cannot be one hundred percent honest with me. I know you're holding back. If you really want to access your visions, you will have to drop the wall you've put up."

Sera heaved a sigh. She couldn't fool this old woman. "I was not surprised."

"Why?"

There was a long pause. Sera had the words at the tip of her tongue, ready to spill out of her at any moment. She had never admitted it, but she had wanted to. She didn't expect a stranger would be the first to hear the truth.

"Because I arranged for it." Sera waited to see if Quila had any reaction before going further, but she wasn't fazed.

"You felt like you could be a better ruler than them," said Quila.

Sera was taken aback by Quila's bluntness.

But Quila was right, Sera was a better ruler.

"Why do you think you did not cry out when your lover died?"

Sera's heart skipped a beat. Everyone knew the truth about her relationship with Thane, but to speak it out loud was another thing.

"Or your closest friend?"

Aiva's purple eyes flashed before Sera. "I don't know," she admitted.

Quila nodded her head. "Because deep down, you know what you must do. They are all attachments... Attachments that you must sever. Remember, 'To save us from the Darkness, cleanse the sky of the clouds.'"

Sera shook her head. "How could any of them be a threat? Gaven's just a child. I'm doing this for him, so he doesn't have to live the rest of his life in a dying world!" yelled Sera.

"A ruler, the Chosen One, must be able to put the needs of everyone else above themselves," said Quila calmly. "If you want to help him, you must distance yourself from everyone you care for, everything you care about. You must be ready to sacrifice it all for the Light." Quila cleared her throat after a long pause as Sera sat wide-eyed, trying to take it all in. "I surmise you had your first vision when your parents died, yes?" After a nod from Sera, Quila continued. "Your first step." Sera found her fingers interlocked, her palms sweaty. All she could think about was Gaven's fate and what her vision might mean. She never felt as out of control as she did now.

"Why did it take so long for the Light to choose me as the Chosen

One?" asked Sera. "Why now? It could've chosen me when I ascended to the throne."

"I don't know," admitted Quila. "Perhaps the Light just knew it wasn't the time. Whatever the answer is, it does not matter. You are the Chosen One now." Quila hid the bag of stones back in her jacket pocket and stood up slowly.

"You carry a heavy burden. No one else can endure it. It's why the Light chose you," said Quila, taking one final bow. "This will be hard, but as you continue, it will get easier."

As Quila finished, Sera's fingers closed around the candelabra on the table. When Quila started to rise from her chair, Sera slammed the base of the candlestick against Quila's head. An intense rush of feeling swept through her. The sense of control flooded back, and she suddenly felt calm again. Blood dripped from the candelabra. Quila toppled over, groaning.

"Please, don't—"

Sera stood over her and rained down several more blows until Quila stopped begging. Every swing felt better than the last. Blood spattered Sera's clothes and the furniture. Satisfied, Sera dropped the candelabra and took a deep breath.

Quila's death was regrettable, but Sera couldn't let her wander around town, knowing what she knew. If even one person knew that Sera had arranged for the King and Queen to be assassinated, it could ruin everything.

Sera's racing heart began to slow. She relaxed her muscles and slowed her beathing. Quila's bloody body blurred before her as visions forced their way into her mind — a Sky District sign, a bakery on third street, and four Knightmares.

She quickly reached into her pocket and pulled out her transmitter.

"Aiva, I know where the Knightmares will be."

FIFTEEN

KOE

Ten Years Ago

In the forest outside the temple, Rus threw a balding, portly, fully naked man onto the ground in front of Koe. They were in a small clearing in the heat of summer with trees all around, five years into Koe's training.

"Today you meet death," said Rus. The portly man whimpered, but being gagged, he couldn't make a case for anything. Koe had known this day was coming. He just didn't think it would be like this: in the forest with his prey handed to him on a silver platter.

"What about the hunt?" asked Koe.

"The hunt is the easy part. I need to know you can finish the job given to you. You've been taught how to kill, but putting it to the test is another thing entirely."

Koe gripped his dagger tightly. For days, he'd mulled over what it would feel like. In the early stages of training, his core shook and he clutched his scarf, covering his eyes at just the thought of taking a life. But every time after, and with every lesson Rus had sent his way, it became easier to accept.

Now, he wasn't afraid—he just wanted to get it over with.

"Who is he?" asked Koe.

"The Seer gave us a target. We do not ask why." Rus pulled the man up to his knees and gave him his signature backhand slap. "Yet I know this man killed his neighbor because his neighbor's plants were hanging into his yard. His neighbor refused to cut them even after he tried reasoning with him, so this man took matters to the extreme. A wealthy merchant from the Leaf District, used to getting what he wants. Does that make it easier?"

Koe hesitated for a split second, trying not to think about it too much. Just to run over and do it.

"Too late, he escaped," said Rus. "If this was a true mission, you'd be chasing him and risk losing him. When you have a target helpless, you end them quickly."

Koe charged, his mind a blank, his dagger by his side. He threw the dagger into the man's flesh, directly into the heart. The man made a few last groans, toppling over with Koe's blade still in his chest. Blood soaked Koe's hand.

"Stab him again."

"He's dead," said Koe, taking another look. The man's body twitched slightly.

"I said stab him again," said Rus more harshly.

Koe withdrew the dagger and stabbed the man once again in the chest, a few centimeters from his initial wound. The body didn't move, no sound escaping. "Again."

Koe did as commanded, hitting the right side of the chest.

"Liver," said Rus.

With each stab, Rus chose a new target. Squirting blood hit Koe everywhere. He was just glad he didn't have his scarf on him today. Koe must've stabbed the man in every organ, every part of his body. By the end of it, the man had forty-seven stab marks.

"Good. You know what it feels like now. You're ready for the hunt."

Present Day

The smell of wine mixed with blood permeated the air outside. Red stained the white snow on the ground, trampled by the fleeing partiers. The bodies of the others were still fresh in the bar behind as the four Knightmares left. Koe half expected more of Wystan's goons to show up for a second attempt at killing them. However, it was doubtful. Wystan schemed, but he wouldn't be the kingpin of the underworld if he rushed into situations.

Jec noticeably trailed behind the three. While he didn't outright complain, he whimpered like an animal who'd been shot.

The civilians around them hid as they walked by. Most had fled once the fighting began. No more lines to get into clubs or bars. No more cheering, dancing or singing. Just the howling wind filled the streets — along with a dead body or two, sick civilians who hadn't been cleaned up yet.

That's when someone caught Koe's eye. He sat in rags, his gray hair all mangled. A few wrinkles were present on his face, including a scar on the right side. Age had been unkind to his neck, and loose skin hung from his chin. He rolled in place on his butt, giggling. If Koe had to guess, the man was on a hallucinogen.

"The Light is with you!" said the man, pointing at Koe and continuing to giggle. The Knightmares kept moving. Fye began to chuckle.

"Whatever he's on, I want some!" he said.

"The Chosen One is alive! Rejoice!"

Zos drew her gun. The blast from the shot sent all the other patrons scattering for shelter. A gaping hole etched itself in the man's forehead.

"Fyrking little flea," said Zos. "Did you know him?"

Koe must've stared at the body for too long, making her think Koe knew the man from his previous life. He didn't.

"No," said Koe, turning around and leaving the body behind.

Zos kept pace with Koe. "Is it something he said then?" she asked. Koe stopped once again, grabbed Zos by the coat and pulled her close to him. He could feel her breath on his face. It was steady and calm.

"We might still be far away from the guards, but do not fire your gun again without asking first. I don't need the Queen's army on us before we even enter the castle." Koe unhanded Zos and walked away. She trailed behind him. Koe kept his ears trained on her movements while hearing an echo of the man's words. "The Light is with you!" He was just high, but something about his finger aimed at Koe when he'd said it didn't sit well with him.

They took the roads less traveled, avoiding several guards patrolling in hoverers as they made it to the Sky District in the middle of the city. No doubt word would travel that four Knightmares were prowling about in Oarlon. The castle would be on high alert. Guards would travel in bigger packs with alarms that could be triggered at the first sign of trouble. With Jec's condition as it was, Koe thought it would be best to avoid another brawl. He had no interest in spilling more blood tonight.

The bakery Wystan told them about sat on the corner of what was usually a busy intersection during the day. "Cake, Please!" was the name of the store. The lights were all off, but a neon sign with the logo of a cake was brightly lit. The snowfall was peaceful here. Lights hung on the trees and around the buildings for the holidays brightened everything, making it feel magical. It was one of the rare instances that Koe wished he was his old self. He could see himself here with Aiva. A few hours earlier, it'd still be dark, but the store would be open. They could come here for dessert after a night out for dinner.

Throughout the years, it had become harder and harder to see Aiva's face in his mind. Koe wasn't sure what it would look like now that so many years had passed. The only thing he could focus on clearly were her calming purple eyes. He could see them now. He could see her here with him, holding onto his arm.

"What are you waiting for? Let's go in!" Aiva would say. He saw her tugging his arm, bringing him toward the shop, but all he could concentrate on was her. "Come on! Just you and me."

"Koe!" said Zos.

The illusion vanished, and Koe found himself back in reality with his fellow Knightmares. "What?"

Koe saw Fye and Zos peering forward at the shop. "Doesn't look like anyone's home. Wystan might've tricked us."

"No, he wasn't lying," said Koe, remembering Wystan's desperate attempt to save Borq. The micro expressions on his face gave no indication of a lie.

Koe went up to the locked door and saw a small bell hanging in the corner. He tugged on the chain, and a small ring went out. A few seconds went by. Nothing. Whatever the case was, Koe's hand slowly moved toward his gun.

That's when a hole above the door opened like a sliding door. A small camera poked out, scanning all four of the Knightmares. Zos drew her gun to shoot it, but Koe grabbed her arm to stop her.

"What did I tell you earlier?" said Koe, squeezing her wrist tightly as she lowered her hand. "We come in peace." The door to the store suddenly opened, and they entered cautiously. Inside were display cases, empty for the night. The amount of price tags for each section clearly marked the wide assortment of pastries they made each day. His stomach growled in response to the residual smell of the sweets. The door to the back of the store clicked and opened on its own.

As they walked forward, Koe made note of the even the smallest details. The purple and white tiled floors. The paint chips in the corners near the ceilings. He was sure Zos and Fye were doing the same. They were scanning for booby traps. It was clear that this Fox person had either been tipped off about them coming or had no idea but was intrigued enough to let four Knightmares inside. If it was the former, then there was a slight chance Wystan had sent them into a trap in a play for revenge. If the latter, then the Fox's confidence must mean she was prepared.

That's when a small girl appeared at the door. Her hair was in braids, and she couldn't be older than eleven.

"Mother's expecting you. This way." The girl showed no fear, no apprehension towards them. She brought them to a set of stairs leading to the second floor where the owner of the establishment must live — presumably the Fox. Koe didn't like all of these factors being up in the air. Too many things were left up to chance.

"Creepy," said Fye. All three of the other Knightmares turned to him. "What? Little girls are super creepy. I'm just saying!" Koe was the only one to audibly sigh, then turned to the stairs. Before he could go up, Fye continued, "Maybe Jec should go first?"

"I'm to be the bait? You think I can't fight?!" Jec's voice trembled. It was clear that he was in overwhelming pain.

"Koe can do it," said Zos. Fye's strategy made sense in a practical way. Jec was easy pickings now. If this was a trap, Jec's sacrifice would help them. Yet, for all his stupidity and brashness, Jec didn't deserve that.

"Zos is right, I'll go," said Koe. He almost volunteered Zos for it, but he needed to control as much of this situation as he could. The stairs creaked below his weight. He heard the other Knightmares close behind him.

At the top of the stairs was a spacious apartment. Based on the couch facing the TV, they were in the living room. The kitchen was right behind them. The room was dim here, but little yellow and white lights on a rope circled around the ceiling. Another strand circled around a pine tree sitting in the corner.

"Mom, everyone's here," said the girl down a hall that presumably led to the bedrooms. The Knightmares spread out in the living room. Jec managed his way over to the kitchen, practically falling onto a chair. Footsteps marched down the hall. A woman emerged, her eyes quickly spotting Jec in the kitchen.

"Well, make yourself at home, I guess!" As she sped past Koe and the others to the kitchen, Jec drew his dagger with his one good arm as she approached. The woman quickly noticed his other arm. "Oh dear, that looks mighty bad. Do you need some medicine?"

"No," he croaked.

"Well, up to you then," she said. Fye wandered over to the kitchen but remained standing. The woman unwrapped a small cake that looked rather plain. White frosting covered the chocolate. Fye leaned over just a little to get a whiff.

"Wow, that smells amazing."

"Please, have some, all of you," she said. Koe and Zos still made no movement. For all their animosity, they were often alike in thought.

"We won't be eating," said Zos as Fye and Jec both inched forward before recoiling back to where they were.

"Are you the Fox?" asked Koe. The woman went over to the sink and turned it on to wash her hands. The bags under her eyes were heavy. She looked rather plain, a little plumped, probably from eating cake often. When she rolled her sleeves up, he could see several tattoos of skulls patterned on her arms. After wiping her hands, the woman pulled out some medicine from a drawer.

"I go by many names. Fox is one of them," she said.

"Did Wystan tell you we were coming?" asked Fye.

Koe wanted to leap over to him and hit him squarely in the face for asking such a dumb question. He should have asked how she knew they were coming. Giving her the option made it easier for her. Koe took a deep breath, relaxing his muscles. Not everything was a trick. Not everyone had ill intentions. She likely wouldn't risk her daughter if this were a trap.

"No, but you wouldn't be here at this hour if he hadn't directed you my way," she said.

"We need to get past the shield, into the castle. He said you could help us," said Koe.

The Fox shrugged. "That's a big ask. I don't usually help out your kind."

Zos dashed over and thrust a dagger to the Fox's neck. "Insult us again, and it will be the last thing you speak," she threatened.

"I don't think so. You need my help. No one else will get you through that shield, and if you're trying to kill the Queen like I think you are, there's no other way."

"Zos, back off," commanded Koe. There was no point in threatening her.

"Then maybe we'll just kill your daughter," said Zos, not listening to Koe or the Fox. "Tell us what we want to know, and we'll consider letting you and the kid live." Koe glanced over and saw the girl standing in the corner near the tree, watching the whole interaction. She didn't even flinch, but Koe wasn't going to let her think her life was on the line. She was young, and he could see her ten years in the future dealing with the trauma of this moment.

"No, we won't," said Koe firmly. "But we won't take no for an answer."

"So, I'm supposed to help you kill the Chosen One? The one who's trying to save us from your curse?" said the Fox. One of her eyebrows perked up into an arch, and a devilish grin formed on her face. "Well, for the right price…"

"You will be compensated—after it works," said Koe.

He knew it wasn't much of an offer, but he wasn't going to let the Fox take advantage of them before helping them.

"I'm sure you'll keep your word. I'll get you in," said the Fox.

Zos sheathed her dagger and took a step back. The Fox glanced over at her daughter.

"Run along to your room, honey." The girl scampered off, closing her bedroom door behind her. Zos walked up to Koe, so close they were centimeters away. She leaned into his ear.

"This is a trap. She knows more than she's letting on. Wystan must be on his way here with hundreds of his goons."

"Then leave and watch the perimeter," said Koe.

"I won't come save you." Zos vanished down the stairs and left.

"Such a happy family," said the Fox.

She moved toward the table, grabbing the cake and offering it up a second time. "Are you sure you don't want some?"

Before Fye could respond, Koe said, "We told you, we're not here to eat, we're here for answers. Now, tell us how to get past the shield."

The Fox set the plate down in the middle of the table. Her eyes fell onto Koe's scarf. She moved a few feet toward him, close enough now that she reached out and felt the fabric in her hand. "Looks like a royal scarf," she said. Her eyes narrowed as she stared at it. Then she shrugged, and all the confusion melted away. "There are two ways to get past the shield. One would be to disguise you all as servants, but that won't work—not with your faces like that. The other is breaching the shield near the sewers. It's not a pleasant trip, but there is a path."

"I want details," said Koe, taking her hand off the scarf.

"Sounds good."

"Now," demanded Koe.

"In the bedroom there's a drawing in my dresser drawer. A map, detailing how to get in and out. You can go look if you like." There was something unsettling about her, but Koe couldn't place it. She was Wystan's friend. That could be it. She was also a mother, he told himself again—a mother wouldn't risk her kid. Yet he couldn't shake the shiver running up his spine.

He walked down the hall but found only two doors: one to the bathroom and one to a bedroom that the daughter had disappeared to. Why weren't there two rooms? It might be odd, but a parent could share a room with their kid. Koe opened the door to the bedroom.

The girl lay on the carpet, shading the shadows on a human figure she was sketching. She quickly shot up, her eyes wide. Her gaze flashed toward the door behind Koe, and he quickly moved out of the way of the door. He didn't want her to think he was going to hurt her.

That's when he saw only one bed against the back wall. Posters of naked men and women were plastered all around, nothing even remotely like a kid's room.

"You live here?"

"This is where Mother sleeps. I sleep out there in the living room," said the daughter. She said it so matter of fact, it almost felt rehearsed.

"You've lived here all your life?"

"Well, I think we moved here when I was young. I don't remember where we lived before, if that's what you're asking."

Why was Koe questioning this girl? She was young. She couldn't pretend. His gaze found the dresser where the map should be, but a rotting, almost nauseating smell pulled him away.

"What is it?" she asked.

"You don't smell that?" Koe asked back.

She shrugged. "You're weird," she said. "I don't smell anything."

Koe sighed and rubbed his eyes. He knew how ridiculous he was being. It made this conversation all the more embarrassing—a preteen kid was making fun of him.

"You don't stay alive in my profession if you aren't careful," said Koe.

"Maybe you should learn to trust people more. People are pretty nice, if you get to know them."

"I wish that were true."

The girl stayed staring at him, trembling less than before. That's when he caught her glance over to the closet. The creeping suspicion of wading into a trap crawled up and down Koe's skin once again. He'd just grabbed for the closet doorknob when the daughter shouted.

"Smoke! Smoke!" she yelled.

Koe paused. "What's going on?" he asked. A terrifying grin appeared on the daughter's face. Her face tilted toward Koe.

"Sorry, but I like money." Then the girl booked it for the hallway, disappearing from view. Koe snatched the closet door open, and a bloody body thumped down in front of him. Gunshots and yelling followed from the kitchen. Koe barely registered anything. He turned the body over to see the face of the Fox. Every hair was identical. Her crooked nose was the same.

How was this possible? Then the answer slammed into him like a wall of bricks. Who else was hunting them, other than Wystan? The Queen. The Queen would send the Assassin of the Shadows—the only person to kill several Knightmares. How did Koe not put it together before? This is why they could never catch the assassin—she was a shapeshifter. Koe's heart was beating faster than ever before. He rushed back to the living room.

He caught a glimpse of the girl's foot exiting the door to the shop below. The window next to the kitchen was broken entirely. Fye's yellow bandana hung from one of the shards of glass. Jec swung wildly at the figure in front of him with his good arm. Koe returned just in time to see the figure duck, holding a sword in hand and thrusting it upward through Jec's chest.

He yelled a bloodcurdling cry. His head lolled back toward Koe, and while he couldn't see Jec's face, Koe knew there was nothing to be done. The figure withdrew her sword from Jec, and his body crumpled to the ground by the chair he'd sat in earlier. Her outfit was entirely different now. Everything she wore looked tactical. Her belt had several different little attachments, all must do something in the heat of battle.

Her gaze met Koe's, and Koe froze. Now the image of her face finally cleared. The scars on her cheek had slightly faded, but her purple eyes remained a maze to get lost in. Yet, unlike the last time they'd seen each other, there was no love in them now.

"Aiva…" said Koe under his breath. Aiva kicked Jec's body.

"Sorry about your friend here. Let's be honest, he didn't have much of a chance."

"You wanted to separate us."

"Well, four Knightmares in one room—even I would have a hard time with that." She pointed toward the window where presumably Fye had left. "I overestimated him. He's not very quick, but I was slow on the draw." Aiva cracked her neck from side to side. "So you must be the great, mighty Koe. I've killed so many Knightmares, but you… Well, I've been looking forward to meeting you," said Aiva. She followed up with a mocking bow.

"Me too," said Koe, almost in a daze. He couldn't believe she was here. Finally. How often had he wondered if she was still alive? If she was even okay. By the looks of it, she was better than okay. Should he tell her who he was? Everything told him to. But that's when Zos flew through the broken window, drawing her gun.

"Zos, no!" yelled Koe instinctively. He quickly wished he hadn't. He would need to answer for that later.

Yet Aiva was ready. She ducked, grabbed a small metal ball from one of her belt attachments and threw it directly at Zos. The ball exploded into a net, ensnaring Zos completely. Zos landed on the kitchen floor, not losing a second before pulling her dagger and trying to cut herself out of it. But the net was electric, and as soon as Zos tried, it electrified her over and over. She yelled in pain, thrashing to get out.

"You Knightmares are weak," said Aiva.

Zos' screams assaulted Koe's ears over and over. He had to save Zos and Fye. As much as he hated to admit it, he couldn't kill the Queen on his own. And right now, telling Aiva who he was might not be enough. She might believe him, but even if she did, would she care? He couldn't risk it.

Koe jumped forward, zigzagging toward Aiva. She drew her gun and fired a few shots, all barely missing. Just before Koe reached Aiva, a tiny flash of light caught his eye: a metal ring on the floor so thin it was hard to notice. He sidestepped out of the way before Aiva activated it.

The ring projected a translucent forcefield, shooting up into the ceiling. It was a perfect way to trap an enemy. Koe turned into shadow, keeping light on his feet.

Aiva flipped backwards onto the table, landing perfectly. She fired her gun in all directions, not knowing exactly where Koe was.

Koe threw one of his daggers into the wall behind her to distract her for a second. It worked. Koe turned visible and slammed into Aiva, sending her toppling out the window. Before she could fall, she grabbed her grapple gun and shot into the ceiling, lowering herself to the ground softly. Koe could have tried striking her with his other dagger or shooting at her, but he didn't do either, and any killer like Aiva would see it coming. Koe took out his second dagger and approached Zos.

A net like this would have a small circle, essentially a battery, that powered the electricity in the net. The only way to stop the current was to find it and destroy it. Zos kept thrashing, almost involuntarily.

"Zos, stay still!" said Koe. He spied the circle on the net, near her backside, but it was damn near impossible to get a clean shot at it with Zos moving. She couldn't hear him now. Koe wasted no time and grabbed the back of the net with his hand. Pain radiated from his hand all over his body. He could feel each individual jolt traveling through his muscles to his brain. His body's instinct was to let go. He couldn't hold on much longer without losing consciousness.

He pulled the net up, Zos and all, off the ground just a few inches so she wasn't covering the battery with her body. Koe quickly sank his dagger into the battery, and everything stopped. Remnants of the electric currents pinged his muscles every few seconds. He sat next to Zos and cut the net with his dagger. Her back was facing toward him, but he could see her body rise and fall with shallow breaths.

"Zos?" She rolled over slightly—her clothes were singed. Smoke rose from each burn. "How bad?"

"Fyrk off," said Zos weakly.

"Stay here. I need to check on Fye." Koe stood up, ready to leave.

"I would have let you die," said Zos, struggling to catch her breath. "I still would."

Even Koe was a bit surprised by it. Did he expect a thank you? No. Maybe a little bit of gratitude. They were on the same side, supposedly.

"Good to know," said Koe. He caught a glimpse of the forcefield Aiva had almost captured him with. He turned it off with a switch on the underside of the ring and placed the ring on the back of his belt, under his coat.

At the window, he brushed aside the shards of broken glass with Fye's bandana and then jumped out, bending his knees to absorb some of the shock as he landed outside. The snow reached his ankles now. He had the flakes to thank for softening the blow.

The commotion hadn't attracted the capital guards yet. Koe couldn't help but wonder if they were deliberately ignoring the situation and leaving it for Aiva to deal with. Fye lay on his side in the middle of the street, a few feet away. He was still breathing and moving. He was facing away from Koe, struggling to stand. His hands were sunk into the snow. Blood dripped from his side.

Koe scanned the area, looking for Aiva. He couldn't see any sign of her or where she'd gone. The fresh snowfall was already trampled, painted with Fye's blood and broken glass, masking any trail she might've left. Why would she leave now when she had them on the ropes? Koe walked carefully over to Fye, still looking around him alertly.

"Fye, you all right?" Koe reached down toward Fye when he heard a voice.

"Koe! It's not me!"

Koe swiftly turned to see Fye gripping his stomach, crawling toward him near the entrance to the bakery. Before Koe could turn back, an elbow rammed into his cheek, throwing him off balance. He fell to his knees as she kicked his legs out from under him. As he hit the ground, the figure he'd thought was Fye changed back into Aiva. She drew her gun and shot at the ground where Koe lay. Koe managed to roll just in time. He wanted to grab his own gun to shoot back, but he couldn't harm her. With a well-placed strike, Koe slammed his boot into Aiva's knee. Aiva recoiled, slipping on the snow. Those few precious seconds were all Koe needed to get back up and flee.

He bolted across the street and down an alleyway as a shot chipped a wood beam on the house next to him. He could hear Aiva's boots thumping in the snow after him. He was counting on her following him. She must know, like he expected her to know, that Knightmares had an advantage in the open and taking your eye off them made it that much harder to fight them. Fye and Zos were wounded. Neither one of them could put up much of a fight, let alone get very far on their own. Aiva could afford to leave them there.

Koe kept dodging through alleys and behind buildings. Every shop sported a neon "Closed" sign as he passed. Shots rang out behind him, but she was far enough away that he never gave her a clean shot.

He had one arm tied behind his back — he couldn't return fire. He couldn't fight. Yet outrunning her would only work for so long until she got a good shot off. He couldn't disappear either — the snow made it easy for her to follow him.

Then Koe happened upon a big, open area guarded by a small fence. Behind the fence was a field of pine trees, each with little strands of lights on them. The ground around the trees still had several sets of tracks from the day's visitors. Shopping for these holiday trees attracted lots of customers.

Koe jumped the fence and disappeared between the rows. A small thud sounded behind him. He silently exited the row he was in and slipped into a different one. All the trees looked the exact same. The light configuration was identical. Weaving between the trees, even Koe wasn't exactly sure where he was in reference to where he started.

A shot rang out, and Koe scurried into another row. Aiva was definitely here.

Maybe he could tell her now? They were alone. The other Knightmares wouldn't know if he spoke to her. They could stop this violence. She might even help them. But why would she be working for the Queen after all this time? They must be coercing her somehow.

Koe quieted his steps, moving slower. He touched the tracks in front of him, feeling the wet coldness seep in through his gloves. Despite the recent snowfall, these tracks were old. She hadn't come by this way yet.

The air was dead quiet, except for a soft wind. Koe found himself at the edge of the trees near where he'd entered. The crunch of snow under his boots was muted but not completely silent. Koe froze in place. Aiva was light on her feet, but even she was having difficulty moving quietly. Koe jumped between the trees in front of him, right where Aiva was. She turned to get a shot off, but it was too late. Koe grabbed her gun and threw it behind him, into the next row.

She threw him off her and tried to get up, grabbing another tool from her belt. Koe somersaulted away as a net flew in his direction, narrowly missing. He rose to his feet, not bothering to stay quiet now. Aiva followed, chasing him from row to row, trying every tool at her disposal to stop him. Her flashbang could've worked, but it landed too far away from him to have any effect. Koe swiftly turned left, and then made a quick right. He spun around as Aiva was at his heels. She drew a silver device that looked like a hilt, activating a long blade that extended from the handle. She swung it at him, the tip of her sword grazing his shoulder. Koe moved in a circle around her, but she kept close. He drew his daggers, parried several of the blows and even attacked back — pushing her back down the row of trees. Suddenly, Koe heard the click he was waiting for.

The forcefield ring he'd dropped in the maze of trees activated around Aiva, trapping her — the same ring she'd failed to capture him with. She cursed quickly and eyed him, surely looking for his next move. The forcefield would protect her from a gunshot, but all Koe had to do was deactivate it from the switch that could only be accessed from outside the forcefield and shoot her before she could react. However, he had no plans to do that.

"Come on then, get it over with," said Aiva. Nothing in her facial expression gave away any indication of fear. Her expression was cold, nonexistent. Her muscles weren't tense anymore. Her breathing remained steady. She was ready for it. Koe wondered if she wanted to die. In Koe's experience, not many people were at peace before the end.

"Did the Queen hire you to kill us? What does she know?" asked Koe.

Aiva scoffed. "I'm not telling you anything," she said. "Torture me all you like. I won't give in."

"It was a nice touch… The cake, the girl. Why would we expect an ulterior motive with you claiming to be a mother?"

Aiva couldn't help a sly grin crossing her face. "People are desperate. You're desperate. When people are desperate, they're oblivious to what's in front of them."

"I know," said Koe, pointing to the forcefield ring. "You're just like us."

Aiva's grin vanished. "Are you done gloating?"

Koe wanted to divulge everything. He'd dreamt of this moment for years—well, not exactly like this. In his dreams, Aiva never wanted to kill him. Now that he was face to face with her, he didn't have the words. It was more than that though. He knew deep down that he was afraid—afraid that she might not be happy to see him. That she would look down on him for his choice to join the Knightmares, despite not having much of a choice to begin with. He couldn't tell her. Not like this.

With nothing else to do but stare, Koe dipped his hat toward her, ready to leave.

"That's it?" she said.

"Yeah, that's it," said Koe.

Koe left Aiva trapped in the forcefield. He had gone against what Rus had taught him so long ago. Aiva had been helpless. Give him any other target and their blood would be sprayed across the snow. She wasn't like any of his past targets. Deep down was the same terrifying dread that had plagued him during those first few days of being a Knightmare, wondering when he would have to kill someone.

He couldn't do it. He rubbed the back of his head, knowing that

Rus would do a lot worse to him if he knew that Koe had left her alive. He tried to tell himself it wouldn't bring any consequences, but he knew that was a lie.

Someone would eventually get her out, and next time, he might not have a choice.

SIXTEEN

QUEEN SERA

The conservatory sat in a glass enclosure at the back of the castle, attached to one of the upper floors. Plants and trees thrived here. The grass was clean cut every day, and the edges trimmed. The Queen's staff had seen to preserving as many plant species as they could. The result was a beautiful aroma of varied smells that could change every few feet. In here, at night, no one was around. Neither Thane nor the council would think to look for her here.

By now, Thane's soldiers would've cleaned the blood from the carpet in Sera's room. Quila's body had been disposed of, and an explanation had been sent to her family. It wasn't a good one: the Queen sent Quila on a business trip. When she didn't return, the Queen would find "evidence" of her death on the road. Whether Quila's family believed it or not, it didn't matter. A conspiracy theory from a poor family in the outskirts wouldn't hold weight with the people. Not when most of the city now prayed to Sera.

The sound of the candelabra striking Quila's head still reverberated in Sera's thoughts. Every hit had sent such a rush through Sera. If only she could rewind time to do it again. Quila's advice was helpful, but it really was her death that made Sera realize how much she had been holding back. Now her visions had returned.

It was her hope for a vision that led her to the conservatory in the middle of the night. That, and she was avoiding Thane. No part of her wanted to sleep with him tonight, and she knew he'd moan about it. To Thane, sex meant they were bonding, coming closer together. For her, it could be fun, but that was it. She knew she could just send him away if she didn't want to. She had done that plenty of times. But then he'd get desperate and emotional, wondering what he did wrong and how to right it. He was so afraid of losing his status. She didn't want to deal with him and his moods tonight. So, she'd sit and wait for a vision and then return to bed when his snores were louder than her boots.

She'd sent Aiva to the bakery from the vision with instructions to kill the Knightmares she believed would be there. Before she left, Aiva convinced her to have the streets cleared. Taking on four Knightmares was risky, yet Aiva believed she could do it. Sera expected a message from Aiva would arrive soon. If not, then Sera lost a friend and her best soldier.

Sera sat down on a bench near a small pond full of fish. She closed her eyes and focused on the emotional release she experienced when killing Quila. Her thoughts shifted to her anger at her parents and their ignorance.

"Show me the path forward. Show me how to save my city," she pleaded.

The darkness dissolved, yet Sera's eyes remained closed. She found herself in the Iron District — somewhere she would never normally go. Snow was falling. The deserted streets were unusual for the district. The moon shone brightly in the sky — perhaps it was past closing time for the bars. She walked through the snow, feeling none of the cold. The wind blew snow against her legs and face, and still she felt nothing.

Nearby groaning caught Sera's attention. She trudged toward the sound. Before her was the Mosquito Bite, but the sign had been mostly blasted away. Wood and glass disturbed the snow. Broken glass laid at the entrance. The door hung halfway off the hinges, bullet holes clearly visible.

Her foot crunched the glass beneath her boot as she entered. The dead bodies of people she didn't know were strewn about. Blood was everywhere, but it had already dried. Sera stopped to examine the body of a woman. There was a bullet hole where her eye used to be. The other eye was still wide open, her face frozen in shock. Was this a surprise attack? Sera inspected a few other bodies, finding cuts and bullet holes on them. It wasn't hard to put two and two together. Knightmares. But why?

A lanky man emerged from the back room and started scrubbing some of the blood off the bar counter. Two men followed a moment later, taking seats on the bar stools.

"Do you want us to go to the bakery? We'll catch them by

surprise," one of the men said. The lanky man shook his head, his crooked teeth on full display as he grimaced.

"No, we're vulnerable. We need to regroup, gather whoever is left and prepare for war."

"With the Knightmares?"

"Yes, you fyrking idiot! They murdered Borq. Nothing else matters now."

"Wystan, I know you want revenge… but they're Knightmares. You saw what they did here," said the other man. This lanky man is Wystan. Finally, a face for the name.

"I don't give a flying fyrk," said Wystan, pointing a finger at the two. "They will die. They will pay. I don't care if it means that every single one of you has to die in exchange." His voice was icy and unforgiving.

"What about the Queen?" they asked.

"She's a false prophet that isn't going to do shit for the air. But let the people believe. They'll live freer, more relaxed, which means more business for us," said Wystan. "And if I'm wrong, then she cleans the air. We just need to stay out of the way for now."

Both henchmen nodded.

"Now, I'm going to put out word for everyone to gather here and prepare. It's critical that we act soon or we'll lose the Knightmare's trail. See to it that every single idiot under my command shows up. Got it?"

The henchmen both saluted and left the destroyed bar, leaving Wystan alone.

Sera watched as Wystan put his head in his hands. A soft cry reached Sera's ears.

"I'm so sorry, Borq. I'm so sorry," he said to himself.

Whoever Borq was, he'd meant a lot to Wystan. Was this the past, present, or future? And why was she finally being shown Wystan when the greater threat was the Knightmares? One of Wystan's men mentioned a bakery. If the Knightmares had indeed arrived at the bakery, this discussion and the fight that destroyed the bar may have already happened. Sera was convinced she was seeing Wystan in the present.

Sera had waited for the Light to reveal to her what she needed to do next. The Light must be telling her that it was time to deal with Wystan once and for all.

To save us from the Darkness
Cleanse the sky of the clouds

Sera could hear a door open and suddenly was pulled backwards, dragged away from the bar and the Iron District all the way back to the conservatory. The door to the conservatory had indeed been open.

As Sera recollected her bearings, she saw Thane in his armor walking toward her. She sighed and muttered a curse under her breath. He was supposed to be asleep.

Even though no one was around, Thane gave a small bow.

"Your Majesty. I'm sorry to disturb you at this late hour," said Thane.

Ugh, thought Sera. He was already upset. He dropped all personality and became incredibly stoic when he was in a mood, like they had never seen each other naked before or had a child together. He usually only did this when there were people around. That, Sera understood. But they were alone now, which meant his weird behavior was because she didn't show up for him. Fyrk him.

"What is it?" asked Sera.

"You've received a message. From Aiva. It's on your secure channel," said Thane.

"Did you listen to it already?" asked Sera, watching Thane's expression closely. Sure enough, he flinched and looked away for just a second.

"It turned on right away. I thought you would want to know," said Thane.

Sera stood up and faced Thane. Her eyes went wide. "Well, what did she say?"

"She claims that one of the Knightmares is dead and two are wounded. She said nothing about the fourth one, just that they got away. All four matched the descriptions you gave her."

Sera paced away from Thane, admiring the flowers as she considered the message. What happened between Aiva and the Knightmares? If it was true and one was dead, her vision of all four of them entering the throne room wasn't a literal vision of the future. Yet three of them were still out there. Her initial relief was replaced by renewed stress. She needed them all dead.

"Should I send the guard to pursue the Knightmares?" asked Thane.

Sera waved him off and paired it with a scowl, like it was a ridiculous question. "No. Wounded or not, the Knightmares will be gone by now. Let Aiva continue to deal with them. Their wounded will need to time to recover, which gives us time to act."

"What do you mean?"

"I want you to take the troops into the Iron District," instructed Sera.

Thane's eyebrows shot up in surprise. "That's... That's Wystan's territory. It's asking for open war. Even if we occupied the Iron District, Wystan will just slip through our fingers. A war will be costly, Sera."

"The Knightmares paid him a visit earlier. I've seen his face, Thane. I want you to personally find him. Find him and kill him. Once we cut off the head, the beast will be confused. The entire underworld will panic. It won't be a war, it will be a massacre." Saying the word 'massacre' in reference to Wystan and his horde felt so satisfying rolling off Sera's tongue.

The underworld had operated out of the Iron District for generations. Wystan wasn't particularly unique compared to his predecessors. Past monarchs had tried to destroy the underworld, but it had become an intrinsic part of the Iron District. A new crime boss always rose up to fill the power vacuum. Sera wouldn't resign herself to this status quo any longer. She wasn't going to permit the underworld and the city to coexist like past kings and queens had. The Light put her on this path. She wasn't meant to just clean the air, she was meant to cleanse the city.

"If we kill Wystan, one of his goons will simply take his place. It's just a vicious cycle, doomed to repeat. I'm not saying we should stand around and do nothing about it, but if we do this, many innocent people will die. If we continue focusing on raiding their operations, we can minimize the risk," said Thane. "We're still making a difference." His objection was noted and quickly dismissed.

"The raids aren't enough anymore. It hasn't been enough for centuries. We have an opportunity here. The underworld is only as effective as their leader. There have been points in history when the new kingpin has been in over their head. Sometimes they're stupid and they fail, resulting in less crime. Wystan is too clever to keep alive. He's evaded us for so long—his operations are organized and precise. We must save the people of this city. No one should need to keep their purse close to themselves while they walk our streets. No one should be walking home at night, nervous if they're going to get home safely. No one should worry that their child may be taken from them while they sleep."

"I agree, Sera, but—" Sera held up her hand to stop him. She hated that he tried to appeal to her personally.

"This is my order. If you cannot obey it, I will find someone who can."

Thane bowed his head. "I will carry it out, as you command," he said quietly. He stood straight up and followed Sera out of the conservatory, back into the castle. Except for Thane's armor clattering the halls were silent. They found themselves back at Sera's room. Thane stood at the doorway, his head down. It didn't seem like he was even going to ask to come in.

"Spit it out, Thane. What's bothering you?" Thane cleared his throat and stepped forward. The light from one of the hallway lamps hit the side of his face.

"I just feel like you've been drifting away from me. I know you're the Queen, and now the Chosen One. Don't get me wrong, I understand that you have many responsibilities. I just want to be there for you... As more than just your captain."

Sera noticed Thane's arm move like he wanted to take Sera's hand in his. Ultimately, he refrained.

"Once this is over and we have saved the world, I will make you king. We will marry, and we will give Gaven siblings." Sera inched forward toward Thane and took his hand in hers. Her gaze met his. She could see his pupils moving slightly. She felt his hand tremble in hers. She couldn't tell whether he was excited or just anxious. He was usually so composed. How could a man like this be king? But she smiled anyway, reached up and kissed him briefly on the lips. Once they parted, she stood at the entry to her room.

"Wake the portraitist and bring her to my quarters. Once the image of Wystan is complete, show it to every soldier. You will find him at the Mosquito Bite in the Iron District. Do not come back until he is dead," Sera commanded.

Thane nodded and bowed again. "I won't fail you," His usual hardened demeanor returned.

This was the captain Sera respected. She left him in the hall and closed her bedroom door behind her, wondering why seeing him vulnerable made her stomach curl. Just a few days ago, she longed to feel his skin against hers. Now, knowing that as the Chosen One she would have to put him at arm's length, distance herself from attachments as Quila advised, she saw him more clearly. He was a groveling boy, desperate to prove himself. She knew now that he was never going to be king.

SEVENTEEN

KOE

After leaving Aiva behind, Koe retraced his steps back to the bakery.
The Sky District was still quiet. Shards of glass crunched beneath his
boots. Just one story above him was the broken window. The blood and
footprints of the fight were still visible on the ground around Koe. Fye
was here when Koe led Aiva away, but he was gone now. His trail led
back into the bakery, his blood marked every stair.

Koe made sure to stomp as he marched up the stairs to let Zos
and Fye know that it was him. No one else would be dumb enough to do
that. In the apartment, he found Fye sitting in a chair by the tree. His
shirt had been ripped open at the abdomen. The fabric was soaked red.
Fye leaned back in his chair with a needle and thread in his hands. He
was stitching himself up. Every few seconds, he squealed or groaned.

Zos was now up. Her clothes were still singed, but she moved
like nothing had happened. Jec's body still lay in the same position as
before. The shadows of the Knightmare were gone, his face laid bare.

They only disappeared when a Knightmare died. Patches of short facial hair scattered across his slightly chubby face. Acne dotted his forehead just above his wide-open, petrified eyes. Staring at Jec's face produced no twinge of sorrow or guilt. He was hardly innocent.

"Stupid kid…" said Zos, looking over at Fye. "That goes for you too."

Fye turned toward her as she insulted him. "Hey! I didn't see you do much better," he hissed.

"All of us should have done better," said Zos.

"All of us?" said Koe, jumping into the fray. He almost wished he hadn't, but he wasn't afraid of an argument with either of them. Neither one had a leg to stand on compared to him. "He's right, Zos. If you hadn't been so desperate, you and I might've had a chance against her," said Koe, turning his gaze toward Fye. "And what happened to you?" Fye muttered under his breath. "Fye. Louder."

"She tried to kill me first. I tried to fight her off. She stabbed me and threw me through the window."

"Did you kill her?" asked Zos, cutting in.

"No. She got away," said Koe.

Zos quickly swore several times. "She's a fyrking doppelganger! A shapeshifter. She could be anyone. Why did you let her live?"

"You think it was my choice? She's a Knightmare killer for a reason," said Koe, lying through his teeth but making sure his voice carried a tone of anger and harshness to give it conviction. "And she made all of us look like fools. For decades, people have feared one

Knightmare showing up. Just one of us made people flee, close their doors and hide, hoping they weren't the target. Hell, even the guards at the outskirts of the city let us waltz in because they're afraid to stand against us. But when four Knightmares go against one assassin, we become children, frantically flailing around like we're playing make believe."

"I'm surprised you care about our reputation," said Zos. Koe happily ignored her comment.

Fye finished sewing himself up and threw the needle and the rest of the thread on the ground.

"Patrol officers will be coming. We should leave," said Zos.

"And go where?" asked Fye.

"We'll go back to Wystan," said Koe. Zos's head twirled toward him. Before she could object, Koe continued: "Wystan didn't do this. The real Fox is dead in the bedroom. The assassin was sent by the Queen."

"But the Queen had no idea we were coming. Unless Wystan told her?" said Fye. "That would be a new one! The Queen and Wystan working together... Makes me want to be thrown out the window again." His shrill laugh was devoid of humor.

"I doubt it," said Koe.

"The Queen's power is real. And it's getting stronger," said Zos, coming to the same conclusion as Koe.

"Yes. If the newscasts can be believed, then she has visions from the Light. She must've seen us coming here and sent the assassin before we arrived. Worse still, the girl that was her 'daughter' was a hired hand, meaning the assassin had time to recruit her, arrive to kill the Fox and establish herself here," said Koe.

"Then we're fyrked! If everything we do can be seen beforehand, we'll never make it close enough to the Queen to kill her. This mission is over," said Fye.

"No!" snapped Koe. His instinct was to walk over to Fye and strike him for making such a weak declaration. "We were given a mission. This doesn't change it. She might've gotten lucky this time, but if the Queen were all knowing, hundreds of officers would be here now. She'd know this conversation. She would know all of our conversations. Hell, she would clean the air. We'll continue our mission."

Koe took a deep breath after he finished talking. He realized he might've come off too emotionally involved. Neither of them believed Koe cared about the Shadows and the threat of the Chosen One. Once again, he'd revealed his hand, but this time neither of the other Knightmares commented on it.

Both were wounded, and they still had no way into the castle. They had no plan. The best idea would be to retreat, return to the Knightmare temple and ask Rus for help. That meant time and the chance that Rus would take this mission away from Koe, and he couldn't let that happen.

"So how do we do this?" asked Zos, crossing her arms.

"Like I said, we'll go back to Wystan. He must have other ways to get inside the castle."

"And risk another fight? We've already been in two we weren't expecting. Maybe you like being backed up against a wall, but I prefer to be the one attacking," spat Zos.

"If you hadn't killed his friend— Fine, if not Wystan, then what do you propose?" asked Koe.

"I don't know, but it's time for some reconnaissance."

"Well then, my idea is now an order. Fall in line and do as you're told," said Koe, stepping toward her. She stayed still.

"I don't think you're qualified to lead this mission anymore. We've already lost a comrade and been ambushed twice. I'm taking charge. Fye... you're with me." Koe watched Fye out of the corner of his eye as Zos rested her hand on her gun.

"I don't really want to get involved..." said Fye.

"You're involved. Choose!" said Zos.

Fye sighed and rubbed the back of his neck. "I'm with Zos on this one. I'm not looking to get into another fight I can't control. Not again."

Koe wanted to scream at both of them. This wasn't going to help their mission.

"You can follow us or you can go on your own," said Zos, about to walk past him. Koe grabbed her arm, and he could feel her wince in his grasp. She must be more wounded than she led him to believe.

"We'll split up. If you find a lead, let me know and I'll join you. If it turns out to work, I'll let you lead the rest of the mission. But if I find a way, you both come back. The mission comes first, understood?"

Zos nodded, and Koe released his hold. She signaled Fye over with a wave of her finger, and they departed down the stairs.

"Don't die, Koe," Fye called behind him, followed by a high-pitched chuckle.

Zos might be right. Wystan was probably a dead end, but he knew the castle, and the castle would be impossible to infiltrate without help. The Knightmares finding a way in or luring the Queen outside would be almost impossible on their own. Wystan was the only person Koe knew who might know someone with the knowledge to get them inside. At least this way, if the Queen truly were able to see them in her visions, she would have a slightly harder time directing Aiva to their locations now that they were splitting up.

Heading back downstairs and outside into the cold empty street was instantly gratifying. The way the cold air brushed against Koe's cheeks in the silent night reminded him how much he craved being alone. It was partly why he'd trained so hard in the temple—to get away. Being sent on solo missions, away from the other students and Knightmares, away from Rus, was a reward in itself.

However, this time, things were different. He wanted to go back to Aiva and tell her everything. His dream of them reuniting and running away together percolated in his thoughts. It was everything she'd spoken of so long ago. He hadn't fully understood it then, but he wanted everything she did.

By now, she'd be gone, plotting her next move against them. While she was a skilled fighter, taking them head on would be unwise. She'd clearly survived for so long by thinking things through.

"Already lost your team?" hissed a voice from the alleyway

behind him. Koe drew his gun and jumped back. He was several yards away from the bakery down the street. He'd been so preoccupied with his thoughts, he hadn't even noticed the shadow with a green tie and vest walking toward him. There weren't many who could successfully sneak up on Koe.

"Are you so lost that you forgot what I taught you?" said Rus almost in a whisper. The air seemed to echo his words ever so softly.

"What are you doing here?" asked Koe. The Seer was never supposed to leave the temple. "If something happened to you, the Shadows—"

"The Shadows wanted me to come. Jec's death is unfortunate. The others have abandoned you. The Shadows worry about you."

"I don't need you watching over my shoulder," said Koe firmly. "Why bother anyway, when the Shadows were wrong? Jec died, barely contributing anything to the mission."

Rus chuckled, a few snowflakes melted against the Seer's crown.

"The Shadows keep the answer from me, but I assure you, it was no mistake. Perhaps he was merely a distraction that kept Wystan's bodyguards or this assassin busy so that you would survive? Do not fret about it, Koe. The Shadows are not worried about the loss of Jec. Now tell me, did you deal with this assassin?" Rus' tone was laced with poison.

"She got away," said Koe.

"Of course she did," said Rus. Distaste dripped from his tongue.

That's when clouds of fire and smoke erupted behind Koe, cutting off their conversation. In the distance, bombs and shouts echoed throughout the city. Koe quickly calculated it was coming from the Iron District. What was going on? Zos and Fye were deliberately avoiding that area. Surely infighting between Wystan's people couldn't cause chaos on that large of scale.

"Leave it, Koe. Rejoin Zos and Fye. Wystan does not know anything else. Stop these unnecessary distractions," said Rus.

"People are dying…" said Koe softly, too quietly for Rus to hear.

The explosions and cries thundered, shaking the earth this time. Koe searched for any means of a higher vantage point. His gaze landed on a ladder just a few buildings over.

"That is not your mission! Focus on the task at hand. The Queen is the only thing that matters," said Rus.

"I know. Zos and Fye will be fine without me. We need a lead, and we need to try everything we can until we find one," said Koe. He quickly climbed to the top of the building. With a glance back, he saw Rus staring at him, shaking his head before calmly walking back into the alley and vanishing. Koe knew Rus disapproved, but Koe needed to be on his own without the others breathing down his neck. He needed to do things his own way. Whatever was happening over there, he needed to help.

Once Koe reached the rooftop, he spied the sea of orange flames spread across the Iron District. The whole city would wake up to the cries of death, see the smoke and fire of war. There was only one possible explanation: the Queen's army had finally gone to war with the underworld.

EIGHTEEN

KOE

Koe yearned for the quietness of the Sky District the moment he set foot on a rooftop on the outskirts of the Iron District. He was never one to run from a fight or fear violence, but the situation here was much worse than anything he'd seen before.

Bodies littered the ground. Snow began covering the corpses. By morning, they'd be buried under a mound of ice. Some hung halfway out of windows, impaled on the broken glass. It was easy to distinguish the Queen's soldiers by the black and gold armor they wore.

Screams echoed throughout the district. Houses were in flames. It wasn't the sight of the carnage that made Koe sick—it was that he could do nothing about it. Skirmishes between the underworld and the Queen were common, but this was unprecedented. Every other person on the street was armed. Why now? Why did the Queen do this?

"Stand the fyrk up, you piece of garbage," commanded a voice nearby.

Koe moved toward the source of the voice and saw a row of six men, presumably Wystan's people, standing in a line with their hands behind their heads. In front of them stood several soldiers with swords and guns trained on the men. The captain of the soldiers, judging by the stripes on his shoulder, was using one of Wystan's men as a punching bag.

"Get the fyrk up!" Each time the captain raised his fist, more blood stained his knuckles.

"Please, stop hurting him!" yelled another of Wystan's men.

The captain glanced over at him and slammed his victim even harder. Finally, the captain sighed and used his handkerchief to wipe some of the blood from his knuckles. The pleading man in the line sobbed, gulping between breaths as he struggled to stand up straight. His friend's face had been bashed in so badly, it was unrecognizable.

"I've had my fun, go ahead," instructed the captain.

Koe knew this was the moment. If he were going to intervene, he would need to do so now. But Wystan's people were hardly saints. If the situation were reversed, Wystan's people would be as cold and ruthless as the soldiers were being now. Better to let the evil fight among themselves.

Instead of the normal firing squad that Koe expected, the soldiers marched behind their victims and drew their swords, slashing into the prisoners' backsides. Wystan's men fell onto their knees as the soldiers kept hacking into them. Some soldiers used their blades to inflict as much pain as they could while keeping their target alive for as long as possible. Others quickly stabbed them in the back. Judging by the locations they chose, the soldiers would miss the vital organs with their blows, like the heart. None of the prisoners were going to die quickly. It would be slow, and they would suffer. The soldiers knew it, and judging by their whooping and hollering, they enjoyed it. The soldiers sheathed their swords and holstered their guns once they were done.

"Come on, time to move on," commanded the captain.

Not so fast, thought Koe to himself. Time to strike a balance and find an answer.

Koe leapt from the roof, drawing his gun and shooting three of the soldiers in the back of the head. Alarmed, the others turned, scrambling to get their weapons back out. Koe sent one of his daggers, perfectly aimed, through the slot of one soldier's helmet, piercing his eye. The force kept the dagger moving, breaking through the soldier's skull and out the back, lodging itself into a second soldier's neck.

Blood and brain matter exploded onto the captain's face. He tried to get his bearings, but Koe was upon him, swatting the gun out of his hand. He placed the tip of his second dagger under the captain's chin.

"Wystan. Does the Queen know where he is?"

"For the Chosen One," said the captain solemnly. His voice was quiet, quite the contrast from a few seconds ago when he was pummeling Wystan's people.

Koe took his dagger and jabbed it into the captain's side. "You can die slowly or I can make it quick. Answer me and you won't have to suffer like the men you've killed."

The captain sneered. "For the Chosen One."

Koe threw the captain to the ground and placed his dagger by the captain's genitals. He began to apply pressure ever so gently. "I'll ask again. Do you know where Wystan is?"

The captain resigned himself to his fate and laid his head back. "FOR THE CHOSEN ONE!"

Koe wanted to make good on his threat, but it was clear that the captain wouldn't talk, so he plunged his dagger into the captain's neck. He stood to leave, and once the captain's death rattle reached Koe's ears, he called both daggers back to him. The best path forward was to revisit the Mosquito Bite. If Wystan had survived the initial attack, there was a good chance that he was smuggled out. But then again, he wasn't expecting this. No one was.

The fighting continued in the streets. While it was clear that the Queen's soldiers were winning, their strategy seemed uncoordinated. They didn't march as a unit or attack with any tactical forethought. They fought one on one in the streets with Wystan's goons and lit fire to buildings to smoke out anyone attempting to hide. Koe narrowly avoided being detected by staying to the rooftops, which were covered in snow and ice. It would be impossible for anyone without his level of training to follow him across the icy, snow-covered roofs.

Eventually the ice and snow became too much for him. Koe slid down a ladder and continued through the side streets. Every so often, he'd come across a lone soldier or thug and dispatch them quickly. Thankfully, the district was in such chaos that it was easy to slip by the bigger groups. The cloud cover gave Koe plenty of opportunities to melt into the shadows. No one noticed Koe's footprints in the snow as he ran across the wide streets.

The entrance to the Mosquito Bite was covered in red. The wreckage was now even worse than before. The body count had easily doubled. Pools of freezing blood soaked the snow. Pieces of ruined gold and black armor were scattered around the rea. The soldiers had visited here, but for some reason, none stayed behind.

Koe moved inside and was surprised to hear a splash. He looked down to see his foot in a centimeter of blood. The wood floors with all the dirt and grime could no longer be seen. Koe carefully stepped over the bodies as he made his way to the bar. He had never seen such carnage before. Earlier, Koe had wondered what was hidden by the closed door he'd spotted behind the bar. Now it was busted open, revealing a stairway descending below.

Two soldier bodies lay at the bottom of the stairs — two bullet holes in both their heads. Someone had tried to hide down here. The passage led to a storage room with several rows of shelves packed with food and water. It was a bunker.

He heard gasping and groaning from around the corner. Even before he got there, he was sure who it was.

Wystan.

Wystan sat against the wall in the back corner. His eyes were half closed. His hand loosely held a gun that rested in his lap. The blood on his shirt marked the wounds in his shoulder and abdomen. His gaze lazily glossed over Koe. Koe wasn't even sure Wystan was conscious enough to notice him until he heard a faint chuckle.

"Come to join me in death, Knightmare? Don't whine about it." Wystan's breathing was erratic, and the color had drained from his cheeks. Koe walked slowly forward, his hand resting on his gun, mindful of the gun in Wystan's lap. With a quick motion, Koe snatched the gun from him and tossed it to the side. Wystan didn't react. Koe knelt down in front of him.

"What do you think death is like, Knightmare?"

"I've never thought about it," Koe lied. He certainly had — he used to imagine an afterlife in paradise, where everything was pure and good. That all changed when he became a Knightmare and discovered the truth. There was nothing.

"Don't lie to a dying man. We're both killers. Surely you've thought about it."

"I don't think there's anything," said Koe.

"Why?"

Koe didn't want to continue this conversation. He needed answers from Wystan before it was too late.

"We went to the Fox and—"

Wystan put his finger to his lips, and Koe stopped.

"Answer. Then we can talk," insisted Wystan.

"I think the afterlife is a dream we made up because we're afraid of the truth. If there's a paradise and humans are there, then it wouldn't be a paradise."

"You're like me then. Best to make the most out of living before going back to nothing again."

Koe sighed. He didn't like the comparison Wystan made between them.

"Don't scoff. You, me, the Queen. We're all the same. There are no heroes, there never were. There are just liars and false idols." Wystan suddenly coughed up a little bit of blood. He wiped it away from his lips and leaned his head back against the wall, closing his eyes. "Before this, I was planning how I'd kill you. Then soldiers showed up and did all of this." He opened his eyes again, this time all the way, and stared hard at Koe. "Please, kill her. Unleash the chaos, and then go fyrk off and die."

"The Fox is dead. I need another way in," Koe pressed, ignoring Wystan's comments. There was a creak at the stairs. Light footfalls reached the ground.

"There isn't any other way. Looks like the Queen was one step ahead of all of us," said Wystan.

"There has to be something! I can't pierce the shield!"

"Maybe she is the Chosen One then," Wystan chuckled. "Or you can always ask him?" Wystan eyes drifted from Koe. He'd heard several people breathing behind him. He'd chosen to ignore it, knowing that Wystan's life was dwindling.

A sword unsheathing with a scrape and the click of a gun loading told Koe his time was up.

Koe turned and stood. Five soldiers were before him. He was trapped. The leader took off his helmet, and despite the passage of time,

Koe still instantly recognized that blond hair and the crooked nose. Thane. Five stripes lined his shoulder. Captain of the guard.

"Thank you for coming, Knightmare." Thane dropped his helmet, unsheathed his sword and grabbed his gun. Koe was speechless. He never expected to see Thane again, especially here, now. "Tell me, where are the other two Knightmares you're traveling with?"

Koe quickly looked at the shelf next to him without moving his head. Between the canned food and bags of dried fruit stacked together, he could see guards lining up on the other side of the shelf, guns at the ready. His options for escaping were limited to fighting his way out. This was a perfect trap—in the corner of an underground bunker in a narrow hallway where the exit and the row next to him were blocked off.

"Captain, you honor me with your presence," said Koe, buying time. He wanted to say his name. His real name. Maybe that would throw Thane off long enough. No, Thane never cared enough about him. Thane took a step closer and held up his blade.

"Tell us now. I won't ask again."

"Why would I tell you? Looks like I'm about to die either way," replied Koe. That's when Koe spied it. His way out. There was a panel on the wall just a few feet away, close to Thane. If Koe was right, he might have a chance.

He took one step forward and put his hands up. Another step, and he could see Thane's grip around his gun tightening.

"One last moment of honor. Something you've never had," said Thane.

"Hmm. When I was young, I remember a boy," began Koe. "He was confident, clever but most of all… a coward. He came from a house of status and played around with the servants. He even convinced one of them to steal something very valuable. Something a princess would own. Then, instead of taking the fall for it, he blamed a servant. He let an innocent boy take the blame, all because he was too afraid to admit it was his idea in the first place. It would've been a shame for him to lose status. Better for someone to lose their life instead." Koe's story gave him enough time to edge himself to the panel. He put his hand on the panel but made it look like he was just leaning against the wall. Thane's body language was steady and resolute, his face hadn't changed a bit. If the story had any effect, he didn't show it.

"Is that supposed to be you?" asked Thane.

"There is only one coward here tonight," said Koe, gripping the handle. "And I'm going to kill him." Koe ripped the panel away, revealing a big lever. Most basements had these emergency levers to turn the power off and on. In a bunker like this, Koe's assumption that Wystan would keep a backup was correct. Before Thane could order his soldiers to fire, Koe pulled the lever down, and the whole bunker went dark.

Muzzle flashes from the gunfire ignited the darkness. Koe jumped through the shelf across from him, scattering cans and dried fruit as he did. His landing was quite loud as food and liquids fell from the adjacent shelves. One glass definitely broke. Koe rolled onto his back, drew his gun and fired in the general direction of the soldiers who had come at him from the aisle over. Bodies thudded against the concrete floor.

With as much haste as he could, Koe rose to his feet and shot in the general direction of Thane and the rest of the soldiers. Cries rung through the bunker, followed by more muzzle flashes and yelling from Thane.

Koe drew both daggers and flung them through the air. They were invisible in the darkness and chaos, and he doubted the Queen's soldiers had trained their ears well enough to listen for them. One thudded into a bag of food, most likely rice or oats by the sound of the tiny grains falling onto the floor. The other ended up somewhere in a soldier.

The sound of flesh tearing was all too familiar.

That's when the lights came up. The soldiers in the aisle Koe was now in were all dead. Two more behind Thane were sprawled out on the floor—a third leaning up against the wall with Koe's dagger in his belly. Koe commanded both daggers to return to his hand. The dagger in the soldier withdrew, letting loose a bloody waterfall. The soldier slowly slumped to the floor.

"Fire! Now!" commanded Thane. Koe dodged, moving out of the way in the nick of time. His dagger found the two remaining soldiers, and with a quick slice to their necks, it was just Thane left.

Thane's gaze darted from left to right—gun or sword. He was only a few feet away. If he chose gun, it would have to be a good shot because he'd only get one before Koe was upon him, and in such close quarters, the sword wouldn't do him much then. Instead, he dropped the gun, tossing it to the side.

"Maybe you have no honor, but what say you?" His hands gripped the sword, and he held the blade out in front of him. Koe imagined the moment: He'd take out his gun and shoot Thane in the leg. Should he stoop so low? The win was too good to pass up, and Rus would be proud of his decision. A fight was not fair. Koe could hear Rus say there should be no hesitation, that his emotions were clouding his judgment. But he didn't understand. Thane played a part in everything that had happened. He was responsible, and shooting him wouldn't be satisfying. Not after the suffering Koe had been through. Koe put both daggers in one hand, grabbed his gun from his holster and dropped it on the ground. He then squared up against Thane with his daggers ready. He wouldn't turn invisible this time. This was going to be a fair fight, and it was long overdue.

Then a gunshot rang out. Thane had a small gun hidden in his sleeve. It was a one-shot gun, but deadly if aimed right. The gun was aimed directly at Koe's chest. A perfect shot to the heart. That is, if Koe hadn't expected a double cross from a coward like Thane. Koe perfectly timed the movement of his dagger into the bullet's path. The bullet slammed into the dagger and was crushed. The deflected bullet went clanging against the concrete floor. Thane's eyes widened. His stance changed from a ready position to preparing to run. Koe didn't hesitate, his blades lashed out at Thane. To his credit, Thane kept up, even in a narrow aisle where a long-bladed sword wasn't the best weapon. Koe thought Thane would crumble after a few blows, but Thane parried them all and even gained enough confidence to attack back.

For a second, Koe thought, 'What if I lose?' He hadn't thought that before. He assumed that the Queen's guard would be like anyone else he fought. Then again, he never really thought anyone except Rus stood a chance against him. But he could add Aiva and now maybe Thane to that list.

Thane went for a killing stroke to the head. He swung as wide as he possibly could without hitting the wall. Koe ducked just in time, then jumped off the wall and sunk one of his daggers into Thane's shoulder. The sword fell from Thane's hand as Koe pulled the dagger out. Thane fell to his knees, out of breath.

"Please, please, don't do this. I have a son. You might not care about me, but how can you deprive a son of his fath—" Koe backhanded Thane before he could finish. He didn't need to hear his pleas. Koe walked around Thane to his backside and placed the blade of one of his daggers on his shoulder.

"Take off your shirt," said Koe.

"What?" asked Thane.

"If you want to live, take it off. I won't say it again."

Thane did as instructed, struggling with his wounded shoulder. Other than a couple of small scars here and there, Thane's back was clean, smooth. He seemingly worked hard to keep himself in great shape and was either good enough to win most of his battles in training or his partners were too scared to beat him.

"If you're just going to humiliate me before you kill me..." started Thane. Koe knew what he was going to say next. "Just end it."

"You're a special case. I won't kill you, Thane. I need you to send a message."

"What message?"

"Your body," said Koe. Koe slashed Thane's back twenty-two times in quick succession. The same amount of times that Sera had whipped Koe back when he was a boy. Now, no matter long he lived, he would always have to remember. Just like Koe did.

With every cut came a scream. Thane slumped over by the sixteenth slash, but Koe kept going until he reached twenty-two. Once he was done, Thane was quiet. Some cuts were small, others were not and yet, his whole back was covered in red. The scars that would follow would intersect and overlap.

"Now, call your soldiers to come find you. Tell the Queen... I look forward to seeing her again." Thane tried to look at Koe, his face twisted in pain. He dragged himself across the concrete and reached out to a transmitter on the ground a few feet away. He pressed a few buttons and then sighed and closed his eyes. His breathing was shallow but regular. If the guards hurried, they would get to him in time. If he died while he was transported, well, Koe was ready for that.

Koe then turned to the other man near death: Wystan. Wystan had seen the whole thing, judging by the fact that he was smiling.

"You are the most interesting Knightmare I've ever met. Your other comrades that attacked my bar, I could see their bloodlust. But you… It's different. You hate that you love it." Wystan pointed to his wound. "Come on, Koe. Add another name to your list." On the one hand, Koe could make Wystan suffer for a few more hours. On the other, he could make sure there was no question that Wystan was dead.

"I need another way into the castle."

"I told you. There is no other way. None that I know of." Wystan's voice was full of conviction. Koe held his dagger up to Wystan's eye level.

"Why do you think you deserve mercy? You've killed hundreds. You've raped and sold slaves for pleasure and money. You partner with pedophiles like Mankar to make a profit off of selling kids. Your drug trade has made hundreds overdose. I have dreamt of this day—watching you die."

Wystan smiled again.

"I've done more than that. I once killed a woman and her baby that was supposedly mine. I set a house on fire that killed a whole family, just to kill someone indebted to me. Then I framed it like an accident. I had such plans. I really thought I was important. I thought I would change things. Turns out, I'm just another pawn in this tale, sacrificed for the Queen and her vision. Nothing can save me now. You know I don't have another way in, but you came back anyway. Scared that innocent people will get caught in the middle of a war? Or did you come back because you wanted to be the one to kill me?"

Koe twirled the dagger in his hand. He needed to decide soon. More soldiers would be here at any moment.

"Ah, it's both," said Wystan, grinning with his bloody crooked teeth. That's when Koe stabbed him in the side. The next stab targeted Wystan's shoulder. Every subsequent puncture missed Wystan's vital organs. Koe did just enough damage to keep Wystan alive, conscious and hurting. Koe sheathed his dagger. The blood oozed from Wystan's fresh wounds, trickling down to the ground in little streams.

Wystan couldn't respond. He was barely able to breath at this point from all the pain. His smile was gone, and his body would soon follow. He was right, nothing could save him. But Koe wasn't going to let him go out easy.

Koe passed by Thane's body, still breathing but now unconscious. He stepped over the dead soldiers and ran up the stairs, on the lookout for the incoming reinforcements. With all the chaos in the basement, he forgot that all the bodies up here were still... here. He escaped back out, into the snow. His lead was a dead end. Literally. As he wracked his brain, trying to figure out what his next step should be, he heard soft weeping coming from the alleyway. He turned the corner to see a young man sitting against the alley wall. He was ghostly pale, with several bullet wounds in his chest. Somehow, he was still alive. That's when Koe recognized him. It was the teenager he'd spared when he killed Mankar. The same teenager that he told to leave this business. Judging by the gun in the teenager's hand, he hadn't listened. Koe knelt down in front of him and drew his dagger, pausing as he sighed. Moments ago he wished he could stab Wystan several more times, but this was much different. Much harder.

The teenager's eyes widened, but his body was too cold and weak to move. All he could muster were two words:

"I'm sorry," he said with a quiver in his voice. With a swift flick of the wrist, Koe's dagger swiped across the teenager's throat. He reached out and closed the boy's eyes.

NINETEEN

KOE

After slitting the throats of a few more of Wystan's followers and the Queen's soldiers, Koe finally found himself in the Leaf District, away from all the chaos. It was much quieter here.

The Leaf District was a residential area, consisting only of houses. Big ones. It was perfect for families to get away from the more urban aspects of the other districts, and the air purifiers were much stronger here. Since it was still night, the lights were out in most of the homes, their windows dark.

Koe scoured various houses, finding all the owners nestled asleep in their beds. It took multiple tries, but he finally found one that was empty. The clue? A 'For Sale' sign on the lawn. Koe wanted to smack himself in the face for not realizing it earlier, but his mind was on other things. Aiva, Thane, Wystan, even the teenager he'd killed out of mercy.

Jec was dead, and Zos and Fye had chosen to separate from him. Koe had been ordered to lead the team, and within a day, he had failed.

They were no closer to penetrating the shield surrounding the castle, and he could barely keep upright, his legs slowly going limp from exhaustion.

Koe hoisted himself on top of a garbage can and then jumped, grabbing the gutter of the empty house. He pulled himself up to a small window on the third and top floor.

Using his dagger, he broke one of the window panes, hoping it wouldn't be heard. The glass shattered, and Koe glanced around.

No dogs barked.

No lights turned on.

He reached through the glass and unlocked the window from the inside.

Though unoccupied, the whole house was fully furnished, and the third floor, where all the bedrooms were, was no exception.

He found a room near the end of the hallway and plopped himself onto the bed. The sun would be rising in an hour. The night began as it ended — terribly. From a bar fight to escaping a shapeshifting assassin, to the start of a war and the end of the status quo between the Iron District and the Crown.

His past was catching up to him now.

Some part of him regretted what he'd done to Thane. Another reiterated to himself that Thane deserved it. At least he didn't kill him.

It didn't take long lying on the bed for Koe's eyes to close fully and for him to sink into the mattress.

He could hear Rus' voice shouting, "Why did you spare him!?"

Ten Years Ago

Whack! Rus appeared before him in the main chamber of the temple with the old Seer present. Koe rubbed his sore cheek. He could feel the imprint made from Rus' knuckles. Koe's first hunt: a failure.

"What happened, Koe?" asked the Seer.

"He… He was… was with his family," said Koe. Another strike hit the opposite cheek.

"He was your target!" shouted Rus. "You finish the job you were given. You do not leave anyone alive!"

"I wanted to do it! I just didn't have a clean shot," said Koe, trying to scramble out of it. Koe's face met Rus' hand again.

"You go through his family if you have to," said Rus. He went to strike Koe again, but Koe caught his wrist in time and pushed it away.

"I'll get it done," said Koe.

"You will not strike, young Knightmare," said the Seer. "Rus gives you the punishment you deserve. We have agreed to give you another chance at your mission. Family or not, you will finish it. Rus will accompany you."

So Rus did.

Koe staked out the house of his target, a man on the outskirts of town. He could hear the family's frequent coughing, especially the younger two. Their hair thin from malnutrition, the children's bald patches revealed rashes and sores on their scalps. Their mother and father took turns sipping from a murky brown bottle they passed back and forth.

As Koe watched, their sips turned into chugging as the evening arrived. The oldest child had bags under her eyes. She spoke of a girl, possibly a sister who had died earlier that year from the air. Most people who had been pushed to the outskirts didn't last long, especially not young or old people with weakened immune systems. How could Koe take more from them?

That was neither here nor there as Rus stood close enough behind him for Koe to hear his breathing. He felt every exhale on the back of his neck, raising the hair there. When the sun finally dropped below the horizon, Rus put his whole hand on Koe's back and shoved.

"It's time," he said.

Koe approached the family, and when they saw him, the kids ran inside. The father stood up, trying to find his balance while the mother chuckled in her seat on the porch.

"Heyyyy, it's a… Knnnightmare," she said with a slur.

"Get out of here!" yelled the father.

Koe drew his gun and pointed, but the oldest child threw herself in front of her father.

"No! Please don't take him!"

Koe paused, knowing Rus' eyes were glued to him. He'd get at least one backhanded slap for hesitating. Koe shot just above the child's head, and the father's back slammed against the door, the weight of his body snapping it off its hinges.

Shrieking, the girl escaped back into the house where the sound of the back door opening and closing reached Koe's ears. The children's cries became more and more distant. Rus approached, his posture straight. He almost glided over, passing the laughing mother and swiftly sending a dagger into her neck to quiet her. He stared at the body of the father and leaned down to his ear. Koe moved closer.

"Goodbye, brother," Rus said, then glanced up to find Koe eavesdropping. "Next time that happens, you kill the kid for getting in the way. You never know who you're going to make an enemy of."

The memory disappeared, replaced by glimpses of Rus shoving Koe's face into a bucket of water and holding him down for his brief hesitation. Then the images darkened and vanished into the abyss of his mind.

Present Day

The sunrays rose in the sky, through the trees and into the house. The sound of hoverers and people talking outside didn't wake Koe. It wasn't until midafternoon that Koe shifted to his side and got up. All the events of the previous night roared back to him.

The fridge and pantry downstairs must've been stocked for an upcoming open house to make the house look welcoming and desirable for prospective buyers. Koe found protein bars in a cupboard and stuffed several in his mouth to find his energy. He then tapped his earpiece transmitter to see if he'd missed any messages. Nothing.

In the bathroom, while he scrubbed his hands with soap and water, he looked up into the mirror. The shadows covered his face, and yet he still thought that even after all this time, maybe he'd see something different. He wiped his hands on the towel next to him, still staring at himself in the mirror.

His hand traveled up to his scarf. He clutched the mildly tattered fabric in his hand and took a deep breath. If only he could turn back time. Maybe he would make a different decision. Not to save Aiva—no, that was something he would never regret. Becoming a Knightmare maybe. When he was a scared boy, on the run, he'd thought it was his only option. It probably was, and logically, he would've died if he hadn't. But what if?

His earpiece buzzed, indicating a call coming through. Koe stepped outside the bathroom and answered it.

"Yes?"

"Hey, it's me," said Zos on the other line. "We have a lead. Can you please meet us?"

Koe paused, replaying the question in his head before responding. "Where?"

"Ocean District, 198 Windford Road. It's an abandoned warehouse. It'll be safe for us there till the sun goes down."

The Ocean District was quite far from the Leaf District. It was literally on the other side of town, closer to the Iron District. It wouldn't be easy to cross the whole city, especially after the news late last night.

"What's the news on the Iron District?" asked Koe. "What's the fallout look like?"

"Don't know much. We've been busy," replied Zos.

Koe sighed. "Okay, I'll be there as soon as I can. Koe out." He ended the call. He marched over to the living room where a large digital display monitor was recessed into the wall. A circular device sat on the couch. Koe pressed a few buttons, and the monitor on the wall turned on, displaying the news. A house for sale wouldn't have many channels, but it would at least have the news to show off the huge screen and sound system.

A newscaster sat with a stoic expression, reporting on the events of the previous night. But no newscaster in Oarlon was neutral. The city and kingdom were in the control of the Queen, and the news followed her orders to a tee.

"Our Chosen One, our Queen, took control of the Iron District last night. We can happily confirm that the underworld kingpin, the notorious and elusive crime boss, Wystan Kerravo, is dead. Most of the underworld has been dispatched. The few prisoners who've been captured will await sentencing by the Queen herself. Here is a direct message from the Queen."

The image transitioned to Queen Sera sitting on her throne. The camera closed in on her. Koe had seen her face multiple times throughout the years, mostly on the news or other royal propaganda. He'd seen how she changed. Her hair was whiter. The black tattoos were bigger. Her skin was still the pale white it always had been. Her eyes still contained the same fury and deception they always had, yet some of the warmth had faded.

Every time Koe saw her, he imagined his hands on her throat, taking the life from her like she had done to him.

He forced his muscles to relax. He hadn't realized that he'd been clenching both fists.

"Citizens of Oarlon. As your Queen, it is my duty to serve and protect you all. I recognize that some of you may be afraid of what transpired last night. I assure you, I only took action because I could foresee the outcome. My power is growing. My visions showed me the face of the man who has terrorized this city for too long. Wystan Kerravo is dead, and his body will be hung up in the city square as a reminder for those who would follow him. The city is already safer, and we will continue to root out those who remain of his former organization.

"This is just one step forward to saving our city. The air that you breathe will soon be clean and fresh. The sickness will go away. Those who plague our city will pay for what they've done. I will not stop with Wystan. I'll find the Knightmare temple and put an end to them, once and for all. My visions are showing me the way. The Light is on our side. I will not fail you." On the last line, the camera zoomed in on her face, revealing that her eyes were a little watery, and while the Queen was a master of deception, this at least seemed to be genuine.

"Now, for the hard news. I will not lie to you... We lost some good soldiers last night. The captain of my guard, Thane Xandos, was severely injured. Thankfully, he is stable and will make a full recovery. Some other soldiers were not so lucky. We will hold a vigil for all involved and for everyone who continues to make the sacrifice to serve this great city. We will prevail against these threats. We will root out this evil, once and for all."

The Queen bowed her head, and the message ended, returning back to the newscaster, who lavished praise on the Queen and her leadership. Koe switched the TV off. It wasn't surprising to see that they'd omitted how many innocent people were killed in the battle. How dangerous the war could be if it spread, depending on how many of Wystan's soldiers lived and moved to other areas. Some of them would hide and hope they were never found, but others would surely retaliate against the crown and continue the fight, even if it meant sacrificing themselves to take out a few innocent people, all to send a message to the Queen.

Koe had business now. He had to get to Zos and Fye on the other side of the city in broad daylight. It wouldn't be easy. He couldn't turn invisible due to the daylight, and with the shadows covering his face, he stood out.

He exited through the backdoor, peeking about first to make sure no one was around. He jumped over the fence into another yard and continued to travel from one backyard to the next, avoiding the busy streets. As he approached the border between the Leaf District and the Sky District, he landed in a backyard that had a small wooden house in the corner with a gnawed bone painted on the front. He instantly recoiled, expecting a dog to charge out and bark or even attack.

Indeed, a dog did wander out. A big rottweiler slowly approached, his fur marked with scars resembling a checkerboard. Koe had treated and seen enough injuries to know a lot of these scars were fresh, and judging by the marks, they were made with a knife. A long chain was cuffed to the dog at the neck, only allowing it to move a few feet away from the doghouse before it stopped her. The dog's tongue hung out, panting slightly at Koe. She lay down as far from the house as the chain would let her, looking up at him with big, beady eyes. Koe advanced cautiously, unable to take his eyes off of her.

He slowly lowered to a crouch, his hand outstretched. He watched the dog carefully, ready to pull his hand back the second she tried to bite him. Instead, she lowered her head to the ground. He pulled off his glove and placed his bare hand on the dog's back, petting her ever so gently. She stirred a memory for Koe: Knightmares didn't have pets, but there used to be a cat who wandered around the servant corridors that would sometimes visit Koe.

Koe's hand traveled too close to one of the scars, and a small whimper escaped the dog. She didn't bark. She didn't even react. Koe stopped his petting, moving his hand farther way from any of the cuts.

"What have they done to you?" said Koe to the dog as if the dog could understand him. Koe drew his dagger, and the dog froze. Her pupils dilated, and the whimpering grew louder at the sight. Koe thrust the dagger into the chain. It wasn't easy, metal trying to break metal. But the chain link was cheaply made, and Knightmare daggers were made out of the best metal around.

It took several minutes of prying with the blade, and the clinking of metal was louder than Koe wanted or needed, but finally the chain broke. Koe sheathed his dagger, and the dog looked at him, frozen, seemingly unsure what to do.

"Go on. You're free." But the dog remained, turning her gaze away from Koe and then slowly sitting up and wandering back into the small house.

Koe turned his attention to the big house, where the owners of the dog resided. He made no attempt to be quiet as he kicked the back door in. Immediately, he heard voices sounding alarmed, wondering what was happening.

Their voices led Koe right to them. A whole family. A father. A mother. Three kids, all younger than fifteen. They were all huddled in the living room, watching the news. Two of the kids were identical in looks. They tried to hide themselves in the couch cushions. A slightly older kid had a bruised eye and hid herself behind her mother. The father froze, but his gaze fell upon a drawer, most likely containing a weapon. Koe walked toward them all, one dagger in hand. He reached the drawer and pulled it open. Indeed, there was a gun inside.

"Why are you here?" asked the father, his voice barely a whisper. "We have nothing of value." His eyes darted from the Knightmare to the dagger and back again.

"I wouldn't say that," said Koe, motioning to the big house around him. "The dog outside. She's been hurt. Recently."

"She got into a fight with another dog," said the father. The kids continued to tremble. Both the father and mother looked like they were trying to stay strong, but they also quivered in place.

"Don't lie," said Koe, taking the gun out of the drawer. The father put his hands up.

"She has a bad temper. We're—"

"What did I just say?" reminded Koe.

The father bit his tongue and took a moment. "My wife sometimes—"

The mother's eyes widened, and she shoved him away from her. "I will not take the blame for you!" she yelled.

A bullet whizzed by them and pierced the wall, silencing both. Koe looked at the kids.

"Tell me who's responsible. Whoever it is, I won't harm them. I just want to know." The girl with the black eye stepped forward, earnestly pleading. "They both do. Please don't hurt them." Tears formed in her eyes. The twins also nodded.

Koe wanted to fire a bullet into both the parents, but that would mean leaving the children parentless.

"Where did you get that black eye from?" he asked. The girl's gaze flew to her parents and back to Koe. She shuffled in place before answering in a quiet voice.

"From falling. Really!" replied the girl. Her gaze darted to the ground, her eyelids fluttered.

"Children, go upstairs. I need to talk with your parents." With nods from their parents, the children all scampered up the stairs, the oldest one putting her arms around them before they closed the door to their rooms.

"Please—" began the mother.

"If it weren't for the carnage last night, the loss of innocent lives I saw, I might've left here with just a threat to return if you continued. But let's face it, there will always be another excuse, another lie. I'm getting tired of it. Maybe this way, your kids will have a chance to grow up to be the good people you should have been… and if not, I'll kill them too."

"Wait, no—" The first shot rang out, and the father threw the mother in front of him. Her face met the bullet, and she crumpled to the floor. Koe shot a few more times, missing the man and now cursing himself for hesitating. Letting the kids go upstairs was his mistake.

The father leaped out of the room while Koe chased him. He heard another drawer sliding open and found the father in between the dining room and kitchen, taking a gun out. The father shot rapidly, and a bullet grazed the sleeve of Koe's jacket. If that shot had been a little better aimed, Koe would've walked right into it.

He waited as the father exhausted his clip and turned to run, then Koe fired a single bullet, hitting the father in the back as he tried to escape again.

No sounds came from upstairs, and it was for the best. The shots would definitely be heard by the neighbors. Guards would come and hopefully discover the bodies before the kids came looking for their parents. With any luck, they wouldn't see a thing.

Koe fled the scene long before any soldiers showed up. He'd have to move more quickly now. The gunshots and bodies would be sure to draw unwanted attention and panic, and the guards, now knowing that a Knightmare was in the Leaf District, would certainly be looking for him.

Crime in the Leaf District was rare. When it happened, those cases always rose to the top of the pile for investigation. The Ocean District, where Zos and Fye were waiting, was the other side of the coin. Crime that happened there was rarely officially acknowledged, let alone investigated. But it also wasn't like the Iron District, where crime was expected to happen every day. The Queen, and by proxy her soldiers, just simply didn't care.

Yet as Koe found his way into the district, with all the buildings tightly packed together, he found many people outside praying and chanting Sera's name, saying she would save them. The newscast had stirred them into a fervor. How could Koe blame them? The air was terrible everywhere, especially here where the houses had the worst filters. There were more people cramped together here than in the Leaf District, where buildings were more spread out. The only silver lining was that they were near the ocean.

The ocean breeze did nothing to improve the air quality, but on clear sunny days in the summer months, families could gather on the beach to tan, swim and hang out. Koe didn't often witness this himself, since he operated mostly at night, but the few times he had, he wondered what it would feel like, letting the sun hit his exposed skin.

Aside from the oceanside restaurants and homes, many of the other buildings were warehouses and places of business. Without the Ocean District servicing the other districts, the whole city would fall apart.

Getting to the Ocean District wasn't easy. It took a lot of maneuvering and skill, waiting for the right moment to move, as stealthily as he could manage in the daylight. Despite his caution, he was still seen by several civilians who would probably report the Knightmare sighting to the Crown.

Zos had checked in again, urging him to come faster. He kept her updated with his progress but avoided giving an accurate time of arrival, just saying that he was on his way.

The sun shined brightly near the ocean, casting an orange glow along the horizon, illuminating a small abandoned warehouse. This was where Zos had asked him to meet. The warehouse was full of tall glass windows stretching from floor to ceiling. As Koe stepped inside, he found himself in a large room, two stories tall. Behind him was a staircase to a partial second floor that oversaw the first. Whatever used to be made here was now long gone. Dust floated in the air while mold and grime infected the walls. The building stood empty, and Koe was seemingly alone. Zos and Fye weren't anywhere to be seen.

Sunlight poured in from the windows. It was still an hour till sunset, and there was enough light to make it hard to find spots of shadow.

Koe walked around the room, thudding every step, making enough noise to be heard throughout the echoing warehouse.

His shoulders tensed as his eyes found a metal ring laying on the concrete floor, only a foot in front of him. Then he spotted a few more positioned across the entire floor. The same ones that Aiva had used, exactly like the one he'd trapped Aiva with. He kicked the closest one away from him, and it skittered across the dusty floor before rolling to a stop.

"Good try," he said. He heard footsteps coming from the ledge above and turned toward them to see Aiva walking out from one of the small offices on the upper level.

"I got you here, didn't I?" she said. She walked down the stairs, twirling a gun.

"I knew it was you from the beginning," said Koe. "Zos wouldn't ask so nicely."

"And here I was thinking the Knightmares actually got along with one another."

"Only when it helps the Shadows." That got a chuckle from Aiva. She holstered the gun and walked toward Koe. He placed one hand on a dagger and one hand on his gun. He didn't want to use them, but he needed to keep up appearances. "You took a gamble—calling me, not knowing if I was with the others."

"Oh, I knew you weren't. Your tracks went off in different directions, and I knew your footprints from following you earlier. That was a good trick you pulled, trapping me. I'm surprised I'm still alive."

"You'll be dealt with later," said Koe, covering for himself. "After we complete the mission."

Aiva shrugged and paced around Koe. "Sounds reasonable—for anyone other than a Knightmare. I would believe you, but Knightmares don't spare anyone, especially a Knightmare killer and agent of the Light. You didn't even care about your friend that I killed. You didn't even wonder how I could call you in the first place." Aiva tossed Jec's small ear transmitter onto the floor and crushed it with her boot. "I doubt you actually cared for him. Or any of them. The cause is everything to a Knightmare. Those rules that you have. You would never grant mercy when it comes to your target, even for a child. Any other Knightmare would've killed me. You didn't."

"So you're curious?"

"No. I'm angry." Aiva walked closer to Koe, and Koe let her, still eyeing her hands. She lifted them both up slowly, moving toward his face. Instead, they landed on his scarf. "Does it still keep you warm?" Every fiber in Koe's being iced over. She knew. She recognized the scarf. Koe's legs suddenly buckled a little.

"I don't know what you mean," said Koe. For the first time in a long time, his voice was shaky. Aiva raised her hands toward his face again, still a few centimeters away from the shadow covering it. Then her hands disappeared into the darkness, and for the first time in a very long, long time, Koe felt another person caress his face, feeling every inch, every scar. He wanted to melt into her arms. The moment he'd always dreamt of stood before him. Tears threatened to fall, and he was glad she couldn't see him. Every feeling he'd pushed away to keep it together came flooding back, cascading in this one second.

"I was right... You are handsome." Tears now formed in her eyes too. "Why did you do this?"

A few tears let loose, and he knew she felt them on her hands. Koe's voice trembled. "I didn't have a choice. The Queen tried to kill me. A Knightmare rescued me... I didn't know what I was getting into."

Aiva softly stroked his cheek with her thumb, brushing the tears away. "It looks like they didn't break you completely. The Light is on your side."

"The Light? It never has been," said Koe. He grabbed her hands gently and held them in his. He hadn't held hands with someone since becoming a Knightmare so long ago. How wonderful it was to feel another human's touch. No battle to be fought. No target to chase down. No evil to fight. Just peace. "It never cared about me. Just you. I was in the way."

"The Light kept you alive all these years," said Aiva.

"Maybe it was love," said Koe. He wasn't sure how he meant it. He always loved Aiva. Aiva was the only person he felt this strongly for. He'd do anything for her. If that wasn't love, he wasn't sure what was. Aiva's expression didn't change at the word love. Whatever she thought of it, she quickly moved on.

Aiva pulled her hands from his, the warmth vanishing in an instant. "I wish you'd stayed dead."

Koe's heart stopped. "Why?"

"Because you've turned into the very thing that haunts my dreams. You kill because the Shadows say so, without any thought for what it does to the families and friends of your victims." She turned to survey the empty room.

"Many are far from innocent, and I know the Queen has her hands full of blood too," said Koe, his voice raising. "She's the one who lashed me twenty-two times, pinned the murder of her own parents on me and then plastered my face across the kingdom so I would be hunted, executed on the spot. I was just a boy!" Aiva swerved back around, her eyes blazing with fire.

"Justifying one target to yourself doesn't mean the rest are the same," she said. "The Knightmares serve the Shadows — the very beings who cursed the world! There's a reason why your kind is made up of outcasts."

"I'm not like them," said Koe.

"Maybe that's true. Maybe you do have a moral code. But you're still a Knightmare. Still a killer."

"Me? What about you? You killed the King and Queen!" shouted Koe.

"It was the only way," said Aiva, not questioning how he knew it. "I'd do it again. Sera was right, the King and Queen were more concerned about protecting their luxuries than they were about the lives of their citizens."

"That doesn't change the fact that she used you. Sera doesn't care about you, she just wants to control you," said Koe.

"That's where you're wrong," said Aiva vehemently. "She never forced me to do anything. We both want to save the world, save Oarlon from this curse. You can't see it because you Knightmares are unaffected by the air, but it's killing so many innocent people. More than ever before. We need the Chosen One to save us. Sera is our last hope."

Koe threw up his arms and paced in a circle, still keeping his ears perked and his gaze on Aiva. He couldn't believe the rage coursing through his veins. He didn't want to fight with her. Not when they'd just shared one of the best moments of Koe's life minutes prior. "Come with me. Let's leave this place. Leave the city. Remember your dream?" Her dream of running away, just the two of them, had been all that kept him going for so long.

"And go where? The air is bad in every city. There's no escaping this. We'll never be able to blend in normally. Even if we did, the air would kill me soon enough. I'm not going to just let people die if I can do something about it."

"Then where were you last night when the Queen, the one you're so devoted to, ordered a full-scale war that killed hundreds just to kill Wystan? Is that really saving lives?"

"If Sera made the decision, she must've seen something."

Koe shook his head and sighed, not believing his ears.

"She's the Chosen One. She will save Oarlon and the rest of the world," she said.

"You're really so loyal that you'll overlook every wrong she's done?" said Koe.

"I trust her heart. Her dedication," said Aiva.

Koe's frustration was palpable. Sera seemed to have successfully brainwashed Aiva. Just another reason to kill Sera—to release her grip on Aiva.

"You criticize the Knightmares for following the Shadows so blindly, yet you follow Sera without a second thought," said Koe, shaking his head. "I thought maybe you called me here to reunite. To put all this behind us and leave. Now I'm thinking I was wrong."

"You spared me. It was only right to show you the same respect." Aiva's voice hardened, and her eyes narrowed. "I wanted one last moment to give you the mercy you never had."

The sunlight was shining on Koe's back, preventing him from turning invisible. He'd never wanted to fight less than in this moment. She'd planned this—the warehouse, the tall, bright windows. She'd made it so he couldn't just disappear. His way out was through her, and he was hesitating.

"But my friend is dead. He died fifteen years ago at the hands of a Knightmare, and today, I'll avenge him," said Aiva.

She grabbed the hilt at her belt, and her blade extended in a flash. Koe drew his daggers. The clash of blades was quick and precise. Koe's duel with Thane the previous night was difficult, but the speed of Aiva's blade and her precision sent him reeling back. Her blade came close to his neck several times, his daggers blocking her sword in the nick of time.

To make matters worse, he was hesitating to attack her. He knew it too. All of Koe's attacks were wild and sloppy but just quick enough that she couldn't use it against him. He couldn't hurt her, even if he did manage to find an opening, which hadn't appeared.

Koe pulled back into the shadow of the wall and immediately disappeared. He had hesitated walking in, hesitated during their entire conversation, and now he was on his toes, barely surviving. But the moment she touched his face had been worth it all, even the ache that plagued his heart now.

Aiva lunged into the shadow, swinging violently, trying to keep him close and avoid losing him. He threw one of his daggers into the ground a few feet away. It was just enough of a distraction to pull Aiva's attention off him. In that split second, Koe let himself become visible once again and jumped through one of the bay windows, summoning the dagger back to him as he dove from the ledge into the ocean.

The cold penetrated the shadows to his skin, making his jaw clench. He wanted to burst out of the ice-cold water, find a heating lamp and stay next to it for days. He swam rapidly away, feeling his muscles slowly freezing up. His heart was racing faster just to keep his body moving. His scarf, soaked and more worn than before, no longer came even close to keeping him warm.

TWENTY

QUEEN SERA

Scars ran all down Thane's back. He was still sedated, his eyes closed.
Sera watched as the needle pierced his skin, sewing it closed once again.
The soldiers who rescued him reported to Sera that the Knightmare had
spared his life to send her a message. Thane had been unconscious since,
but the doctors reassured Sera that he would make a full recovery. The
medicines they gave him would get him back on his feet soon. The cuts
were all superficial. He could be back to leading the army within a week.

While her heart remained steady at the sight of him alive, back in
the deep corners of her mind, she wanted to yell until he woke up.
Without her captain to lead her army, the underworld war would be
harder. The Knightmare threat against her life was still present. If they
got to her, the world would be doomed.

She took a breath and shook her head, even though there was no
one there to see it. Her guards were outside. She only had herself to talk
to.

The people were clamoring in the streets, throwing their hands up and clapping at the news of Wystan's death and his underground operations coming to a stop. Of course, they didn't know that some stragglers escaped, and there had been a significant number of innocent bystanders killed. There were voices of dissent, mostly family members of the fallen, but they were quickly drowned out by the praise the rest of the city gave to Sera and the kingdom. She had taken a big step toward her goal. The people's faith was being rewarded. People were seeing results.

The Knightmares were her next target. As long as they were out there, she couldn't focus on the poisoned air. She'd been trying to force her visions to reveal the solution to the curse, but she kept running into a wall. The vision showed the Knightmares instead, always the same thing every time: Knightmares in the throne room. Now there were only three, but the end result of them killing her was the same.

A knock at the door interrupted her thoughts.

"Come in," said Sera.

The door opened to one of her guards who bowed right away. Gaven bolted inside, wrapping his arms around Sera's waist and burying his head against her stomach.

"What's wrong?" As soon as Sera said it, she regretted it. Gaven looked up to her with his big eyes as wide as can be.

"Is Daddy going to be okay?" Thankfully, Gaven didn't seem to notice Sera's inconsiderate question.

"Oh, yes. He's going to be back on his feet soon. Don't you

worry." She stroked the back of his head and continued reassuring him. Her gaze turned toward Thane, and she moved her back away from the window, opening the view to Gaven.

Gaven jerked back when he saw his father on the operating table. The doctors weren't done yet, and any time they touched Thane, Gaven froze. He still wasn't used to the sight of blood. Sadly, he needed to get used to it.

"Your father was very brave. He took down a lot of bad men, making the world a safer place. However, there are some called Knightmares. Do you know anything about them?"

Gaven nodded rapidly. "Daddy told me about them. They look like shadows come to life."

"Yes, they are soulless creatures, designed to kill. They take no mercy and have no honor. Your father is lucky he survived."

"A Knightmare did that?"

Didn't she just explain that to him?

"Yes."

Gaven walked up to the window and put his hand on the glass. "I wish I could heal him."

Sera smiled. Gaven had a long way to go before becoming king material, but he had Sera's instinct to help others. Hopefully, by the time he became king, he wouldn't have to work as hard as she did. Her hand rested on his shoulder.

"We will make them pay. I promise."

The room went silent. A cold shiver tickled Sera's neck.

Something was off. Gaven turned to her and stared into her eyes, but he said nothing. Sera scrunched her eyebrows and tilted her head. "Are you okay, Gaven?"

The door behind them blew off the hinges by a force so powerful that the wall itself cracked. A loud clang echoed through the hall and the room. Sera turned back to see the operating room was now empty. Thane and the doctors were nowhere to be seen. She took a step behind Gaven, putting her hands on his shoulders. Then three shadowy figures entered the room. They were the same figures she had seen in her prior visions.

"Guards!" No response. It was deathly silent.

Sera backed up against the window. She looked to Gaven, but his face was expressionless. She shook him, but he didn't respond to her, remaining void of any emotion. Sera took a deep breath, and her heartbeat began to slow. This was a vision.

The Knightmares surrounded them. The largest one attempted to grab Gaven, but Sera pulled her son away before the Knightmare could. Sera moved back, holding Gaven in front of her as a tall, skinny Knightmare reached for him and missed. She felt the stare of the Knightmare with the white scarf and hat. Though she couldn't see his face, she recognized him.

He was in all of her visions.

She looked at the Knightmare, and a moment later he vanished, reappearing right in front of them. He grabbed Gaven, who remained unresponsive. His eyes didn't show any sign of life. The Knightmare hoisted him up in his arms as Sera tried to grab Gaven back, but her hands passed through Gaven and the Knightmare like they were ghosts.

Suddenly, the floor beneath Sera's legs turned into quicksand, and she immediately began sinking. She tried to scream out, but no sound left her lips. She watched as the Knightmare walked out with Gaven in his arms. The other two Knightmares simply vanished. Sera slowly sank under the floor, drowning.

Once the last speck of light disappeared, Sera jolted back to reality. Gaven was by her side once again. Her chest was heaving. Gaven tugged on her hand.

"You okay?"

"Yes, yes, I'm fine." But she wasn't. This was a warning. She needed to act. She quickly told Gaven to stay and left the observation room to find her guards.

"Call my transport immediately."

The guards did as she commanded. Her parents had a second, secure location north of the city. They'd often disappeared there. While Sera rarely visited, it was still relatively unknown and very well guarded. Perhaps it would help in her predicament now.

When she returned, Gaven was staring at her. He didn't say anything, but she knew he was wondering what was going on—why she had been so startled moments ago. She tried not to shrink away from his questioning eyes. Her hands were shaking ever so slightly in fear of what could happen to Gaven, but she also felt a sense of revelation. She realized in this moment that maybe, deep down, Thane's near-death experience had rattled her. Seeing what happened to Gaven in her vision and what that had genuinely done to her told her she still had more attachments than she cared to admit. If she was going to follow Quila's advice, she needed to distance herself from Gaven and Thane.

She took Gaven by the hand and led him out of the observatory. After a few quick calls and commands to her staff, the Queen soon sat in the back of a bulletproof enclosed hoverer. The four back seats in the hoverer faced each other. Gaven sat opposite her, playing with action figures. Sera kept the privacy shield up to separate the guards driving the vehicle from them.

Clash! Clash! Gaven slammed the action figures into each other multiple times. He made small noises that Sera couldn't make out, but he was clearly on another planet while orchestrating his story.

"Gaven."

Gaven paused his story and saw Sera's eyes shift to the right, staring at the seat next to him. He sighed and put his figures down. "I just thought we could have some you-and-me time. I might not be able to see you for a while."

"Why's that?" Gaven asked, sitting beside her.

"You know the bad men who hurt your father? Well, I have to stop them."

Gaven nodded and twirled his thumbs together. "You won't end up like Daddy, will you?"

"Stop thinking that," snapped Sera. She'd had enough of his worrying for one day. "Your father will be fine. I will be fine."

"I'm sorry, Mother, please don't hurt me."

This caught Sera off guard.

"Why would I hurt you?" she asked, her voice softening.

"You're sending me away. You're punishing me. It's because I wasn't strong enough in the dungeon, wasn't it?"

The dungeon? Then it clicked. Gaven was referring to the man she had tortured below, that she had Gaven electrocute.

"No, not at all. I'm sending you away to protect you."

Gaven reached over, his hand hovering over hers. He tried to touch her, but his hand passed through hers. She was only a holographic image projected into the hoverer from her throne room at the castle. Sera wanted to accompany her son, but she knew she had to stay. There was too much to be done. She compromised, projecting herself into the hoverer for as long as she could. It would be several hours until Gaven reached the vacation home, she could at least comfort him as he departed the city.

"You'll be back before you know it," said Sera, smiling.

"Where am I going?" asked Gaven.

"Our vacation home. It's secure and unknown. You'll be safe from danger."

"I just want to go home," said Gaven.

"Gaven, please stop complaining. I'm doing this for you. To keep you safe. I love you so much, but I'm not just your mother. I am the Queen, and it's my duty to help everyone. Please understand," said Sera.

Gaven shrugged, scooted over to the window and looked out as they passed through the city on their way to the northern gates.

"Who's that?" he asked.

The Queen couldn't move from her position to look. She pressed her transmitter to contact the driver. The privacy barrier retracted into the car.

One of the guards propped himself up and turned around.

"Yes, ma'am?"

"My son says there is someone out there," said Sera. The guards shrugged and scanned everywhere they could see.

"Probably just a citiz—"

A large blast erupted in front of them as one of the escort hoverers exploded. The remaining three hoverers halted. The flames and wreckage were visible from the windows. There were no survivors.

Yelling voices intermixed with the clanging of bullets on metal. The Queen's hands shook, and her world seemed to spin out of control. Sera couldn't tell what was happening.

"Commander, report!" said Sera frantically.

The Commander, who was driving, shook his head.

"I don't know. We're being attacked!" yelled the Commander. Both the Commander and the second guard exited the vehicle. The sounds of a struggle followed.

"Mother? I think it's the Knightmares," said Gaven, staring out the window.

Sera's throat suddenly felt tight, constricting more by the second. She watched as Gaven peered outside, trying to see what was happening. She quickly tapped some controls on her armchair in the throne room.

Reinforcements would now be on the way, but more than likely, they wouldn't get there fast enough.

"Gaven, tell me what's happening."

"I just see… blood. Lots of it." Gun shots rang out, hitting the hoverer but stopping short of penetrating it. That didn't stop the assailants from trying. Over and over, the gun fired, hitting the same spot on the rear window with incredible accuracy. However, the glass was barely damaged. Then Sera heard two voices arguing, trying to unlock the door from the outside. Gaven threw himself to the other side of the hoverer and gasped.

"It's them! It's them!" He curled up in a ball and buried his head into his knees.

"Gaven, I need you to remain calm. Can you do that for me?" He shook his head without looking at her.

"Gaven," started Sera more forcefully. "Look at me." Slowly, he did. Tears rolled down his cheeks and his lips trembled.

"How many are there?" She asked. The cracks on the glass were spreading now, covering the whole window like a spider web. The door rattled, and the voices on the other side became louder. It would take another ten, fifteen minutes for the reinforcements to arrive. They would surely get through by then.

"Maybe three. I don't know," Gaven whimpered.

"Okay, good. That's good." Sera watched her son's eyes, wide as can be, locked on the door. She placed her hand on the left armchair, trying to recall the buttons she needed. She keyed in a sequence and held her finger above the final button, ready to press it. The door to the hoverer flew off, and sure enough, she could see at least two Knightmares. She recognized them from her dreams immediately.

One of the Knightmares drew a gun and shot at her, but the bullet went right through the hologram. Sera flinched, touching her stomach where the shot would've hit her. Gaven covered his ears and closed his eyes. Smoke rose from the hole in the seat.

"It's a hologram! It isn't her!" yelled the Knightmare with a male voice. The other one hissed, firing a shot at Sera as well just to make sure. Sera flinched again. Her heart was pounding, despite knowing that she wasn't in any real danger.

"Fyrk!" yelled a woman's voice, slamming her fist against the hoverer.

Sera knew these voices. She'd heard them in her visions.

The male Knightmare turned his attention to Gaven.

"He's real," he said. Gaven backed as far away as he could, making himself as small as he could. He looked to his mother in terror.

"Help me!"

"Hey, look at me," said Sera, fighting back tears. "You are going to be okay, Gaven. Just focus on my voice." She pressed the button. A loud beep sounded. Both Knightmares looked at one another as the hoverer exploded.

Sera's connection was terminated.

The throne room was full of a heavy silence. Not even the sun dared to disturb the scene, hiding behind an overcast sky.

She knew they would have killed him anyway. This way, at least two Knightmares were out of the picture. But her heart was gone. Pain snaked through her body. Her chest was hollow, her vision blurred, her breathing erratic.

Then her cries could be heard throughout the halls, reverberating throughout the castle and beyond. Not even the people on the other side of the world could escape her wails.

She closed her crying eyes in agony. When she opened them again, she was in a fog covered field. A ray of light pierced through the fog, and indistinct whispers from a soft voice reached her ears. She couldn't make out what it was saying. But she knew. She knew that whatever laid just past the fog was the answer to breaking the Shadow's curse. She was so close, but her chest welled up again, heaving between sobs, and she couldn't stop the tears from falling. At no point had she ever thought there was a price too great. She never thought she would question the sacrifices necessary to save the world. Until now. The vision wavered and dissipated.

Sera walked down to the medical facility a few floors below. There Thane rested on a bed with a mattress full of a blue gel. The gel was for comfort, so he wouldn't have to sleep on his front or side if he didn't want to.

She ordered the medical staff out. The doctor said something about Thane being conscious, but she didn't pay them much attention.

She took a seat by Thane's bed. His eyes flickered open, and he gave her a half-hearted smile when he saw her.

"I didn't think you'd be here. Don't you have better things to do?" he said a with quick wink. When Sera didn't smile back, Thane lifted his head up slightly. "Hey, I'll be okay. I'll be back on my feet soon enough. I'm going to make those Knightmares pay."

Of course, he thought it was about him. At least he was right, she would make the Knightmares pay.

"Thane... I had a vision about Gaven, so I sent him to my family's vacation home up north to keep him safe. On the way, the convoy was attacked by the Knightmares. They killed him, detonating an explosive device meant for me."

All the color from Thane's face washed away. He shook his head slightly.

"No... Please say you're lying."

"I was in the convoy via hologram. I saw it all."

Thane broke down. Sera had never really seen Thane cry before. His bellows matched the ferocity of her own screams earlier. He was like a dying cat yowling alone in an alley. He tried taking her hand, but she withdrew from him. She knew he wanted comfort. She did too, but there was no comfort to be had.

There was no going back now. She was on the path, and she would see it to the very end.

TWENTY-ONE

KOE

The air was hot as Koe sat in a small laundromat, covered in blankets.
His wet clothes were drying in a dryer and had been for the last half
hour. Besides the blanket, he was completely naked. No one would
know since the shadows covered every part of him, but even so, he was
exposed in a way he didn't care for.

While he was mostly warm now, he could still feel the chill of the
ocean freezing every muscle. He had trudged in the snow for a while,
trying to keep himself warm in his soggy clothes, but they'd started to
freeze and stiffen. His chest tightened. He knew if he didn't get
somewhere warm, he'd go into hypothermic shock. Thankfully, a few
minutes later, he'd spotted a big faded sign that read 'Laundromat'
nailed above a door. As he entered, the people inside screamed, almost
diving out the window to get away, leaving enough coins for him to dry
out his clothes.

It was almost comical, he thought. But he was too busy to laugh.

His mind was stuck on how much of a failure this mission had been already. They'd barely gotten anywhere, and now he was sitting alone, naked, under someone else's blankets that had been left in the dryer.

Aiva's rejection still burned his heart, but he wasn't going to give up hope. He knew what the Queen was like. What she hid deep down. The day he was framed, he saw firsthand how ruthless Sera was. He imagined enduring that kind of brutality for years would break anyone. He never considered himself the lucky one, but maybe he was.

His transmitter beeped. At first, Koe thought it might be Aiva, but he reminded himself that he changed frequencies and sent a message to Fye and Zos to do the same. They hadn't picked up when he tried to reach them, but he figured it had to be them.

"Koe here."

"We need to meet. Now," said Zos breathlessly, like she was on the run.

"What's going on?"

"Can't explain here. Meet us at the Arctic Hotel. Basement. As soon as you can." Koe pressed his transmitter to end the call. He sighed and rubbed his forehead. Could this be another trap? No, Aiva destroyed Jec's transmitter. It had to be Zos. If it was Zos, then why did she sound exhausted and even... nervous?

To make matters worse, the Arctic Hotel was in the Crown District. The Crown District sat just south of the castle and overlooked the other districts below. Anyone who was a royal but didn't live in the castle itself lived there. Anyone who was high up, traveling from another city, stayed at the only hotel. The Arctic Hotel — known for gambling, champagne and prostitution, though no one would ever admit that last one. The hotel was where anyone with more than a dime to their name went to spend their ridiculous wealth.

Koe had been there once on a past mission. It was heavily guarded. Everything in the Crown District was. He'd been sent to kill a wealthy trader from overseas who was transporting drugs into the city for Wystan. No one could prove it, and either the Queen didn't know or didn't care enough to intervene.

Infiltrating the hotel was only possible through the use of old underground tunnels that led into the basement. Not many knew of them, but as the hotel grew more popular, the Knightmares passed that info along from generation to generation. On that particular night, it came in handy. Koe rode the service elevator up, snuck past some hotel staff and made his way to the trader's room, where he slit her throat.

Once Koe's clothes were dry, he threw them on, the warmth doing little to alleviate the shivering of his body. They didn't feel like clean clothes, since he hadn't washed them. He could still smell the ocean on them, but at least they weren't drenched.

As Koe ducked and dodged through the city, he couldn't help but reflect on how often he'd been doing this in the past few days. On a typical mission, he would go directly to the district where the target was, kill the target and then leave immediately.

He didn't want to admit it, but if Sera was the Chosen One, then there was no possible path to kill her. At least, not until she fulfilled the

246

prophecy. The Light would be protecting her, and she could see their plans before they even made them. If she was able to wipe out Wystan so easily, the Knightmares would be next.

Koe clenched his hands as he slipped into an alley, evading a patrol. He was entering the Crown District and would have to be on guard now. But he couldn't avoid the thought of Sera winning and the thunder that shook his core. How could he have suffered the lashes, being framed, and Rus' brutal training, just to end up failing?

"Did you hear that?"

Koe froze behind a dumpster. He was on the border between districts now, and the patrols were heavy. Three soldiers marched together on foot on the main street while Koe hid.

"No, I didn't," said another. The third one began violently coughing.

"You okay, Angun?"

Angun tried to reaffirm he was between coughs. "This air, being outside all day. It's getting worse."

"Don't worry, the Queen will save us all soon enough. Have faith, my friend," said the first guard.

Koe rolled his eyes. Could he kill them now? Kill the first one because of his stupid beliefs, Angun because he was already sick, and the last one… well, because she was a part of it.

"Come on, let's move on," said the second guard. Their feet sloshed in the snow, away from Koe's hiding place. He returned to the street, checking for more guards before crossing. Halfway across, a spotlight caught him as he bolted to the other side. Yelling broke out in the guard tower above, and a piercing alarm blared throughout the district that could probably be heard across the entire city.

This wasn't what Koe needed right now. The three guards that had passed him had turned around, drawing their guns. Koe threw one of his daggers like a boomerang. The dagger whisked through the air, slicing their throats in succession. Their bodies hit the ground as the dagger returned to his hand. At least he got something he wanted.

As Koe hastily ducked behind a building, his boot hit something that sounded metallic. He crouched and dusted aside the snow to reveal a grate below him. With the adrenaline flowing and the sound of more soldiers nearing, he yanked the grate up with ease and jumped into the darkness below.

He would have to enter the hotel through the sewers anyway — he just wished it didn't have to be so soon. The whiff of feces made him want to vomit whatever was left in his nearly empty stomach. Between this and the frigid ocean swim, he couldn't wait to bathe.

The shouting above kept Koe moving through the tunnels. Patches of light filtered in from other grates above him, helping him navigate the darkness. Each turn, each patch of moss or dent in the tunnel wall sparked his memory of his first journey through.

As the minutes went by, the voices faded. At this point, he knew they weren't coming for him. Trying to fight a Knightmare in the dark would be difficult. But now they knew he was here, the Queen would reinforce the district and Aiva would certainly hear about it.

The sewer was a well-designed maze that was easy to get lost in. Every turn required Koe to recalibrate where he was and what direction he faced. He quickened his pace as he drew closer, landing at the grate leading into the hotel. He pushed it and slid it away as he hopped up into the basement of the hotel.

Muffled music from the floor above played as Koe pulled the grate back into place. He took out his gun and kept it by his side just in case.

The basement, like the sewer, was a maze of rooms. There was a big laundry room that had mostly towels and sheets rolling about in the washers. There was a breakroom and locker room for the staff. Several rooms were chock full of storage items. Koe could guess that they were full of things like gambling chips, spare tables, alcohol, anything that the guests visiting might need.

Yet one thing was missing: people. While the basement was hardly crowded the last time he was here, Koe still had to sneak past a bunch of staff to reach the service elevator. Now, the rooms were eerily quiet. He felt like he'd been duped again.

A wet streak of red painted the floor, leading him to the next room where the door was left ajar. Koe nudged it open with his gun. He could hear a small whimper. The light flickered on and off by itself. According to the nameplate on the door, this was the general manager's office.

A big desk lay in pieces on the other end of the windowless room. Some of the tiles on the wall were broken. Lying against the wall were several bodies, all in the hotel staff uniforms they were forced to wear. One looked like a bellboy, another was probably a receptionist, and a few were maids. The last one was in a suit and tie, probably the general manager himself. All of them had been stabbed several times. Judging by the mess outside the room, they'd been dragged in here.

A small click behind the door made Koe slam against it, crushing whoever was behind it against the wall. He swung around the door and aimed his gun, ready to fire, when he saw Fye groaning and clutching his shoulder.

"Don't shoot!" he said. He was breathing heavily. Fye's right arm was bandaged heavily, but patches of blood were slowly soaking through. Most of his clothes had been charred away, and Koe could imagine the burns that Fye must have underneath.

"What happened?" asked Koe, holstering his gun. Fye lifted his good arm and pointed to the corner across from them. Part of the broken desk obscured his view, but now Koe could see where the whimpering was coming from. It was a small boy with pale skin and white streaks in his hair, like Koe's scarf. He had a few black markings on his face. It was impossible not to know who this boy was. Son of the Queen and Prince of Oar, Gaven.

Gaven curled up, facing the wall, trembling and shaking. His gaze shot toward Koe, and instantly, he tried to make himself smaller.

"You kidnapped the Queen's son?" snapped Koe. "Are you an idiot?"

The door pushed open, and Koe lifted his gun only to find the newcomer was Zos, looking as disheveled as Fye. The bottom of her jacket was burnt away on one side, singe marks lined the edges. With one finger, she pushed the gun out of her face.

"We ambushed the Queen's personal convoy, expecting her to be in there."

"She sorta was," said Fye, jumping in.

"She was a hologram, sending her son away into the mountains. She detonated an explosive device. We barely got out of there in one piece."

With the shadow covering her, Koe couldn't see how hurt Zos was or wasn't, but if she was, she didn't show it. Her posture was tall, her movements swift. There was no sign of weakness. Unlike Fye, who groaned every few seconds.

"You should've known she wouldn't leave the castle. That's what you were waiting for?" asked Koe.

"We saw an opportunity. I don't see you offering a solution to get past the shield," said Zos, crossing her arms. Koe then turned to the boy huddled in the corner. The only reason they would take him but not kill him was if they were going to use him.

"You're going to try and draw the Queen out, aren't you?" asked Koe.

"Yes," said Zos.

"Why would she come for him when she already sacrificed him to take you both out?"

"You underestimate her love for him. For her son."

Nikai

"She's not like anyone else!" yelled Koe. "If she was willing to kill her son once, she'll be willing to do it again. No matter how much she loves him, she doesn't love him enough." A small cry came from the corner. Koe immediately regretted raising his voice. He didn't regret his words, just that Gaven had heard them.

"She won't sacrifice him in front of the whole city. We'll send word out to the media that we are holding the Prince captive. The media will report it, and the Queen will have no choice but to save face. They will do whatever we tell them to, and once we get the Queen out, we will kill her and this will all be over," said Zos.

Koe took a step closer.

It wasn't a bad plan at all. It was actually a very good one, except for one minor detail.

"You're forgetting who you're dealing with," said Koe. "The Queen might seem like she's playing by the rules, but she'll order her troops to stop us at all costs. You've just trapped us in a building, dangerously close to the castle, thinking we have the upper hand, but the truth is — we have no advantage. We need to leave now and figure out another way."

Zos shook her head. "She doesn't know we're here," she said. "The crash site is still far away but... we couldn't move fast enough. The kid wouldn't stop crying, and Fye here has a hard time moving, so we stopped here. Once we decide on a meeting location, we'll take the boy there to meet the Queen. And once we're sure she's there, we kill her, and then him."

"And what about them?" Koe pointed to the dead bodies along the wall. "Someone is going to notice they're missing, if they haven't already."

"Which is why we need to decide a place soon!" urged Zos.

"This was your plan. You figure it out," said Koe. If Zos really wanted to be the leader of the team, then she needed to make the hard choice. Koe didn't care. He was sure the plan wouldn't work anyway.

He sighed and walked away, toward the boy. He had his face pressed against the wall, seemingly hoping to disappear into the next room. Koe knelt down in front of him. Tears were still falling from his face. He looked younger than Koe was when Koe was banished.

He was shaking so badly, Koe instinctually reached out to put a hand on his shoulder. The boy gasped and shuddered. Koe pulled back but scooted closer. Gaven was the Queen's son, and Koe should be happy to see his mortal enemy suffer. But she wasn't suffering. An innocent boy was suffering.

"Don't be afraid. We're not going to hurt you," said Koe.

The boy stopped trembling for a second. "You're a Knightmare, aren't you?" he asked, barely audible.

"Yes," said Koe. He wished he could say that their reputation was overexaggerated, but he knew that wasn't the case. "I'm sorry you're a part of this. I'm sorry for what I said about your mother not loving you."

The boy didn't respond.

Koe sat against the wall next to Gaven. He couldn't halt the sadness building in him as he watched the boy, forever changed by this ordeal. Koe was just a servant boy, and Gaven was a prince, and yet, their tears were the same.

The elevator way down the hall dinged, and Gaven quickly used every ounce of energy to scream, "HELP!"

Koe slapped his hand over Gaven's mouth as he continued shrieking. Zos ran out the door. A groan and then a body thudding against the ground followed.

"Hey! Stop. I know. I know," said Koe.

Gaven's cries softened. A few of his tears soaked Koe's glove.

"I'm going to take my hand off you now. Do not scream." When Gaven nodded, Koe removed his hand.

"Next time you scream like that, I'll cut out your tongue," said Zos, returning with her bloody dagger in hand.

Koe held up his hand to her. "He's just a boy. He's scared."

"Big fyrking deal," said Zos. "This isn't daycare." She turned on her heel and went back to Fye.

Gaven tried to hide his face. With tears streaming down his cheeks, the boy whimpered. He looked exactly like what Koe must've looked like every night when trying to fall asleep in the Knightmare temple. Curled up, eyes closed, hoping that once he opened them, he'd be somewhere else, in a different life. Koe propped himself up, clearing his throat.

"I was like you once. I worked in the castle." Koe heard Fye and Zos stop their little conversation. Koe was confident they were listening.

"Your mother cast me out for something I didn't do. She tried to kill me. She took my best friend away from me. I know this must be hard for you, but it's for the best. She doesn't deserve you."

The boy's crying stopped, and a long silence followed. Koe hadn't tried to be supportive of someone's emotional needs since before he was a Knightmare. Rus would beat him to a pulp if he heard the speech he just gave to Gaven, but seeing Gaven act the same way he had so long ago triggered a yearning, gnawing desire that Koe couldn't hide away.

"It's true though, isn't it?" asked the boy, looking directly at Koe. His voice was a little stronger. "She detonated the explosion?"

"Yes. She only cares about her mission and herself," said Koe. "Everything else is expendable." Koe thought of Aiva and how devoted Aiva was to Sera. The Queen was a master manipulator. Koe was just glad to see Gaven opening his eyes a little to her selfishness.

"I've seen her do something terrible," said Gaven. "She made me do it. I didn't want to, but she said I had to. I... I..." Gaven started bawling again. Once again, Koe placed his hand on Gaven's shoulder, and this time, the boy didn't move away.

"You really are like them, aren't you?" asked Zos, having silently returned to their side of the room. The venom in her tone was more present than ever before. "Soft spot for a kid, huh? Even the Queen's spawn?"

"Not now," said Koe.

The mission, all the events from the past few days, even Aiva, weren't worth thinking about. Rus always warned Koe about attachments. It's why Koe got in trouble for helping others out when he wasn't ordered to. He couldn't help but feel protective toward Gaven, just like he'd always wanted someone to look out for him when he was young.

"We need to decide on a meeting place now!" said Zos.

Koe stood up and matched her stance. "Then choose!"

Behind him, the crying from the boy changed to a groan. Gaven stretched his legs out and clutched his side. Since he'd been huddled up, Koe hadn't noticed that a piece of shrapnel was protruding from Gaven's stomach. While it wasn't a big piece, for a small boy, the wound was bad.

Koe placed two fingers on Gaven's neck and felt his pulse, finding it faint. Now taking a closer look, he realized Gaven looked pale.

"He needs a hospital. We can't help him here."

Fye's shrill laugh bounced around the room, albeit not at full volume, due to his weakened state. "Brilliant plan! There goes our leverage!" he said.

"If he dies, we lose our leverage all the same," said Koe.

"Then we'd better make a plan fast," said Zos.

"He won't make it much longer, and there's no way we can do this if we rush it," said Koe.

Zos chuckled and threw her hands up in the air. "We already contacted Rus. He's on his way," she said. "He believes in the plan. Do you want to tell him how you threw away the Shadows' most important mission for just one life?" Fye stood up as straight as he could, drawing a dagger in support.

"Don't do what I think you're going to do, Koe," said Zos. She rested a hand on one of her daggers. Koe wanted to put his hand on his gun, but that could end up escalating the situation. Ultimately, he refrained, raising them instead.

"You're right. I have lost sight of what's important. I want the Queen dead more than anyone. No matter the cost."

Fye sheathed his dagger, and Zos took her hand off hers.

Koe lowered his hands, stepping forward. "Where do you propose we go?"

"I suggest we move to the Sky District. This time—"

Koe got close enough to her to throw three punches, two to the face and one to the gut. With Zos bent over and disoriented, Koe grabbed her and threw her across the room into the wall, where she landed right on top of the pile of bodies.

Fye, taken aback, went for his gun, but Koe reached him first and kicked it out of his hands. A gunshot went off, loud enough that it might be heard from upstairs, even with the music and partying above.

Koe wasted no time. Fye was bigger and stronger, but Koe was faster and uninjured. Every punch that Fye threw, Koe ducked or moved in time. He focused his jabs on Fye's injured arm. Soon, it wasn't even a fight, it was a beatdown. Koe slammed Fye over and over until he was on the ground.

Koe swerved around to see Zos still struggling to get up. He had hit her pretty hard. She was winded, and being thrown into a wall wasn't helping either.

Koe ran over and picked Gaven up, being careful not to make the wound worse. Surprisingly, Gaven let him do it without a struggle. Koe hoped that Gaven was beginning to trust him, but more than likely, Gaven's wound was making him weaker and he was only going along with Koe because he had no other choice. Everyone else wanted him dead. It was just like when Koe had been forced to go with Rus so long ago.

"I can't let him die," said Koe. He knew he had betrayed his comrades, knew he could be sentenced to death for it, but he was one of the last skilled Knightmares left. He might lose whatever tiny bit of respect the others had for him, but he'd never cared about that. After Gaven was safe and the Queen dead, Sera's spell over Aiva would be gone, and they could finally leave Oarlon behind.

Gaven held his hand over his wound as he bounced ever so slightly up and down in Koe's arms. Koe weaved through the hallway and pressed the elevator button at the end, tapping his finger on Gaven's back repeatedly. The body of the servant Zos had killed by the elevator still lay on the floor. Koe turned his back to it, shielding Gaven from the sight, though he wasn't sure what difference it made after everything the boy had already witnessed.

Gaven fidgeted in his arms, avoiding looking down at the shard poking out of his stomach. As the hum of the elevator descended toward them, Koe laid Gaven on the ground, took off his scarf and wrapped it around Gaven's wound, tightening it to stem the bleeding. For years, Koe had kept it so clean, and now he could see the blood soaking through it. But that was a small price to pay.

"You're going to get into this elevator, and you're going to ask the first person you see for help. They will take you to a hospital. Your parents will find you, I promise."

"No, please. I don't want to go back."

"You have to. You need help, and the castle has the best team of doctors in the city," he reassured Gaven.

"I don't want to see her!"

"This isn't up for debate!" shouted Koe. He instantly regretted raising his voice and softened his tone. "I'm sorry. You'll be okay."

The elevator door beeped and opened. Koe softly nudged Gaven in and pressed the button before stepping back. As he did, he heard a scuff behind him. He turned and saw no one in the dark hallway, but his hearing detected the quiet sound of footsteps pattering toward him. Koe threw himself back in the elevator as Zos revealed herself. Her dagger whistled by his throat, barely missing.

The elevator doors reopened, revealing Zos standing in the doorway. Koe pushed Gaven into the corner behind him, grabbing Zos' wrist and yanking her off balance before she could stab Koe.

She stumbled into the elevator with them, and the doors closed. The elevator rose. In those few seconds, Zos' attention turned to Gaven and back to Koe repeatedly, trying to throw Koe off balance. He kept parrying her blows, pushing her around and away from Gaven as much as possible in the cramped space. Her dagger, aimed for Gaven's face, cut across Koe's shoulder instead. The scratch barely registered.

When the elevator reached the first floor, several partygoers were waiting to get on, only to find Koe shoving Zos out of the elevator. Her body tumbled onto the golden floor. Shocked, the guests dispersed, yelling as they rushed away from the Knightmares.

Koe grabbed Gaven and pulled him toward the main area, full of rows and rows of tables filled with cards and poker chips. On her feet again, Zos threw her dagger at Koe's head, barely missing him and slamming it into the gold-colored wall.

Newly lit cigars were left smoking on the ground, cards and drinks abandoned, as their owners tried to flee toward the front of the room, away from the fight. In the periphery, Koe heard the elevator chime again. He turned to see Fye jump down in front of the main doors, taking a few shots at the runners in front before they could get out.

The rest of the partygoers scurried behind tables, behind the bar or the big golden pillars that sectioned the room. Fye charged in, clearly hurt but still very able to aim and fire a gun.

Koe grabbed Gaven and ducked behind a table as poker chips and green felt flew into the air from the bullets striking it. Beneath the table was a woman, another guest of the event, covering her head. A few men and women were behind her, trying their best to stay out of the way. Her eyes widened as she saw Koe.

"This is the Queen's son. He needs a hospital. If I distract them, can you get him out?" asked Koe urgently. The woman nodded, looking toward Gaven and recognizing who he was. Koe drew his gun. He tapped softly on the scarf at Gaven's waist. "This will keep you warm."

With a powerful jump, Koe backflipped onto the table, firing at both Zos and Fye.

Hotel security guards soon entered the shootout, engaging with Fye near the entrance. The hired security was a joke, but the Queen's soldiers would no doubt be here within minutes. Fye made quick work of the guards, but it was long enough of a distraction for Koe to jump on him, stabbing him several times in the back. Fye grabbed Koe and threw him onto the ground.

"You fyrking backstabber. I'm going to enjoy killing yo—"

Koe shot two bullets into Fye's shoulder, sending him through the glass doors outside. He twirled around to find Zos standing in the middle of the room.

"You have betrayed the Shadows, and I will not let you desecrate their love, even if it's the last thing I do," she said, pointing her dagger at him.

"And when you die, the Shadows will abandon you like all the rest," said Koe. He gripped his daggers.

They stared at one another, neither making the first move. Koe played out every scenario he could in his head: if she struck with her left versus her right. If she dropped her dagger and went for her gun. If she threw her daggers. What form would she use? High or low? For every scenario, he thought of a counter. He could only imagine what Rus would say if he were here. He'd be disappointed that Koe had taken up arms against a fellow Knightmare. But if this were an enemy, the only thing he'd say is, "No student of mine would lose."

Several seconds passed with Zos and Koe moving slowly closer together, then Koe charged. His attack was swift. Both Zos' hands grabbed her daggers, clashing against Koe's. He slashed one of her wrists, and one of her daggers clattered to the floor. Before Zos could react, Koe drew two more cuts, going high, then low. One cut on her shoulder and one to her calf. Zos fell to her hands and knees. She moved to get up, but Koe grabbed her, pulling her up and into a headlock.

"This is how we fall," said Zos, twitching to get out of his grip.

Koe plunged his dagger through Zos' heart. Her death rattle followed, and when she stilled, Koe released his grip. The shadows slowly faded from around Zos' body as blood trickled from her mouth onto the floor. Her brown eyes were wide open, unmoving. Her black hair was short and unkempt. Her gaunt face bore several scars from past battles.

With the fight finished, all the partiers were scampering to leave or had already left. Koe checked outside and saw an imprint of Fye's body in the snow with a blood trail leading away from the hotel. Koe sighed, ready to return to the basement and disappear into the tunnels below.

That's when Gaven hobbled out from beneath the battered table, all alone.

"Why are you still here?" hissed Koe.

Gaven shook his head. "I don't want to go back."

TWENTY-TWO

QUEEN SERA

Before she saw the messenger, she heard the hurried footsteps thudding across the tile floors. Sera's advisors were all around her, preparing her late night speech about her son's death and the terror the Knightmares had inflicted. Sera and the council all turned in unison when a lowly messenger girl, no older than fifteen, entered the chamber. She looked to be a servant by the state of her ragged clothes. She bowed her head and did not raise it to meet the Queen's gaze.

"Your Majesty, I apologize for the intrusion. I was sent here to give you word from the Arctic Hotel."

"What about it?" asked Sera. Her eyes narrowed, unsure why the hotel would be of any concern right now.

"There was an attack. I wasn't told the details, but many of the hotel's patrons were killed. There were Knightmares... fighting each other."

Sera approached the messenger and used one finger to lift the

servant girl's head up to face her. There was a spark in Sera's eyes. Not
of happiness or hope, but of anger.

"Did you say 'Knightmares'?" She emphasized the 's' at the end.
If Aiva killed one a few nights ago and she blew up two, there should be
one at most.

Unless the Knightmare cohort sent more.

"Yes, Your Majesty. Three were reported but—"

Sera held up her finger, silencing the girl. "What were they
wearing?" she asked. The appearances of the Knightmares from her
visions were imprinted on her mind. She needed to know if the two who
attacked her son's convoy were still alive.

"I don't know, I'm just the—"

The Queen grabbed her face with one hand, pinching her cheeks
and mouth together. "Don't say it. Go, run along." Sera let the servant
girl go. Before she could think of a plan or return to her council, the girl
blurted out:

"Your son is alive!"

Sera's heart skipped a beat. Her hands were suddenly clammy. It
couldn't possibly be true. Could it? She reeled back toward the girl, their
faces inches apart.

"You're lying!"

"No, no, that's what I was told. I know nothing else!" The
chamber went silent. The council members froze. The girl's voice did not
waver, her expression steady. This was the truth, and Sera couldn't
believe it.

With a wave, the guards escorted the girl away. Sera immediately turned on Hanna, grabbing her by the arm and pulling her so close Hanna could taste the virulency in her voice.

"I want security footage of what happened delivered to me at once. Whoever saw my son still alive must be brought here immediately. Understand?"

Hanna nodded, whimpering in surprise at Sera's grip and intensity. Sera let go and stormed away from the advisors, who struggled to catch up.

"Wait, Your Majesty, what about the speech?" Hanna called, coming to her senses.

"Find me the evidence first! I need to know." The Queen waved dismissively at the councilors following her. They all stood in place, silently waiting for her to disappear.

Sera walked out and made her way to the balcony of her bedroom. As soon as she stepped out, she could feel the smog in the air. There was no glass enclosure over the balcony. Most people were used to the poisoned air, but since the air inside the castle was filtered and purified, breathing in the poison caused her every organ to tense up.

She wanted the burning pain in her lungs.

She coughed, leaned on the stone barrier and looked out over Oarlon. If it was true, and her son was still alive, what would he think of her and what she did? How could she face him again and tell him that she loved him?

Behind her, voices were getting louder. She turned to see Thane, still in his hospital gown, arguing with the guards at the balcony door.

"I need to see her!" shouted Thane as loudly as possible. Sera had to admit, seeing him be so brave in the face of so much physical and emotional pain was relieving. She knocked on the glass door to get the guards' attention. She gestured to Thane to join her outside. The guards moved as he pushed the door open. His eyes were focused. There were no tears.

"I want to go after him."

"You can barely stand. Sending you in would be sending you to your death, and right now, I can't let that happen."

Thane went down on one knee. Pain flooded his face. He grabbed her hand like he was going to propose.

"He's our son!"

"And I will send our very best to get him back. Right now, we know very little. Knightmares fighting against each other? Why? We need answers. My soldiers have surrounded the hotel. We will get him back. Now, go rest." She wasn't really sure of anything that was going on, but she figured that if she looked like she knew what she was talking about, Thane would trust her. Thankfully, it did break down his defenses a little. He rubbed the back of his neck and looked off, lost in thought.

"I just... I don't trust them!" His gaze flicked back to her.

That's when Sera realized something: this wasn't about saving Gaven. This was his chance at vengeance. This was his chance at the throne. What better way to get it than to gain recognition for saving the Prince? The war with the underworld was largely being kept out of the public eye and off the television for many reasons, one being that Sera didn't want anyone to know of the collateral damage. This was different, though—this was one mission. One mission against the worst foes the world could imagine. If he won and rescued the Prince, everyone would clamor for him to be king.

How could she yell at him after what she did to their son? She only did what was necessary for her to find the cure, to break the curse. It was a selfless deed. Thane's desire for vengeance was selfish, but she couldn't tell him no. Her guilt stopped her.

"You can go," said Sera.

"Thank you, Sera. I will bring him back." His voice was strong, his eyes determined.

"Bring him home," said Sera.

His smile dropped, and his eyes dimmed. He nodded, bowed and shuffled away before Sera could change her mind.

Sera returned to the safety of the castle interior. Her chest loosened as she breathed the purified air once again. Hanna stood waiting for her and bowed immediately as she walked back in. She held a digital pad.

"We have the security camera footage you requested."

The Queen gestured with her head to go on. Hanna turned on the display and held it up for Sera while the video played.

The Arctic Hotel's main floor held games, a bar and lounge areas. They were all familiar to the Queen. She'd never stayed a night at the hotel, but she'd visited when making public appearances. Not many of her subjects wanted her there though, they acted odd and performative when she was in their presence. Even the people visiting the city got swept up in the spectacle. Although to be fair, she was the Queen and could order anyone executed on the spot if she wanted. She took a deep breath. This was what it was like to be a royal. No one understood it. No one understood what it meant to be the Chosen One either. That was the burden she had to carry.

The video began, showing a gun fight erupt as a Knightmare shuffled Gaven off to a hiding spot at the far side of the room. Meanwhile, several of the hotel customers were gunned down by the other two Knightmares, who seemed to be trying to reach Gaven. Sera caught sight of the white scarf she had seen in her dreams tied around her son. A splotch of red marked the scarf, near his stomach. The Knightmare was protecting her son. Why?

As the video played, she saw the other two Knightmares fall. The first one disappeared out of camera shot. A quick cut to an exterior camera showed the Knightmare standing up and limping away, bleeding terribly as he did. He had been moving weirdly the entire fight. Sera supposed he was hurt. She hoped it was from the blast. The display switched back to the previous camera where the two Knightmares faced one another, daggers drawn. Within seconds, they charged, and the battle was soon over.

"Play it back," said Sera. She'd been so focused on the Knightmares, she hadn't paid attention to what Gaven did during the fight. Hanna rewound the footage back to the beginning of the fight. Sera watched as a woman next to Gaven waved him over to follow her. Some of the others were taking advantage of the Knightmares being distracted to escape. Gaven simply shook his head. The woman tried again, going to grab him, but he pulled back. The woman looked to him, looked to the fight and fled.

"Fast forward to the end of the fight." Now the dead Knightmare was laying on the floor, and the victor faced Gaven. Sera could only imagine what they were saying to each other. The Knightmare's face was forever hidden in shadow, but Gaven's reactions were plain to see. "Zoom in on Gaven." Hanna used two fingers to zoom onto Gaven's face. The display took a minute to adjust and refocus, showing a clear image of Gaven's face.

She watched as Gaven fought to hold back his tears, shaking his head and stomping his foot. Now that they were zoomed in on him, she could see the blood spot on the scarf was bigger than she originally thought. He needed help soon.

The display shut off, and Hanna put it down by her side.

"The Knightmare took Gaven after that, went to the security room and shut down all the cameras. We have no eyes in the hotel."

"My son doesn't have much time. Get me on camera, immediately."

Hanna bowed and left the Queen. Sera walked back to the throne room. A camera crew was there in minutes, setting their equipment up. The Queen waved off their fancy lights and told them she needed to record now.

After a flurry of activity from the crew, they gave Sera the signal that they were broadcasting. The Queen spoke.

"Citizens of Oarlon. Today, I saw a vision of my son being taken by the Knightmares. In an effort to save him, I sent him to a secure location. In transit, the Knightmares attacked, blowing up the convoy. I thought my son was lost. I was wrong. Those monsters kidnapped him to use him against me, to stop me from saving our kingdom. Their mistake was letting us know where they are. We have already killed one Knightmare, and another is in the wind. Only one remains with my son. We will find the one that fled. We will hunt him down and kill him. To the Knightmare that holds my son, I say this: surrender my son, and I will give you a fair trial. All I want is my son back where he belongs. You have no idea what I would do for him." Tears flowed down her cheeks. She could barely contain herself. Sera signaled with her finger off camera that she was done, and the crew cut the broadcast. The tears stopped, and she breathed normally again. The elevator opened up behind the crew, and the sound of muddied but familiar boots echoed in the chamber. Aiva had returned.

"You're all dismissed. Leave me. Now." The crew rushed to carry out their equipment as fast as possible. After a moment, it was just Aiva and Sera.

"Any trace of the Knightmare who fled?" asked Sera.

Aiva shook her head. "He made it to the forest." She took out one of her guns and flipped it around in her hand. "I wouldn't worry about him, he was bleeding heavily."

"Then why is he still a problem?" said Sera as she pounded her fist into the armchair of her throne. Her eyes widened, and she leaned forward, gritting her teeth. Aiva was unfazed. She kept twirling her gun.

"Your boneheaded soldiers got in the way," said Aiva.

"Is that all? Or is your mind on something else?" said Sera, every word sizzling in the air.

"I'm more concerned with the Knightmare that has your son."

"He's the one that got the best of you."

"I plan to return the favor," said Aiva.

"Who is he?"

Aiva paused, her stoic expression breaking for only a moment. Sera's question briefly broke the rhythm of her twirling gun.

"His name is Koe."

Sera knew the name. Some Knightmares became famous for one reason or another. But that's all he was, just another Knightmare. It was actually Sera's father who once told her, "Do not believe in the folk tales. Everyone exaggerates who the Knightmares are. They are just people, hiding behind the shadows. They might be monsters, but they still bleed. They are nothing to fear." It was one of the only intelligent things he'd ever said.

Aiva continued, "He is one of their best."

"Then why did he turn on his comrades? Have you ever seen a Knightmare do that? Why does he have my son?" said Sera.

Once again, Aiva paused, finally holstering her gun.

"No, I've never seen that."

"Care to speculate?"

"I have no idea," said Aiva. "All I know is that I'm going to kill him and get Gaven back." Aiva turned to leave, but Sera said one last thing, making her stop in her tracks.

"Your main priority is to kill the Knightmare. If my son gets in the way, do what you have to do."

Aiva turned back to Sera, eyebrows arched. "What's going on?" she said. "What are you not telling me?"

Sera avoided Aiva's piercing gaze. "It's nothing. I gave you an order, Aiva. Just stick to it."

Aiva's eyes narrowed, but she tipped her hat, turned for the elevator and left. Sera stroked her chin, replaying the image over in her mind of Gaven following the Knightmare on his own accord.

If Gaven went willingly, then he wasn't fit to be a prince.

He *betrayed* Sera, his own mother.

But Sera was forgiving, and if Gaven was returned to her, she would help him find his place again.

It was a terrible thought, and her heart cringed at the thought. Yet as she did, her face became stone. She didn't care.

TWENTY-THREE

KOE

The basement was closed off. The Queen's soldiers had created a perimeter around the hotel, which meant the nearby sewer tunnels were also being guarded and Koe couldn't escape the way he'd come. The soldiers weren't entering the hotel yet, but there was no doubt: Koe was trapped.

With Gaven in his arms, Koe's plan was to go to the roof, but as Gaven wove in and out of consciousness, Koe realized they wouldn't make it there in time. After the fight, he'd detoured to the security office and disabled the cameras permanently, but the delay had only worsened Gaven's condition. Without the cameras, it would take the soldiers searching the fifty-floor hotel one by one.

Koe exited the elevator to the fifteenth floor, remembering from his previous visit to the hotel that each floor had a suite at the end of it.

With a swift kick, the lock to the suite broke and Koe carried the boy in. Any other day, Koe would've admired the plush carpet and the wide, open windows looking out onto the city. One of the rivers flowing down from the mountain weaved by the hotel on the west side.

Koe set Gaven on the table, which thankfully was big enough for a small child to lie down comfortably. Gaven kept his eyes open at Koe's urgency, but judging by the severity of the wound and how long it had been, Gaven's chances of survival were low. He really should've gone with the others outside. Koe had minimal medical training and no equipment other than a small medical kit he'd found in the bathroom, consisting mostly of bandages and cotton balls.

Koe turned the stove on, the flames erupting in a circle. He drew his dagger and placed the tip fully into the fire before returning to Gaven. He untied the scarf and lifted the fabric of Gaven's shirt away from the wound, taking a closer look at the jagged shard. More blood oozed from the wound, staining Koe's gloves.

"It really hurts," squealed Gaven.

"You really should've gone with them," said Koe, but that was neither here nor there. Even if he yelled to the guards where to find Gaven, he wouldn't make it to a hospital now. Every tick of the clock on the wall slowed down as Koe watched the tip of his dagger turn orange.

When he couldn't take it anymore, Koe swept up the dagger. He placed his fingers gently on the shard, knowing it would need to be a quick pull.

"You're going to be all right, but this is going to hurt," said Koe. Before Gaven could whimper again, Koe snatched the shard out with a clean tug. The trickle of blood turned into a river.

"Don't yell," said Koe as he placed the searing hot dagger against Gaven's flesh, sealing the wound. He threw his other hand over Gaven's mouth as a sharp cry escaped. When Koe lifted the dagger away, the blood no longer flowed, but he had just marked the boy forever.

Gaven's eyes were closed, but his chest rose and fell. Koe scooped him up in his arms and laid him on the couch, throwing a blanket over him. Only time would tell now. Koe's gaze returned to the old clock on the wall, the long hand moving millimeter by millimeter. The ticking banged in Koe's ears louder than the commotion from a crowd outside. Every minute that went by made it harder to escape. Koe took his hat off and set it down on the coffee table next to the chair he plopped himself in. He knew he should be trying to find a way out or preparing himself for the moment the soldiers found them, but his heart told him to watch the boy before him until his eyes opened again.

Even with his reputation, Koe knew going back to the Knightmares might earn him a death sentence after what he'd done and there wasn't anywhere else to go. Now this kid was in the same boat. His tattoos were too well known for him to disappear among the crowd. Both of them would have to go off grid, somewhere far away where no one could find them.

Aiva's purple eyes and her three scars flashed in Koe's mind. He'd always imagined it would be her coming with him, the two of them leaving Oarlon behind. Maybe that was still a possibility after the Queen was killed. Yet, looking upon the boy, for the first time, Koe asked himself if he really did want to kill her.

It was a silly question; of course he did, if given the opportunity. But maybe saving her son would be enough. Save Gaven and leave it all behind, as he always wanted to, with someone who had been betrayed just like he was.

The hour passed, and finally Gaven blinked. The light in his eyes slowly returned.

"It hurts," said Gaven, wincing as he moved slightly.

"It always will," said Koe, moving toward him and putting a hand on his shoulder.

The barking of distant voices sounded from down the hall. He needed another miracle.

Koe went to the door, drawing his gun. Through the peephole, he could see soldiers in the hallway, checking each room. There were about five, easy enough to pick off. If he were alone, he'd seriously consider the idea. He could disappear to another floor and throw the guards off by turning invisible. His chances would greatly improve if he were alone. But a firefight with the kid nearby wasn't an option.

"I need you to stand." Koe offered his hand to Gaven, palm up. Gaven took it, and Koe helped him to his feet. The boy winced at the newly closed wound, but Koe thought he looked less pale than before.

Koe circled the room, considering his options. The ceiling above was tiled like the floor beneath them. No way to cut into it. The vents around them were too small, and anywhere like a closet or under the couch would be an easy find.

"You don't have a way out, do you?" asked Gaven. He couldn't even see Koe's face to know, but he was correct. "You can leave me. It's okay."

Koe knelt down in front of him. He knew what he should say: "It's the only way, but I promise you, I will find you again." But Koe couldn't say it.

Instead, Gaven went on, "My mother said we should be afraid of the shadow men, but you don't seem so scary to me."

"I'm… not a good person, Gaven," said Koe, almost choking up. Everything he had done as a Knightmare had left its mark, more so than the twenty-four lacerations on his back. He'd always believed himself to be doing it for the right reasons, and that helped him sleep at night. But here, this boy was looking up at him as some sort of hero, and that thought made Koe squirm inside.

"Then why did you save me?"

Koe cleared his throat, still very much aware of the noise outside growing louder every second. "Doing a few good things doesn't absolve one from everything else they've done."

"My dad says that a kind heart is all you need," said Gaven.

"Not in our world," said Koe. He put a hand on Gaven's shoulder. "But it certainly is worth something." Koe then pointed to the bedroom. "Go hide, and don't come out until I tell you to."

"You're not going to leave me?"

"No."

Gaven presented Koe's blood-stained scarf back to him. "You should have this," he said.

Koe smiled, but remembering that Gaven couldn't see it, he gave a small nod instead as he took the scarf back, wrapping it around his neck. With all the killing Koe had done, all of his clothes had some blood on them.

Gaven raced into the bedroom and shut the closet door. Koe drew his daggers and took a sharp inhale. A kind heart? How could he live up to Gaven's expectations when he was about to murder all the guards on the floor?

The door broke off its hinges, and wood splinters flew in every direction. Koe turned invisible as the guards shuffled in, wandering around the room, looking for any signs of him. They found Gaven's blood on the table, gathering around it to look for other clues.

When they were all distracted but before they had the chance to call it in, Koe appeared behind them. Fresh blood was added to the dried blood, drenching the table in red. Not one cry left the soldiers' mouths. A few more walked in nonchalantly to assist their comrades' search, and they too were unprepared for Koe's assault. Their bodies crumpled to the floor. Koe sent his daggers flying through the hallway at two more guards, piercing their chests.

The closet door opened, and Koe beckoned Gaven to follow him.

"Close your eyes." The kid had seen too much carnage already. He didn't need more images to haunt his dreams.

Koe led Gaven out of the suite. They could go the elevator route or the stairs. On Koe's gut, he chose the stairs — more maneuverable. There was a small chance that there was a deluxe hoverer on the hotel's roof, a way for wealthy patrons to leave without encountering the regular guests. No doubt it would be heavily guarded, but probably less so than the soldiers outside the lobby on the ground.

The stairwell was cramped, and Koe kept glancing up and down. He could hear soldiers below, but the way up seemed to be clear. Gaven kept pace with Koe, even with his shorter legs. Every five floors or so, they'd stop so Gaven could catch his breath. He pressed a hand to his side, and Koe worried about his wound. There was nothing he could do about it now. For Koe, the adrenaline overcame any desire to stop, but if he focused, he could feel his muscles tiring and his throat dry.

On floor thirty-six, the door opened right above them. Koe's hand covered Gaven's mouth to keep his heavy breathing from being heard. They stayed still and heard a single pair of footsteps heading their way. Koe readied his dagger, only to find the light footsteps belonged to an older woman in a maid's uniform with the Arctic Hotel name sewn above the breast pocket. Seeing them, she squealed and covered her head while she sat down on the step. Gaven grabbed Koe's other hand and squeezed it, hiding himself half behind Koe.

"Please don't hurt me," said the old woman. She'd seen them, and as soon as they left, she would tell the soldiers where they were. Koe could tell that Gaven was afraid by how he hid behind him. He couldn't help but wonder if Gaven was afraid of what he would do to this innocent bystander.

"Go. Don't tell anyone we're here," said Koe. Even if Gaven weren't here, he'd like to believe he wouldn't hurt an innocent person.

Other Knightmares would have slit her throat the moment they saw her. Maybe he could live up to what Gaven saw in him.

"Thank you, thank you," said the old woman, standing up. As Koe sheathed his dagger, he saw a flash of purple in the old maid's eyes. With a swift kick to the chest, Koe forced the old woman back as her body twisted, bones cracking, changing shape to another being entirely. The wrinkles softened, the scars etched back into her face.

Aiva slammed backward into the stairs and hit the wall as Koe grabbed Gaven's hand, pulling him onto the thirty-sixth level.

"That was Aiva!" exclaimed Gaven. Koe's gaze never settled on the doors they passed, knowing there wasn't time to hide in a room now. Aiva would be on their heels within seconds.

"Gaven, watch out!" Koe instinctively ducked, grabbing Gaven as two bullets flew toward his head. He swiftly covered Gaven with his whole body, drawing his gun but stopped. He wasn't sure why—whether it was Aiva's purple eyes or Gaven's whimper against his chest.

"Don't," said Koe, spinning around to face Aiva. Both their guns were raised. "Let's not end this here with him."

"Gaven, come with me now," she ordered.

Gaven poked his head out from behind Koe, pushing himself out and toward Aiva.

"No, I don't want to go back to her!"

"She's your mother!" said Aiva sternly. "This isn't up for discussion."

"Gaven…" said Koe slowly. "She has orders to kill me at all costs.

Even if you're in the way." He was only speculating, but his guess seemed to be correct as Aiva's expression didn't change. Then her hand holding the gun twitched and her eyes wavered for a second.

"Gaven, whatever he's told you is a lie. He was sent here to kill your mother. You know the stories of the Shadows! This man serves them. He is not your friend," said Aiva.

Gaven shuffled around, facing Koe as Koe dropped his arm, holstering his gun.

"Is that true?

"Yes," said Koe. "But I gave it all up—to save you. And if you still want to, I'll take you far away from this place, and I'll never let anything happen to you."

"No, you won't," Aiva said, drawing a few steps closer.

"I told him to go, tried to get him help," said Koe. "He stayed with me. Aiva, please, have mercy. Let us go, and you'll never see me again."

"You like it… having someone to save," said Aiva. "But you're a killer, a murderer. You're part of the Shadows, and he will never be safe with you no matter where you go."

"Then come with us," said Koe, standing up straight, his arms by his side. Holstering his gun was a risk, but his breathing was steady—he was giving Aiva a clean shot. "Help me protect him."

Aiva let out a loud groan. "You don't get it! You get so easily attached, and then you can't let go. After fifteen years, you still think we're going to live our lives like we're fourteen again? No. The world doesn't work like that," said Aiva, taking another step forward. "You're just looking for someone to save so that they can save you from the void you can't fill. There's no riding off into the sunset. If you'd wanted that, you would've gone the first minute you could, but no, you stayed with the Knightmares because you can't let go. You've been with them longer than we knew each other — than you served at the castle. Don't you see that the boy who was my friend died? And you're just a shadow of him."

Koe slumped under the weight of her words, pushing him to one knee.

"I don't want to —" started Gaven before Koe put a finger on his mouth.

"She's wrong," said Koe. "Don't listen to her. I will get you out of here."

The elevator doors opened and out came a soldier with blond hair. His sword was extended, and the rest of the troops filed in behind him. He walked up beside Aiva.

"Daddy!" said Gaven, his eyes brightening for a second. Thane didn't seem to hear him as he locked eyes with Koe.

"Good, you're still alive," said Thane, twisting his blade in his hand. His gaze traveled down toward Gaven. He took a step forward when Gaven took a step back. "Gaven! Are you hurt?"

"He was hit by a shard after the explosion," said Koe.

"You Knightmares really have no honor," said Thane. "Taking an innocent child hostage. Give me my son back, and I'll make it quick." Thane held up his sword, the blade between his eyes.

"Gaven wants to go with him," said Aiva.

"What?" said Thane, dropping the tip of the blade to the ground. "No. Gaven, come here now!"

"The Queen detonated the explosion to kill him," said Koe. Thane's eyebrows lifted, his eyes widened just a little. He hadn't known. "He's not going back."

"Aiva, take him out. Now," said Thane. Aiva paused, readjusting her grip. "Take the shot!" But no shot came.

"She hesitates because escalating this with Gaven in between all of us will risk his life, despite her orders," said Koe. "How can you serve the Light when it asks you to go against your moral code? He's just a kid." He looked toward Aiva, knowing she only killed or hurt people who arguably deserved it.

"Gaven, please. Come here, right now!" said Thane. "I am your father!"

Gaven took a step forward, but Koe grasped his shirt and pulled him back. "He's just like your mother. He's killed hundreds of innocent people in the Iron District because he wants to be king. He'll do anything to please your mother."

"Stop putting lies into my son's head!"

Gaven spoke softly to Thane. "You lie like her," he said. He pulled back toward Koe. Soldiers from behind Thane aimed their weapons. Koe grabbed Gaven's shoulder and backed up with him. They were at the end of the hallway now, where another set of elevators were. Behind Koe was a glass window overlooking a small table with flowers.

"Soldiers, kill the Knightmare!" ordered Thane.

Koe reached toward his gun, but that's when he saw the flash of the muzzle — too late. A bullet ripped into his left shoulder from Aiva's gun. It was a clean exit, but fighting with his left arm would be out of the question now.

Gaven threw himself toward Koe. Everything slowed, even the bullets heading toward them. Koe reached for Gaven, seeing he was in the line of fire. But with his gaze trained on Gaven, he didn't notice Aiva had drawn her sword and charged. Koe's fingers extended, reaching toward Gaven to pull him close and turning his back for the bullets to hit his own body instead.

Koe could only imagine Queen Sera's smug satisfaction: seeing Gaven returned to her and knowing that the Knightmares who were sent after her were dead. Aiva would report that Koe was the boy Sera had framed so long ago. His entire life, all his goals and dreams, would end in a hotel hallway.

But as long as Gaven lived, his life would be worth it.

Koe's fingers had just skimmed the hair on Gaven's arm when a force crashed into him. Aiva's sword exploded into Koe's chest, ripping through him and bursting out the other side. His breathing came in gasps as Aiva pushed him back, the sword still lodged in him. He kept his arm outstretched toward Gaven.

Three bullets pierced Gaven's torso, sending him flying into the air. Koe couldn't find the breath to yell, but his bleeding heart cried out to every muscle in his body.

Gaven's screams echoed in his ears, the same ones he'd heard coming from his own lips the day he was whipped.

Blood was dripping from both his wounds and onto the hilt of the sword. Koe's vision blurred, his head dizzy. Both the bullet and sword must've missed his heart, but he could barely get enough air to function.

Aiva withdrew the sword, sending another jolt of agony through Koe's body. Without hesitation, she slammed a well-aimed kick into Koe's chest, propelling him back against the window. The glass shattered, and before he fell, Koe saw the last bit of light fading from Gaven's lifeless eyes. The chill air whistled louder and louder as he plummeted toward the ground. The pain disappeared as the darkness consumed him.

TWENTY-FOUR

QUEEN SERA

One of the servants tightened the strings on the back of Sera's black dress and bowed before leaving the Queen alone in her room. The door was left open. She stared out the window overlooking the garden where the other servants were aligning chairs and sprinkling a walkway with flowers towards a grave.

The service would start soon for the Prince. Sera put a dagger in her sleeve, knowing she would need it in a minute.

Thane sauntered in, running his hands through his hair. There were black bags under his eyes from the sleepless nights following Gaven's death. She had no idea what Thane was going through. He'd been retiring to his own quarters in recent days.

"Did you read my speech?" he said. He walked over to a tray which held a pitcher of water, poured himself a cup and gulped it down.

"Yes, it's well done," said Sera.

"How are you?" asked Thane, running his finger around the rim of the cup. Sera sat on her bed and cleared her throat. There was no point in lying.

"I already miss him. I wish it didn't have to be this way."

Thane suddenly threw the glass, and it shattered against the wall.

"That's all you can say? Your words are so hollow, people will wonder if someone replaced you with a machine. I wonder!"

If anyone else had talked to Sera like that, she would have them lashed. Interestingly, she appreciated Thane's insult. This was truly him. He wasn't groveling at her feet nor pretending to be her stoic captain.

"I loved him, I really did. This is bigger than all of us. I have to save this city, our world! Let me remind you that you fired the gun. You ordered it." Sera stood up and faced Thane. His anger slowly vanished, and he backed into a corner as Sera approached.

"Yes, Aiva told me it was your decision." Sera was inches away from him now, and she put her hand on his face, forcing him to look her in the eye. His eyes were full of anguish and uncertainty. "As hard as it was, you made the right choice." She softly pressed her lips against his, and when she moved away, the fire was back in his eyes.

"Then make me king," he demanded.

"We're dispensing with the pleasantries, are we?" asked Sera, pointedly facing him at all times. "Good. You've been saying you love me without meaning it for such a long time. I can't believe I fell for it." She sat on the bed and sighed. "I am never going to make you king."

Thane went over to the door, locking it. He tried to keep his composure, but Sera's words made his blood boil. He turned toward her and drew the hilt of his sword. With a flick, the blade extended from the handle. He placed the tip of the blade right at her neck.

"If you're really the Chosen One, then I won't be able to cut your throat."

"You'll be sentencing everyone to their deaths."

"I don't really care much anymore."

His role in the death of his only son, his failure in combat and now losing his chance at the crown had truly broken his spirit. Sera had taken his last bit of hope away.

"What if I told you I saw this very moment in a vision yesterday," said Sera. "Not that I needed to—I could see it coming. You're too predictable, Thane. When Aiva told me what you did to our son, I wasn't surprised. No matter how much you loved him, there's nothing you want more than the throne. The biggest difference between you and me is that I will sacrifice my son for the good of the world, not for my own selfish desires."

Sera pulled out the the dagger hidden in her sleeve and clashed the blade against Thane's sword, pushing it away from her neck. Before Thane could swing back, Sera was on him, her dagger pressed up against his neck in turn. The blade dug into his flesh, the drops of blood sliding along the edge of the dagger before falling to the floor. Thane backed up, hitting the wall and groaning. The cuts he received from the Knightmare a few nights back were still fresh.

"I saw this moment. I saw every scenario you would try. Everything you would say. Drop your sword."

The clatter of the blade dropping to the floor broke the silence between them.

"Fine," croaked Thane. His once proud stature was nowhere to be found. His back was arched, and he could barely hold himself up. "I hope this was all worth it." He tilted his chin in a bow.

"I really did love him," said Sera, stepping back and removing the dagger from his throat. Thane swiftly retreated to the door to leave, but not before turning back to Sera.

"I did too."

Thane walked the passageways aimlessly. His dreams were all ruined, and there was nothing for him now. At some point, he would serve Sera one last time.

A single candle was placed by the coffin of the Prince in the castle garden. Every royal official was in attendance and the funeral was televised. The camera crew stayed as silent and out of the way as they possibly could. Gaven's body had been cleaned before his burial, and now that they were preparing to lower the casket, the lid was secured in place. Sera thought he would be happy to know that he was buried in the garden—the most beautiful place in the castle.

Hanna slipped a note into Sera's hand as the proceedings continued. Written on it was eighty-three percent. Sera took a deep breath of satisfaction. She had asked Hanna to give her the percentage of homes in the kingdom tuned in to the funeral. This was beyond what she had hoped for. It could only boost her popularity.

Sera had been afraid for a moment that Gaven's death and her inability to save him might hurt her reputation as the Chosen One, but the day after the hotel incident, she'd cleverly spun the death, declaring that the Knightmares are after her because they're afraid of what she'll do. She told the people of Oarlon with such satisfaction, "I saw four Knightmares after me, and today, I can confirm that all four are dead." Yes, they only had two bodies, but one fell from thirty-six floors after Aiva stabbed him, and another had left such a long blood trail that it would be a miracle if he had any blood left in him at all.

Thane, wearing his armor loosely, had to be helped up to the podium. His hair was even messier than when she'd seen him earlier. A small twinge of pain resonated in her heart. Whatever they had, it was over. Their eyes met, and he quickly looked away.

"Citizens of Oarlon," he said quietly. "As captain of the guard, it is my duty to protect everyone and everything in Oarlon. Days ago, I failed." He shuddered and tried to stand a little taller. "The Prince was a beacon of light, of hope, a symbol of our future," he said with strength returning to his voice. "If I'd known how the future would play out, I would've done it all differently." The last line deviated from his pre-written speech, clearly a dig at Sera. She just kept her stare leveled at him, knowing there could be a camera on her.

"That's all," he said, and walked down from the podium. Scattered polite applause came from the rows and rows of people watching. Sera stood up after Thane plopped himself down in his chair and almost tipping over from the indelicate force.

As Sera walked toward the podium, the guards lowered the casket into the ground and a beautiful voice sang out an ancient song of love and tragedy. The words, the voice, and her memory of Gaven smiling flipped a switch in her heart. Tears poured from Sera's eyes. She struggled to hold it in; she could be gloomy but she couldn't lose composure. Not with all the cameras on her.

But she couldn't help it. She hastened past the cameras, using her guards to shield her from the camera's view. She saw Hanna's jaw drop and her eyes widen, trying to wave her down, but Sera didn't care. Not now.

She barricaded herself inside the castle in one of the many empty hallways. She could hear guards take up their posts outside the closed doors. She leaned against the wall and slid down to sit. She was so useless right now. Why couldn't she get it together? Staring at the floor overwhelmed, she eventually recognized two boots before her. She looked up to see Aiva with her arms crossed.

"I don't know why this is happening," said Sera.

Aiva dropped her arms to her sides and sat down next to her. "You're the Chosen One and the Queen... but you're also just like everyone else."

"Am I? When I thought he was gone before, I cried for him. This time, it's not so much that he's gone... it's that so much of me went with him," said Sera, wiping away the last of her tears. "My visions are clearer, more frequent, but I can't help but wonder why the Light wants me to sacrifice everything."

"The Shadows are selfish. They only care about their own desires. To break their curse, it takes someone who's truly selfless. The Light chose someone who can put the world's fate above all they love."

"But what happens afterwards? If I succeed?" asked Sera coldly. Any desire for tears was gone now, replaced by the void where her heart should be. Her questions came from the last few remnants of the broken pieces of her heart that she knew now were slowly fading.

Aiva stood up and offered her hand to the Queen. Sera took it and stood, facing Aiva.

"You'll find your way back," said Aiva. "For now, you have the biggest weight on your shoulders. Focus on your duty, and figure out the rest later," she said steadfastly.

"You're right," said Sera. "The Knightmares are still out there. They all need to be destroyed. Once they are, there'll be no obstacles in the way."

"Underworld resistance fighters keep popping up," pointed out Aiva. "We're fighting two wars and the captain of the guard is too weak to lead the fight."

"They're scattered. They pose no threat, but you're right. Thane is weak. You will take his place. Not officially. Wipe out any insurgents that get in the way while you continue the search for the Knightmares. Fortify the border. The Knightmares will no doubt come back soon, and we must be ready for them. I will work on finding their stronghold in my visions. It is just a matter of time."

Aiva smiled and bowed. "For Oarlon. For you."

"Thank you, Aiva, for understanding," said Sera. "All this time, and you're still the only one who does."

"I'm an agent of the Light. I will protect the Chosen One at all costs. We can't let the Shadows burn the world."

TWENTY-FIVE

KOE

Eight Years Ago

The sixteenth kill lay at Koe's feet. Another death on his hands, another face to remember. This one was in the Crown District—wrinkled skin, gray-and-white poofy hair with a diamond necklace around her neck. Koe knew nothing of her or her life, just that she was the target the old Seer had given him.

Koe stared out the window while his lifeless victim lay in a pool of blood at his feet. The castle stood before him in all its glory. Every time he laid eyes on it, he thought of Aiva. Koe knew he should be getting back soon or they'd start asking questions. A small creak, almost impossible to hear, sounded behind him.

"Still checking up on me?" asked Koe. He turned to see his mentor, Rus, emerge from the shadows, his green tie catching the light of the streetlamp outside.

"You tried to infiltrate the castle last night during reconnaissance. You almost got caught." The shields had been momentarily down for a huge party of foreign dignitaries arriving to greet the Queen, a rare event that gave Koe an opportunity to sneak in. Yet Koe could only be invisible for so long, and hundreds of soldiers were on duty.

He made quite a commotion when he was spotted. He would never admit it to Rus, but he barely got away with his life.

"I saw an opportunity to take out our enemy," said Koe. "She is an agent of the Light."

"You saw an opportunity for revenge," said Rus. "The Shadows did not deem the Queen a threat."

Koe didn't flinch. He stood perfectly still as the spite dripping from Rus' words could be heard a mile away.

He stepped over the body and faced Rus. Koe was still young, but after all his lessons from Rus, the viper before him didn't shake him to his core any longer. "I killed your brother, the man who turned you in to the authorities. He lost his business because of you. That wasn't enough for you. You wanted vengeance. Why do you criticize me for the same desire?"

"The Shadows showed his death. If I really wanted vengeance, I would've done it myself. No, you aren't looking for revenge. You look for love."

Rus moved closer. Now that Koe was taller, his spit hit Koe's chin. "You went for the girl, the one you cried out to in your sleep when you were a boy — Aiva." Rus paused, and with a sigh, he continued, "We are not tools or instruments. We are death, and death does not long for love. Just the next target." He took a step back and gave Koe a glance up and down. "You have taken all my lessons well, except for one."

"Don't suddenly pretend to care," said Koe.

"Care if you die? No, someone else would replace you," said Rus.

"Then why are you still trying to teach me?"

"The Shadows brought us together for a reason. They made you, Koe. Yet you want to be the boy you were. You still don't realize that the Shadows are the only thing you've ever needed."

Present Day

The distant sound of a voice rang out. A twinkling light shone through the darkness like a star finding its way from another galaxy. The light grew brighter and brighter until it was unbearable to look at. The light started to form an image—an outline of a person in the periphery. Koe grunted with great effort, realizing he wasn't dead. The details of the man beside him were slowly filled in—the green tie, the crown on his forehead. Rus.

Koe tried to speak, but no words came out. He moved his head inches, examining the room around him. The Knightmare temple's columns came into view next to the familiar torches of white flame, burning, everlasting. Beneath him, he knew there had to be something, but only air brushed up against his back.

He recalled the hotel, the fight with Zos and Fye, the

conversation he had with the boy... Gaven... who was now gone. While Koe couldn't move, the tears slid from his cheeks. The sword breaching his chest was nothing compared to the pain of seeing Gaven fall to the ground, lifeless. He wanted to scream, to shout. How could Thane do that? Why did Aiva stop him from saving Gaven? He was just a boy.

"You're awake," said Rus. "Do you know where you are?"

Koe tried to nod his head to no avail. He attempted to raise his arm — to raise any part of him. Nothing. He was of able enough mind to know that his body was broken. Every ounce of strength focused on pushing what little air he could get to exhale a 'yes'. It was so soft, he wasn't sure Rus heard.

"You've been out for several days. You would be dead if I hadn't saved you. The Shadows' last bit of magic is the only thing keeping you alive," said Rus. "I know what you did to Zos. Fye is alive but barely. How the Shadows could still accept you, well... I do not question them."

Rus lifted his hand like he had done so many times to backhand Koe across the face, but instead, he put his hand on Koe's forehead.

"Open your mind to the Shadows. Let them in. Only they can heal what's broken."

Shadows from under Koe slowly transformed into five fingers, crawling up Koe's body. The fingers merged into one sharp blade hovering over one of Koe's eyes.

He couldn't look away, couldn't move. The blade plunged deep, and shadows covered his eyes in darkness.

He tried to shake his head, tried not to think about what

happened, but his mind couldn't escape the vision of Gaven's lifeless eyes as he fell.

"Don't fight it, Koe," growled Rus. Koe's mind centered on Gaven, rewinding the clock back to when he'd first arrived at the hotel. A warm tingle covered his body. Whispers of an ancient language caught his ear. Rus' voice chanted softly along with it, echoing the whispers.

He led the Shadows through the fight with the other Knightmares, to the chase, to the hallway. But along the way, he couldn't help but think about his time as a servant boy in the castle so long ago. When he killed the Knightmares, he thought of Rus and all his training and everything Rus had imprinted on his brain. Every hit, every lesson.

When he got to Aiva pointing a gun at him and stabbing him, Koe couldn't help but think about all the times that Aiva, as a kid, would hang out with him. Their last memory together as kids came to the forefront—Aiva telling him her dream of running away from it all. And when he finally broke free and went back to what had happened in the hallway, he could only see Sera manipulating him as a boy and the scars on his back that would never heal.

Hours and hours went by, and Koe relived all those moments over and over again. At this point, the Shadows knew everything, but it was hard to think of anything else.

Then they slowly moved away, and the darkness cleared from his vision. Rus stood, his voice still quiet.

"Your body was broken. Specifically, your spine. Must've been from the fall into the river, though any of those wounds would've killed you," said Rus. "The Shadows want you alive. So now you'll rest, Koe. You might not be dying anymore, but your body has been through a shock," said Rus, moving swiftly out of the room.

Why did the Shadows want him alive? He'd betrayed his fellow Knightmares, and he never fully gave himself to the Shadows. But if even Rus didn't know, there was no chance of Koe figuring it out.

Koe's eyes slowly closed. His dreams were filled with every decision he'd made, reliving and redoing them to choose something else each time. So many 'if's.

The next morning, Koe sat up, his muscles still creaking like an old machine that hadn't been used in a long time. He looked down at himself, having finally regained enough energy to take in his appearance and surroundings. His boots were off and so was his coat. His hat and scarf were gone. He still wore his undershirt, now with several bullet holes in it. His exposed hands blended into the shadow table. Carefully, he placed his feet on the ground, putting his weight on them and immediately keeling over.

Rus walked in, finding Koe like a fish on dry land, flopping around as he struggled to get up.

"Calm down," Rus said, standing over him but not leaning over to help. "Find your footing."

Koe stopped flailing about, lying still and feeling every lash on his back. He rolled over, his hand pushing against the cold stone of the floor. His muscles seized, trembling as he pushed himself to his knees. One foot, then another. Koe's body swayed, so he grabbed the wall inserts of one of the torches to hang on to. He could feel Rus' gaze on him, judging him.

"Come," Rus said.

The door opened, and Koe, using the wall for support, stumbled his way out, his knees buckling with every step. Rus led him into the next room, an isolated chamber with a couch and some chairs. Koe practically fell over onto the couch.

The fire roared, warming Koe, who hadn't realized how cold he'd been. The comfort of the cushions pulled Koe in, his mind finding a small moment of relief.

The door reopened, and Koe instantly looked down at his hip where his gun would be. His hand was slower, but it managed to get to his belt, only to find nothing. A big figure with his shoulders hunched and his arm in a sling pushed his way in.

"I want to see him!" yelled Fye. Rus threw a jab into Fye's shoulder where Koe had shot him. Fye toppled over, shrieking.

"I told you, the Shadows want him alive," said Rus, leaning down. "They didn't say anything about you. Interrupt again and you'll regret it."

Fye dragged himself out of the room, whimpering as he did.

Rus took a seat opposite Koe, who had now sat up, trying to hide his diminished state.

"So..." said Koe, "Are the Shadows so desperate they need a

traitor?" He saw the backhand coming a mile away, but his reflexes were still slow and the pain that radiated through his cheek burned ten times more than it normally would.

"Do not insult the Shadows. They just believe in you. Yet you turn your back on them, even now, after all this time," said Rus.

"This has never been my home," said Koe, finally saying it aloud. "I never wanted to be a Knightmare. Every day, I've thought about leaving."

"Yet, you didn't," said Rus.

"It was more convenient to stay," said Koe, omitting how every night he thought of running off only to imagine looking over his shoulder for the rest of his life, waiting for Rus' dagger in his back.

"This is a setback, I'll admit," said Rus. "Killing Zos, one of the only Knightmares here worth the reputation… Fye is in little condition to do anything useful, and the Queen's power is growing. She will find our temple soon, and she'll send whatever is left of her army to wipe us out."

"Then the Light has won," Koe shot back, knowing full well that would spark another slap, but Rus refrained this time.

"The Shadows have a secret—one I don't even know about. We're not out of the fight yet." Rus stood, straightening his tie and vest. "The one you whisper of—Aiva. The Shadows tell me she's responsible for what happened to the Queen's kid. I guess you couldn't deal with her. We'll be sending other Knightmares to take care of her, as the Shadows have named her another target to wipe out. I will let you know when it's done."

In the past, that would have sent daggers into every fiber of Koe's being. Hearing it now, not one muscle twitched.

"You're sending them to their deaths," said Koe.

"Do I detect a flicker of joy in your voice?" said Rus.

"No," said Koe truthfully. "That dream is gone."

"Good. You're finally learning the most important lesson I ever taught you."

TWENTY-SIX

QUEEN SERA

The chill wind blew against the citizens huddled together in the city square in the Sky District. The clouds up above blanketed the sun, making the world under them a dull gray. Snow mixed with mud had been scooped to the side of the road. A thin layer of brown water covered the square.

In the center of the square was a new structure that had been built in less than a day by order of the Queen. The design was simple: a large, wooden rectangular platform held up by wooden beams with an arch over the platform and three ropes tied into nooses dangling about halfway down it. Sera stood proudly off to the side, her guards around her. Thane stood by his lonesome on the other side of the platform, struggling to stand up straight. Patchy facial hair covered his face for the first time ever. He had reeked of booze before coming here, but Sera paid no attention to him. Aiva had stepped up in his absence of leadership, and to no surprise, found results. Of course, a lot of her successes had to do with Sera's visions. Now they were here to show the people their progress.

In the weeks following Gaven's funeral, the people's faith had wavered. The death toll from the campaign against the underworld was getting harder to cover up, and soon, it was impossible to insist that the war was going smoothly. Even the Leaf District had suffered some attacks from the remnants of Wystan's organization.

But Sera's visions roared, guiding Sera's soldiers and Aiva as the tracked them all down. The war all but ended overnight, and other than the gloom of the clouds and the cold of the winter, this truly was an occasion to remember. Sera even had a few surprises in store for the audience.

Sera stepped forward to address the crowd. They had been scanned before entering the city square to make sure no one carried any weapons. Sera inhaled the poisonous air — almost gagging as the air filled her lungs. She could feel the venom killing off her cells, slowly rotting her down. The palace air was a luxury, even if the machines couldn't filter out all of the poison.

"Citizens of Oarlon. I know the last few months have been hard. But real change takes great sacrifice, and today, my friends, we have finally come out the other side of this dark tunnel. The war with the underworld is over. We have won."

Cheers erupted, warming the air and the hearts of everyone in the crowd. At least everyone that she could see. She imagined there were still a few citizens that disagreed or were wary of her still, but she either didn't see them or didn't want to. Clearly, the majority was with her, and soon, the rest would follow.

"Today, I present you with the last of the resistance!"

Guards escorted three men in chains up to the platform, positioning them all in front of the nooses. A black hooded guard, who Sera knew to be Aiva in disguise, wrapped the nooses around the men's necks. All three men had dried dirt and blood on their faces. Their eyes were sullen, and their bodies were like Thane's—barely able to keep upright.

Sera had starved them for several days, giving them only sips of water. She didn't let them sleep. Of course, they had fresh lashes on their backs, some of which Sera administered herself. As the crowd shouted in anger at the three men, one of the prisoners spat at the audience, which only made Sera's smile brighten. One last act of defiance. One last act to show the people that the men here weren't worthy of sympathy. For the people, they were just an evil that needed to be defeated. And Sera had done just that.

"These monsters are among the worst. We spared their lives because they do not deserve the dignity of dying in battle!"

More applause sounded throughout the city square. Cameras recording the event were everywhere.

"We have confirmed that all three of these men have murdered, raped, and pillaged our city. We can't change what they've done, but we can administer our justice here today!"

The loud boom of voices and clapping would've made Sera want to plug her ears if she wasn't enjoying it so much. She gave a small nod to Aiva, who pulled a wooden lever, and the platform beneath the men's feet gave way. Their bodies squirmed in the air as the crowd grew louder and louder. Once their final breath had run out, the crowd quieted down once again. Sera smiled and held up her hand.

"But this is not the only offering I give you. Behold." She gestured to the side, and three Knightmares walked up to the platform in a line. Chains snaked around their bodies, holding their arms against their chest. Every few seconds, a jolt of electricity travelled along the chains, sending smalls shocks throughout their bodies.

The crowd murmured, the ecstatic faces that Sera saw just moments prior were gone. All that was left was fear. Sera raised her hand again, showing no sign of concern. She would be the reassuring voice. She had the control.

"Citizens, please. These Knightmares will not harm you. They are well under control."

With one glance, Aiva kicked the biggest Knightmare, the one they called Fye, onto his knees. The two others soon followed.

When Sera first saw Aiva bring a captured Fye into the throne room, a fire burned through her whole body, threatening to consume the entire city of Oarlon. He was supposed to be dead, but here he was, alive. What would the people think? She had declared him dead already. She took a deep breath and reminded herself that she could use this as an opportunity to claim another victory over the Knightmares. She would dress him up differently, and no one would know. Her guards stripped him of his purple and yellow clothes and dressed him in all blue as he cursed and shouted. But that was just the beginning.

Aiva had found the Knightmares on her own, without Sera's visions. Fye had been able to flee back to the stronghold and return with four more Knightmares. Aiva dispatched two of them and captured the remaining three all on her own. She had a few more scars on her arms and shoulders but paid no attention to them. She truly earned her moniker: the Assassin of the Shadows.

All in all, it was good news. The Knightmares had sent their best, and they had failed. They sent what little left they might've had, and they too failed. Now the cult would fall. Unfortunately, even torture couldn't reveal the location of their temple. The Knightmares' loyalty to the Shadows survived even the most brutal forms of punishment. It's why any time a king or a queen tried to extract the location from their prisoners, they never could. Monarchs in the past had considered burning the whole forest down, but even then, the Shadows might extend their power to protect the temple from discovery. To wipe them out, they needed to know the exact location.

Now, the three captured Knightmares were of no further use. They would face their death.

"The Knightmares have terrorized our city for centuries," began Sera. "Their plague of violence and fear is almost as bad as the curse that affects our air. But they are getting desperate. If I have proven anything to you, it is that I follow through on my promises. I killed Wystan and destroyed his operations. The Knightmares are next." The gloom of fear departed, and the applause and cheering resumed in full effect. When the cacophony subsided, a high shrill laugh erupted from Fye.

"You think this will do anything? The Shadows will kill you, and regardless of where I am, I will be smiling."

Sera smirked.

"Your numbers dwindle. The Shadows are weak. Soon your grip on our land will be broken, and you'll be just a terrible memory." Sera nodded to one of her guards, who drew his sword and presented it to Sera. She took the handle and rested the blade on Fye's shoulder. "Citizens of Oarlon, through interrogation, we have discovered the identity of this Knightmare. He is the Butcher of the Bells. You might remember him. This is what crime gets you. A rope around your neck —" Sera pointed with her sword over to the hanging men. " — or your identity erased and a blade at your throat."

"It's too bad you don't release these chains and fight me yourself," said Fye as another jolt of electricity shook his body.

"What say you?" shouted Sera to the crowd.

The crowd bellowed in unison, "KILL HIM!"

Sera threw her arms back, the sword behind her head now. She swung down hard. The blade severed the back of Fye's neck, slicing smoothly through the veins and arteries and emerged from his throat, a stream of red following it.

Fye's head rolled off the platform into the crowd. The people in the front jumped back, disgusted but also cheering. Sera nodded to Aiva, who grabbed a big ax and executed the remaining two Knightmares. An overwhelming sensation of pure bliss tingled down Sera's spine. Her eyes rolled back in her head, and she threw her head up toward the sky.

The forest on the outskirts of Oarlon appeared before her. The trees of the forest uprooted themselves and moved to create a straight path forward for Sera. She couldn't see her body at all when she looked down. It was like she was floating in the air with nothing tethering her to the earth, not even gravity. An unseen force propelled her forward. She knew she wasn't walking; she couldn't feel her legs moving. It was as if she were hovering like a ghost, being pulled by an invisible rope. The trees and bushes moved aside, their trunks leaning away from her. Their branches were like arms arching over the path, creating a tunnel with what little leaves they had in the winter. As she passed, she realized the trees were cowering away from her.

A building at the end of the path grew larger and larger as Sera travelled. Despite the darkness that surrounded it, she could tell it was a small fortress. Not even the sun's rays could penetrate the inky black. As she approached, the door to the fortress opened and out poured a wave of darkness followed by the outlines of many figures. Suddenly, soldiers from behind Sera emerged, running at the Knightmares with their swords held up high. Gunfire erupted and blood soon spilled, but one by one, the Knightmares all fell, and the darkness surrounding the fortress vanished. She looked down at the dead soldiers and Knightmares. The surviving soldiers hoisted their swords in the air and yelled in triumph.

But at the fortress entrance, there stood a circle of soldiers bowing their heads to the ground. One by one, they departed until Sera could see what they had been paying tribute to: the body of Thane, stabbed in the back.

Sera had no tears for Thane. It had to be done.

The vision slowly melted away, and she found herself suddenly back in the present, standing on the wooden platform while the crowd cheered and chanted her name. She smiled and waved Aiva over to her. Together, they left the platform as the crowd began dispersing into groups. They would celebrate long into the night.

Sera's guards cleared the way for her return to her hoverer. Thane tried to join, but Sera waved a few guards over to him. They escorted him to his own hoverer without question.

Once in Sera's private hoverer, with the roof and doors fully closed, Aiva returned to her natural self, scars and all.

"A good show," said Aiva.

"An even better one is on the horizon. I've found the Knightmare's temple," said Sera.

"You had a vision?"

Sera smiled malevolently. "Yes, I know how to get there. When we return to the castle, I will show you. You will lead my army. I've already seen your victory."

Aiva stroked her chin and leaned back into her seat. "Even a victory will be costly."

"As all things are."

"What about overseas? Someone might think we're vulnerable," said Aiva.

"No, I have not seen any movement overseas. In visions or by spies. No kingdom would interfere with the Chosen One, not while the air is poisoning them too. They wouldn't succeed, and they wouldn't dare try. There are enough believers in the world who would turn against their ruler for even thinking of killing the Chosen One," said Sera.

"I believe it," replied Aiva.

A long silence followed. Sera straightened out her dress while watching Aiva look outside the window at the passing scenery.

"Can I ask you something?" asked Sera.

"Always," said Aiva.

"Do you have any regrets about your life?"

Aiva clicked her tongue and shrugged. "After I killed your parents, would you have let me walk away if I'd wanted to?"

"Of course," said Sera without hesitation or remorse.

Aiva didn't act surprised. "I was always being used, whether it was for my gift or for emotional support. I gave up on my own dreams long ago. At least with you, I deliver justice for those who can do nothing. I'm proud of what I've done." Her purple eyes found Sera's stare. "But no matter the mission or the people I've protected, I can't save the people of Oarlon from the sickness all around. I've seen it destroy their souls and their loved ones. I've watched them suffer and die in the streets. I've seen the hope go out of their eyes. If I die soon, then the only regret in my life would be missing out on breathing in fresh air and seeing hope in a child's eyes."

Aiva looked at Sera for any sign that Sera knew of her fate. Sera leaned in and lowered her voice, even though it didn't matter in the privacy of the hoverer.

"I need you to do something for me. I have another attachment that needs clearing." Aiva nodded for her to go on.

"Make sure Thane does not survive the battle. After what he did to Gaven..."

Aiva took out her pistol and twirled it around in one hand. For Sera, it wasn't really about Gaven, but she knew Aiva would need a moral reason. In reality, Sera needed him off the board, once and for all.

"Will that be a problem?"

"I can do that," said Aiva, her eyes narrowing for a moment. She kept twirling the gun; sometimes she would stop and the barrel would point at Sera.

"He was your friend a long time ago," said Sera.

"Friend or not, if he's a threat to you, then I'll do what I have to," said Aiva.

TWENTY-SEVEN

KOE

Fye's decapitated body slumped to the ground, lying in a pool of his own blood soaking the wooden platform. Koe watched with binoculars from a rooftop far away. This was the first time he'd ventured outside. Every day, his hands grew steadier as he ate, his legs pushing himself up without stumbling. Rus hadn't even stopped him from leaving the temple, even when the other Knightmares objected. Rus had confidence he would return. At least, the Shadows did, and Rus would never question them.

As he recovered, Koe continued to avoid the other Knightmares, and by Rus' orders, they stayed out of his orbit too. Not even Rus visited him much. They were too busy plotting, trying to find Aiva and take her out of the game before moving to Sera again.

Every time Koe entered the meeting room to hear them talk strategy, all the other Knightmares would stare at him. His reputation and skill had drawn their attention before, but this was much different.

They saw him as a traitor, someone who didn't deserve to be there, let alone alive.

Koe stood his ground, keeping his ears open for news, what the Shadows were saying and what the spies reported back.

Evidently, none of it meant anything as all the Knightmares, including Fye, fell into Aiva's trap. Less faces to stare at him, and yet according to Rus, these were his friends who were going to fight against the Queen.

Koe slid down the ladder, landing in the slushy snow. He grabbed his scarf and pulled it tighter as the chill wind blew against him. Not even the sun piercing the clouds warmed his skin.

He didn't know why he kept the scarf anymore. By all accounts, he should've thrown it away by now, cut it to shreds and let the wind scatter it around Oarlon. But each time he reached to take it off, he merely tightened it again.

He wasn't sure what he was going to do now. He had no allies, his dreams were lost and the hope of vengeance against the Queen grew dimmer and dimmer. His gun rested in his holster, and Koe's hand hovered over it, ready to pull it and put it to his own chin. How easy it would be to end it all here. The Queen's blue eyes, her grin, her white hair pulled back appeared before him. His heartbeat rose, but he pushed past the image, leaving the Sky District and heading toward the outskirts.

His hoverer rested in a barn with half the roof missing. The wood was covered with moss, rising up from the ground and infecting the lumber like a cancer. The barn sat by itself a stone's throw away from a few other broken-down houses. The outposts were still far away but were now all unguarded as every soldier had been recalled to fight the war against the underworld while the rest guarded the castle and its Queen. The death toll must be high for the outposts to be abandoned.

Just behind the barn, over a small hill, lay three houses similar in their dilapidated state to the barn, except for the hole in its roof. Koe caught sight of a man, his arms shriveled nearly to the bone, carrying a body toward a rectangular hole — a grave — six feet deep. A rusty shovel lay on the ground to the side. The man kissed the forehead of the body before dumping it unceremoniously into the hole. Koe walked toward him, unsure why. The man's hair was filled with mud, and his clothes were torn. Upon seeing Koe, his eyes brightened just a little. A first for someone seeing a Knightmare.

"Death has finally arrived," said the man with a sad smile. "I am ready when you are, Knightmare."

Koe wandered over to stand beside the grave with the man, peering down to see a young girl's body at the bottom. She had the same button nose and hair color as the man beside him. Her head held a nasty gash, caused by some blunt-force instrument.

"Your daughter?"

"Yes," said the man. "My son died a few years ago. It's just me now."

"I'm sorry," said Koe. With a blink, the girl's body turned into Gaven's, and after another second, it changed to Koe's own as a boy.

"Another fallout of the war," said the man. "The Queen said she would save us. That she would cleanse the streets, clean the air. But what is there really left to save?"

"People still have hope," said Koe with a sigh.

"Hope is a lie," replied the man cynically. "Do things ever really get better? Problems don't go away, they just change."

"Wasn't it worth it? The time you spent with them?" said Koe.

"No," said the man after a pause. "They were my everything, but all their lives, they suffered. Not just from the air. I helped bring them into this world, and for what? To live a half life? A painful one too?" The man wiped away tears running down his face. "Will you give me peace, Knightmare?" The man's eyes looked at Koe, both bloodshot, half closed. It would be mercy.

Koe pulled one of his daggers from its sheathe. He stared at the blade, twisting it in the sunlight as it reflected the light into his eyes. One swift flick, and the man would fall into the grave next to his daughter, but after staring at it, Koe put it back.

"No," said Koe. "Peace doesn't exist, not as long as the people who did that to your daughter are out there." Koe moved from the man's side toward the barn once again.

"Please, don't go. Please! End it," cried the man desperately. Koe kept going, focusing on the winter chill. He grabbed his scarf once again, tightening it around his neck. All his life he was told to let go, leave it all behind, but there was nowhere to go. Nowhere to escape the pain.

Flames lit up the forest, the humming sound of hoverers crashing through the bushes. A small army of soldiers were making their way from the city toward the Knightmare Temple.

Koe sat on his haunches as the snow piled atop his hat. He would sit and wait now for the forest to burn and the soldiers to reach the temple. His Knightmare comrades were going to die today and so would most of the soldiers. After the dust had settled, he would have his vengeance.

TWENTY-EIGHT

KOE

There was no secret path to follow back to the Knightmare temple. The Queen's army had destroyed the path with fire, burning the trees and the roots below the ground. Even the falling snow and the little of it that had settled on the ground couldn't slow the fire's destruction. The smell of ash still filled Koe's nose. He barely noticed it now though, as the smell had been so prevalent as of late.

Bodies of the Queen's soldiers hung over every tree stump, slowly burning away as the fire melted their flesh. The sight was just more of what Koe had already witnessed since setting out on his mission to kill Sera.

Soldiers, some as young as thirteen, lay lifeless. Their scrawny arms would barely have been able to carry a shield or swing a sword. An easy slaughter.

The sound of battle echoed far away. Flames danced on top of the temple. By now, all the Knightmares would have evacuated. With the sun out, there would be no chance of disappearing, even if they wanted to. But the Knightmares knew the forest better than the army did. They knew how to kill, even the ones who were just in training.

Yet as Koe moved through the snowy forest toward the sound of cries and clanging swords, he found a couple of Knightmares who'd joined the ranks of the dead. At one such, he leaned down and checked the sword gash across the chest. Down by the Knightmare's feet was a forcefield ring, used to ensnare enemies. Aiva's handywork.

As the flames destroying the temple grew and grew, Koe couldn't help but stare into the blaze. A small weight lifted from him, knowing he'd never have to set foot in that place again. He was glad to see it burn. All of it was coming to an end.

As the center of the battle came into view, Koe evaded a pair of rookie Knightmares dying at the hands of a larger group of soldiers surrounding them. He watched as another tore several soldiers apart, only to lose an arm and then their head. But the Queen's army wasn't doing much better. The ranks of soldiers were thinning.

Two squads regrouped after three of them pulled their swords from a Knightmare's back, the Shadows leaving his portly form. Koe watched from afar as one soldier barked orders, only to be ambushed by four Knightmares before he could organize his squad. One Knightmare died instantly while the other three sliced and diced a few soldiers. The clash of swords and gunshots rang out through the burning forest. By the end of it, only one Knightmare with a nasty gash in her right side struggled to stand.

Koe moved toward her, silently creeping up behind. She was breathing heavily, holding her wound with her hand to apply pressure as blood oozed through her fingers. She clearly didn't hear Koe's approach. As she turned around, she jumped back in surprise, her back slamming into a tree.

"It's you." The disdain in her tone was louder than the gunfire.

"Where's Rus?" asked Koe, watching this young Knightmare, known as Hec, turn her head and glance down at her gun in the snow.

"He's down by the lake, fighting off the leaders," said Hec.

"How many do they still have left?"

"Not many. But we don't either."

Koe nodded his head, keeping his eyes on her gun in the snow.

"Come to watch?" she asked.

Koe shook his head. "No. But I'm not here to help."

He picked up her gun, dusting the snow off it, and proceeded to shoot her.

After tossing it away, he approached the lake, completely iced over at this time of year. Four Knightmares remained, trying to disappear in the shade as one squadron of troops were trying to regroup. One Knightmare ducked, dodged and killed in the same manner as Koe. His moves were quick and precise. The shadow crown still clung to his head. Koe could hear the commands Rus made to himself as he slit a soldier's throat and ducked underneath another's sword.

Not far away, Aiva chopped the head off a Knightmare who moved slowly, his blood smearing the ice. With gashes along his stomach, it was clear that Aiva had already softened him up, made him feel the pain of losing before taking his life.

Thane stood further back, resting on one knee with his sword piercing the ice. Both hands clung to the hilt. Koe could see his breath leave his mouth in the chilled air. He had blood-soaked clothes and only wore one shoulder pad; the rest of his armor had been ripped away, revealing a few noticeable cuts along his side. But as one Knightmare killed two of his soldiers, Thane ripped his sword out of the ground and clashed with the Knightmare. With a few quick parries, Thane moved backwards, seemingly tiring. As the Knightmare grew cocky at this apparent sign of weakness, Thane's energy bounced back and his sword met the Knightmare's neck.

Rus paced the lake, watching as Aiva killed his last remaining ally with ease. Rus in turn picked off three soldiers, leaving himself, Aiva and Thane as the only ones left alive.

Aiva didn't immediately jump to attack. She took a glance over at Thane. The crown on Rus' head was a dead giveaway that he was the Seer.

As Thane and Aiva geared up to fight Rus, Koe knew he couldn't sit back any longer. Revenge was his. He jumped down from his perch onto the frozen lake, making a loud thump, the ice cracking a little under his weight. All three turned as he walked toward them, head high. His scarf blew in the wind, and all was silent. No battle cries left. No victory yells.

"You…!" shouted Thane, his voice trembling. "You can't be

alive…" He quickly turned to Aiva. "He can't be!"

Aiva's eyes narrowed at Koe, like she was trying to find a discrepancy in the way he dressed to determine it wasn't him, that it was another Knightmare pretending. Rus simply huffed. Just as Koe could pick out Rus in a battle from far away, Rus knew how Koe moved. He'd taught him. There was no hiding it from Rus, but Koe wasn't trying to fool anyone.

"Good. Let's finish this together," said Rus, gesturing around him with his dagger. Koe looked upon each body lying on the lake.

"I'm not here to aid the Shadows, Rus. I'm here for them," said Koe, looking toward Thane and Aiva, "And for you." Koe held his dagger up and pointed at Rus.

"You would disobey the Shadows after they saved you, gave you a home? Even now, they whisper to keep you alive!" yelled Rus.

Koe walked between Rus, Thane and Aiva, keeping his ears open for any sudden movements but remaining calm and slow himself. Before he had his revenge, he needed them all to understand.

"But I had a home — in the castle. I was friends with a girl. When a boy of the royal kingdom convinced her to transform herself into the Princess to steal goods, I took the fall. Because I loved her."

Thane's eyes grew wide, his grip on his sword loosened so he had to grab it before it fell on the ground.

"You… The servant boy…"

"Can't remember my name, can you, Thane? Did you ever think about what happened?"

Thane could barely keep his eyes on Koe, but to his credit, he shook his head truthfully. "I remember your face. Not from the wanted posters but as you were taken away. I can't forget that."

"Nor I. Nor every burn, cut or lesson you made me learn," said Koe, turning to Rus. The ice cracked a little beneath his feet as his boots slammed into it. "Or the pain of my best friend turning into a monster, not even in charge of her own destiny."

Aiva chuckled and shook her head. "Stop making yourself into the victim, Koe. I don't cling to a fantasy like you do."

"She's right, that's always been your problem," sneered Rus. "You dream of the future instead of the here and now. You make decisions based on your past, ruining the life you chose."

"I didn't choose any of this!" yelled Koe, matching Rus' intensity.

"You did. When you tried to save her," said Rus. "It was a choice. You could've kept silent, been a good little servant and probably lived a fine life in servitude. You chose to sacrifice yourself that day, and no one is going to wipe your tears now."

A long silence followed, the cold air surrounding them all. Koe flexed his fingers one at a time to keep his hands warm. He could feel the urge to grab his gun and let loose. What had started as the perfect setup for his revenge had begun to turn against him. The power he had when he first arrived was slipping away, and he would not have it.

"There's a lot of things I regret. I don't think this will make the list." Koe drew his other dagger.

"So we all die here today and the only one who benefits from it is the Queen herself," said Thane, drawing up his sword to hold the blade between his eyes.

"What does that mean?" asked Rus, stepping a few feet to the left to get a better view of Thane from behind Koe.

"It means that the Queen wants us all dead," said Koe.

Aiva scoffed, dusting the thought off her shoulder. "Not us," said Aiva, but no one could miss the side-eye she gave Thane.

"My orders were to kill you after we destroyed the Knightmares," said Thane, angling his blade toward Aiva now and backing up into his own corner on the ice. "I'm certain she told you the same."

While they spoke, Koe stepped quietly away from the middle of the ice until all four paced in a square, each keeping the same careful distance from the others.

"She needs me," said Aiva, a subtle bitterness accompanying her words.

"We're the last two she cares about," said Thane. "Without us, she'll have no one and she'll be free."

"Don't waste your breath, Thane. She's too under Sera's thumb to care," said Koe.

"You're just saying that," said Aiva. "Always plotting, Thane."

Thane then stabbed his sword into the ice, harder than before. Cracks formed, spreading toward the others. Koe kept watch. It was hard enough to keep track of the other three, but now he had to make sure the ground wouldn't go out beneath him.

"We might hate each other. We've certainly destroyed each other," said Thane, pointing to the battle around him. "But all of us have been betrayed by the Queen. We could fight here and now, and maybe one of us would be lucky enough to return to the palace and end the prophecy. Or we could join forces and make sure that Sera is exposed as a fraud," said Thane. Everyone paused in their movements, considering his proposition.

"You've been around her for years. If you wanted her dead, why have you not done it?" asked Rus, pointing with one of his daggers.

"He wanted to be king," said Koe. "That's all he'd ever cared about."

"Not true," said Thane. "My son—"

"Aren't you forgetting?" exclaimed Aiva. "She's the Chosen One! She's going to save Oarlon. She'll save the world! Can't you feel the air getting worse and worse?"

"I don't care. If she's our savior, we're better off without one," said Thane.

Koe was almost impressed by Thane's reversal. He suspected part of him was scared of a fight between all four of them. Thane was by far the least skilled. The more Koe thought about it, the more he saw this as a desperate attempt to survive somehow. That was Thane, always finding a way.

"If she is the Chosen One and has seen everything that has happened up to this point, she will see us coming," said Rus, seemingly onboard with the idea. Rus did prioritize the mission above all else.

"She doesn't see everything. There's still a chance. A better chance if we all unite," urged Thane. "I can get you into the castle. You may kill me after, I don't care. I just want to see the life leave her eyes."

"An interesting proposition," said Rus, stroking his chin and mulling the idea over.

As the two discussed, Aiva's eyes fell on Koe. She must be wondering what he felt. He truly didn't know himself. Taking Sera's life was his ultimate purpose, the goal he'd had forever. Well, other than saving Aiva and leaving Oarlon with her. But that 'fantasy', as she'd called it, was gone. It made sense that if Thane could get them into the castle, then they should unite and kill Sera. They could try to kill each other after. Yet the idea of siding with any of them caused Koe's stomach to twist and turn violently.

Aiva wouldn't turn against Sera, no matter what. She wouldn't go along with this plan, which meant that as Thane and Rus were coming to an agreement, she would be in their way. As good of a fighter as Aiva was, she wouldn't last against Rus and Thane together. But more so, Koe couldn't let Rus or Thane kill her. That was for him alone. They were all for him alone.

"I suppose I just have to trust you?" Rus asked Thane, a hint of doubt bleeding into his tone. A subtle flash of hope crossed Aiva's eyes.

"Trust the man who killed his own son for Sera?" asked Aiva. "He'll kill you the moment you turn your back."

"Then I wouldn't turn my back," snapped Rus. "But she makes a valid point. Why would you help me?"

"Aiva's right. I did kill my son. I deserve to die. I can only hope that you and Sera kill each other, and then I can take my own life in peace." Thane breathed a heavy sigh and stood straight, regaining some of the usual strength in his body language and voice. "Believe what you want. I'm not going to go on and on, trying to convince you. All I'll say is this: this is the only opportunity you'll have. Take it or leave it. I don't care."

Rus took a long pause and sheathed his dagger. "I've been reading people for a long time — seen people lie and tell the truth. You really believe you deserve to die."

Thane's face was wrought with remorse, but Koe had trouble holding any sympathy. He was there when Thane gave the order to kill Gaven. Even if he now regretted his actions, the boy was still dead and Thane still needed to answer for everything he'd done.

Koe returned his gaze to Aiva, who had turned to look at him. Thane and Rus had struck an uneasy alliance, and now it was time for Koe to choose. He almost spoke, uttering the words that he'd join Thane and Rus for now.

But as he peered into Aiva's eyes from afar, he could see the same girl he grew up with. The same person he fell in love with. He was so sure she was playing on his feelings. At least, he suspected it, but seeing any genuine warm emotion from her felt foreign.

Rus and Thane now eyed both Koe and Aiva. Rus walked toward Aiva, drawing his blades once again.

"She won't change her mind, Koe. You side with her, she'll stab you in the back," he said. "Remember, the Shadows are the only one who has truly ever cared about you, Koe!"

Koe kept his gaze on Aiva, and hers remained on him. His anger toward her churned inside, but Rus and Thane's alliance was more problematic than it was potentially helpful. Koe twirled one of his daggers in his hand.

"I know she will. That's why I have to make the best decision for me." With a quick and accurate throw, Koe's blade left his hand, humming straight toward Thane. The captain of the guard tried to move in time, but the blade tip sliced his shoulder. Blood squirted out onto the ice.

Now that the temporary truce was broken, Aiva, without hesitancy, engaged with Rus, clanging sword and daggers together. Their moves were quick and precise, neither one gaining the upper hand. Thane clutched his bleeding shoulder with one arm and his sword with the other. Koe recalled the dagger he'd thrown back to him, cutting the back of Thane's calf. He fell to one knee, barely able to hold his sword up.

As Koe approached, Thane's body quivered, his breath shaky. Finally, he dropped his sword and got on all fours, drops of blood running from his shoulder onto the ice.

"That's it? No fight?"

"What's the point? I can't beat you," said Thane.

Koe leaned down onto one knee in front of Thane and lifted his head up with two fingers under his chin. "You once told me I would be a good memory after my death, that these were the consequences of my actions. I want you to know, your son despised you so much he wanted to go with me: a stranger whose face he couldn't even see. You were passed over for the throne. Sera hated you. You died with nothing. Rest assured though—you will be remembered, but the only good memory of you will be this."

With a quick flick of the wrist, Koe jammed his dagger into Thane's chest. A huge cry echoed across the lake. As quickly as he'd stabbed him, Koe withdrew the dagger.

Thane's breathing became haggard and heavy. His upper body tipped forward, and he fell stomach first on the ice. His face twisted toward Koe, choking on his own blood. Koe watched as the life left Thane's eyes. He could still hear the clash of metal and the grunts of the other two behind him. Their sounds faded into the background as Thane's last guttural grunt hit Koe's ears. The sound of a beautiful melody had ended. If only Koe could kill him again.

His head turned toward the other two. Rus gripped his daggers tight, and with a swift kick to her chin, he drove Aiva backwards, causing her to fall and lose her sword. That's when Koe noticed something by Rus' feet.

A small black ball sitting atop a little mound of snow above the topmost sheet of ice. Then he noticed more and more of them. As Aiva had been fighting, she must've thrown them all around.

As Koe watched, Rus noticed them too and swiftly sidestepped as they all exploded at once. The ice split into chunks, each platform becoming unstable and wobbly. Koe shielded his face, thankfully far enough from each of the small explosions that he wasn't affected.

Rus, on the other hand, hadn't moved far enough away and his whole arm was engulfed in flame. He dropped his dagger, letting it fall into the lake water below. His whole arm followed as he submerged it to extinguish the flames. He let out an ear-splitting cry as he withdrew his arm. All the clothes on his arm were gone, singed from his flesh, exposing the shadows beneath.

Aiva rose up and scampered off the ice, apparently fleeing the duel. Rus leapt on the scattering ice pieces after her, turning invisible in the shadows, but Koe knew how Rus moved. Every beating created a memory. Every memory echoed throughout the years. And every echo tortured him at night.

Koe hopped on the moving ice pieces just behind Rus. He made sure to stay light on his feet, the sound of him landing on each sheet of ice was similar to a Knightmare dagger being thrown through the air — almost impossible to hear.

When Rus reappeared once again in the sunlight, Koe was upon him, sinking his dagger into his back and tackling him onto the ice. Freezing water sprayed out around them as Koe's weight crushed Rus' back. Koe withdrew his dagger, flipped Rus around and stabbed him in the chest before Rus could react.

Rus' cries were unlike him, shrill with pain. In all the time Koe had known him, he'd never once heard Rus cry out for help.

Koe pushed the dagger deeper into Rus' heart, through all the torture and memories, stabbing him over and over again, blood flying everywhere. He hit every vital organ, and every time the dagger broke flesh, Koe had another flash of Rus' backhanded hit. With a final stab, Koe withdrew the dagger and pushed Rus off the ice sheet, into the freezing cold water.

Koe never considered what Rus' face looked like until now. He could only imagine Rus' eyes wide, the blood dripping down his chin. His body slowly sank, and Koe watched until the darkness swallowed Rus as the shadows around him left.

The Seer's crown floated to the surface, whispers echoing from it. Koe reached out to take it but stopped just before doing so. He had a bigger concern.

There was still one left. Aiva stood by, watching from the shoreline. Her gun was pointed at Koe, but any urgency to dodge out of the way disappeared upon seeing her arm tremble as she tried to steady her aim. Instead of shooting, she ultimately dropped it. Koe walked toward her slowly, hopping across the ice sheets and finding no trouble balancing from one to the next. When he was close enough to talk, she took a heavy sigh.

"You know, Thane was right," said Koe. "About Sera. He wasn't lying."

Aiva nodded, clutching her side. "I know." She dropped her head. "Even so, I can't... I can't kill her. She's the Chosen One. I don't agree with everything she's done, but I won't doom everyone. So just get it over with, Koe. I can't beat you."

Her hand withdrew from her abdomen, and Koe could see the deep gash in her side. Rus had gotten her. Koe paused. He knew he should be able to kill her, but seeing trickles of the person she used to be and not the cold-hearted assassin made it all the more difficult to draw and send a few bullets into her chest.

"I'll make it easier for you," she said. With a series of quiet grunts and cracks, Aiva's bones shifted in place, her shoulders widened, her hair turned white. Tattoos of falling stars appeared across her forehead. She was now Sera.

"Well, what are you waiting for?" Sera's blue eyes pierced into Koe's heart. He walked forward, putting his hands on Aiva's arms to help keep her upright.

"No, let me see you," said Koe.

Aiva morphed back, slower than usual due to her wounds. Her eyes met his. Koe traced his fingers over her scars.

"I never cared about the scars. The purple eyes. Your powers. I even felt bad for you, being brainwashed by Sera."

Aiva opened her mouth to object, but Koe drew his dagger and set the tip below her chin. "But you stopped me from saving Gaven." Koe shoved the dagger into her chest. Aiva let out a gasp, choking on her breath just as Thane had. "You were right—the boy I was did die that day. So did my friend Aiva."

Koe watched as the light in her purple eyes darkened for the last time before withdrawing the blade and letting her body fall into the snow.

Slowly, Aiva exhaled her last breath into the frigid air. Koe sat down next to her body amid the carnage of the battle. The Knightmares were gone and Sera's soldiers with them. Only a lone shadow remained.

TWENTY-NINE

QUEEN SERA

It was on the tip of Sera's tongue. The solution to the poisoned air was staring at her in the face as she sat on her throne under the golden dome, alone. The castle was a lot less guarded than before. Too many of her soldiers had died. She'd known it was going to happen. She foresaw Thane's death, the Knightmare's and even Aiva's. She hadn't wanted to give up Aiva, she was such a loyal servant. A friend. But the more she cleared away, the more she could see. The more she let go, the closer she got. Their sacrifice would mean Sera's detachment from all belongings — freedom to really focus on her destiny.

When she saw that Aiva and Thane left with the last Knightmare, she'd thought they would dispose of him and then dispose of each other. But the Light sent her exactly what she needed — a killer.

Once her army left the palace and she had given her orders to Thane and Aiva, another vision appeared before her. The Knightmare named Koe, alive and well, walking calmly through the forest.

When Koe killed Thane, Sera saw the life leave his eyes. She was there, a watchful, omniscient presence, pitying him and rejoicing that she wouldn't have to hear him complain again.

When Koe killed his fellow Knightmare, Sera smiled — there was almost nothing better than watching enemies kill each other.

When Koe finally killed Aiva, Sera realized he was the boy she had framed so long ago. Aiva knew who he was too, but she hadn't told Sera about it. Another reason Sera wasn't as sad as she might've been over Aiva's death. Sera gave Aiva life, yet she had hidden the truth from Sera.

She knew Koe would be coming for her. Anyone else would be terrified that a Knightmare was coming after them, but not Sera. Not anymore. With her growing powers, she knew every step he would take to get to her, everything he would say and everything she would say back. She would kill him, and with his death, she would discover the secret to saving the world.

Sera relaxed on her throne, letting her back settle into the soft cushion. Destiny was a funny thing. If only she knew when she was young — that this slave boy and her destiny were more intertwined that she realized. The irony.

He was coming for revenge after all these years… and he would fail. She almost felt bad for him.

The elevator doors opened, and a few guards marched out, bowing quickly to Sera. Their faces were blank, but Sera could see the cracks in their resolve. Their loyalty, much like the loyalty of the people of Oarlon, was breaking. They could not see what Sera did, what she was doing. They only saw their fellow soldiers dying and the people suffering from the air.

Hanna and a few other advisors quickly scuttled into the chamber behind them. Hanna took center stage, trying hard to maintain eye-contact with Sera.

"My Queen, the caskets from the battle are being brought behind the shield wall. The families are accompanying them. Many have wondered if you planned on saying any words. We believe it would be in your best interest to reassure the people that this is part of the plan."

Sera interlocked her fingers over her lap and sighed. "Words can't help anymore. By this time tomorrow, the people will know how I will save them. I have seen it."

"But Your Majesty, the people need you now," said Hanna, with desperation filling her words. Her voice shook like a sick puppy trying to call out to its mother.

"This is the way it needs to happen. I have foreseen every action. I know what you are about to say… I know your brothers all died for the cause. I know your heart aches. This is the cost of saving the world."

A few tears broke from Hanna's eyes to run down her cheeks. Unable to maintain her composure, Hanna started to speak.

"Do not say it, Hanna. Do not make it true."

Hanna stood tall, cleared her throat and started again with more conviction: "Then I resign as your advisor. I wish you and the people of Oarlon the very best."

As Hanna dipped into one final bow, Sera signaled the guards to grab her. Two guards moved to Hanna's sides, each grabbing an arm and bringing her to her knees.

"You're right, the people are losing their faith," Sera began. "Even after tomorrow, as I save Oarlon and clean the air, people will wonder if I went too far. So I must send a message. Anyone who abandons me or loses faith will suffer. Who better to present that message than the Queen's own personal advisor?"

Hanna stopped struggling. She turned to her fellow advisors and then to the guards.

"None of you believe in her. I see it. I know it. Come on, let's take her out before she kills us all! Let us savor what time we have left."

Sera could see the minds of her soldiers and advisors racing, trying to decide what to do. She already knew their decision—she just needed to give them a little push.

"Keep me alive and there is still hope. Kill me and you will have certainly doomed the world." Sera relaxed in her seat. Renewed conviction crept onto each face before her. Her advisors bowed, and her guards gripped Hanna tighter.

"Don't do this! She's a false prophet!" shouted Hanna.

"You forget, Hanna, that faith is hope. And just a little spark of hope can be enough." Sera nodded to the guards. A third guard drew his sword, and before Hanna could squeal again, he chopped her head clean off.

"Put her head on a spike for all to see," directed Sera.

The guards nodded, and the rest of her advisors left in a hurry. Now she would wait for the boy out for revenge. He was the final piece in her long quest for salvation.

THIRTY

KOE

Hiding in a casket under a dead soldier was simple enough. The Queen's soldiers, the ones who had avoided the battle, had been ordered to pick up the fallen. The Knightmares were to be strung up so the people of Oarlon could see that the order had finally been brought to an end. Most likely it was a gesture designed to make the families of Oarlon feel like their sacrifices weren't in vain as the caskets of dead soldiers arrived.

A small crack in the casket yielded the only light available to Koe. The body on top of him made the cramped space harder to breathe in, but Koe kept his breaths shallow and steady, focusing on his mission. A nasty odor told Koe the dead man had defecated.

The occasional jostle of the casket confirmed he was still moving. He clutched the scarf around him with one hand and one of his daggers in another. He'd fight his way out when the casket was opened. By then, he'd be within the shield wall.

Even with the army engaged, the Queen still had her personal guard, so he'd use the tunnels that ran through the castle to make it to the top. He still remembered all the routes. He'd find the Queen, dispose of anyone around her and then he'd savor his kill: cutting her thousands of times so she would know an ounce of his pain and suffering.

He ran his hand along the smooth wood of the casket, pushing any and all thoughts of failure from his mind. He didn't believe in fate. Aiva was wrong—Sera wasn't untouchable, even if she was the Chosen One. But his thoughts became a hand, grasping his heart and tightening its grip. He'd spent too long waiting for this moment to lose now.

He retreated to his memories of Aiva and him as kids, looking at the sunset and wondering what else was out there. The retreat was short lived as the casket was opened unexpectedly and dumped out before Koe knew what happened. The soldier's body and his thumped to the black metallic floor. He could feel the daylight shining down on him. The echo of their bodies hitting the floor reverberated throughout the room. He didn't have to look up to know where he was.

The dome.

The throne room.

On his hands and knees, Koe looked up to see Sera sitting on her throne. He couldn't believe he was here, more so that she'd brought him to her. She must've seen him in a vision. Her power had grown, and now he was on the back foot instead of her. Two guards, the ones who had brought him here, nodded at her as she flicked her wrist, signaling for them to leave. The metal of the dead soldier's uniform grated against the floor as they dragged the body away. Koe almost didn't register the scraping. He couldn't believe his eyes.

Seeing her in the flesh brought a mountainous wave of shock crashing down on his heart, electrifying every part of his body. He noticed her white hair, the adult features that he'd seen on the broadcasts, her blue eyes, still as chilling and calculating as ever.

"Do you need help?" she asked.

Koe picked himself up, his eyes darting every which way to find traps or hidden figures. Nothing. At least, nothing he could see. So why bring him here? What was her plan?

"Those were my first words to you, don't you remember? They were right here in this very room."

She knew who he was.

"Aiva tell you?" asked Koe.

Sera just smiled and shook her head. "No, I see so much now. Every event that led you here, I watched it like a moving picture. The poor servant boy. Framed, beaten, abandoned. Turned into a shadow, yet still just a boy wearing a scarf to comfort his broken heart."

Koe touched his scarf and pulled it off his neck. "It's yours. I've come to give it back."

"How thoughtful," said Sera sarcastically.

"I can't tell you how many times I've imagined this day. You were a fool to bring me here," said Koe.

"You came to kill me. I know. It's why I brought you here," said Sera. "You think you're in control, but I know your every move.

Everything you're going to say. Everything I'll say in response." Her eyes flashed to Koe's feet as he moved a half step back. An evil grin formed on her lips as she stood up.

Without a second thought, Koe threw one of his daggers at her head, but she casually dodged, and the dagger embedded itself into the golden velvet behind her. Koe tried to call it back, but the dagger was lodged too deeply into the metal of the throne. He dropped his scarf onto the ground and drew his gun, firing directly at Sera, who simply danced around the room, effortlessly dodging all of the incoming bullets.

Anger swelled in Koe's chest, bursting out in a primal yell as he emptied the clip. Gone was the meticulous, cunning warrior. The enemy in front of him tugged at his pain like no other, and logic went out the window. The chamber was riddled with bullet holes as Sera stood smiling before him.

"I wouldn't do what you're thinking next," advised Sera.

Koe threw his remaining dagger up into the air, crashing into the glass dome and shattering it all. Glass rained down upon them both, neither of them flinching. Sera took a step forward, her boot crushing the glass into more pieces.

"This ends with me killing you, but please know that your death is the final key I need to unlock a vision of how to save the world. Make this easier on yourself and let's finish this now. Think about how many people you'll save."

Koe recalled the dagger he used to break the ceiling and rushed at Sera, swinging for her head, legs, body, anything. She ducked and dodged with her hands behind her back. She backpedaled, and for a second, Koe thought he was a predator boxing in his prey. Except her expression hadn't changed. He threw the dagger once again, but her head moved just in time and the dagger hit the wall behind her, clanking to the ground.

Koe ran at her, preparing to tackle her, when her foot kicked upward and little bits of glass flew in his face. His momentum was already too fast to stop as he closed his eyes, crashing on the ground. Shards of glass dug into his hands as he pushed himself back up to his feet. He used his arm to wipe at his eyes, thankful none of the glass had pierced them.

"If you can kill me so easily, why are you waiting?" asked Koe, facing her once again.

Sera just shrugged. "This is what the Light has shown me. If it gives me the answer I seek, I will play the game."

Koe recalled his dagger once again and rushed at her, trying not to let her mind games get in his head. But he sliced only air once again until Sera moved her arms in a quick motion, hitting a pressure point that caused the dagger to drop from his hand. Before it touched the floor, Sera grabbed it and sent it straight into Koe's gut.

A soft groan tumbled from Koe's mouth, and the sting of failure radiated through his body, more biting than the pain of the dagger. His muscles relaxed, and he fell onto his knees. The scarf lay between them as Sera knelt to one knee to meet his gaze. Koe's blood soaked the scarf as he reached out, bundling it into his hands.

"Even behind a shadow, you stay true to the boy that grew up here. What a tragedy." Sera put a hand on his face, her hand disappearing underneath the shadow. "I can't see it."

Seeing Koe glance up at her made her continue: "Your face. I can't see it being the same." Koe chuckled.

"What's so funny?" asked Sera, seeming more puzzled than one might expect from someone who knew every word he was about to say.

"I trained my whole life just to be here and kill you. And now… I've failed." Koe's heartbeat was fading. He couldn't even feel the dagger in his gut anymore. He couldn't help but wonder, as he stared at Sera's eyes — was all of this worth it?

Sera put a hand on Koe's shoulder and smiled, an almost kind, genuine smile. "I know. Your quest is over. You can finally rest."

As the blood dripped from his wound, Koe's spirit slowly began to leave his body, yet his hand around his scarf tightened.

"Be at —"

A quick motion, the sound of fabric ripping and a soft gasp. Sera's eyes grew wide. She looked down to see a long, pointed shard of glass, like a dagger, protruding from her chest, right through her heart. Her gaze locked on the the bloody scarf wrapped around the glass. Shreds of it hung off the makeshift dagger, the other half on the ground in front of her.

"No! No, this wasn't supposed to happen —" she managed to croak out. Koe pointed to his wound and withdrew the dagger with a groan.

"You missed my heart."

"No… This… No, my visions. Everything I sacrificed… to find the secret to save the kingdom."

Koe took a deep, painful breath and picked up the largest piece of his scarf. Everything inside was empty. Every lesson meaningless. He thought of what it would feel like to watch the Queen die. Now as he watched it, he felt nothing.

Sera looked to the sky as the sunlight poured in, her eyes widening in surprise. "I see it now. The cure for the air… It's a flower. West of Oarlon… A rare black-and-white-stemmed flower." She turned back to Koe. "Please, for Oarlon, save them."

Koe dropped the piece of scarf and used his dagger to slice a clean red line across Sera's throat. Sera toppled over, gargling in her last moments. Koe struggled to his feet and hobbled toward the elevator, not looking back as Sera lay dying on the floor, reaching out to him in one final plea for Koe to listen to her. The torn and bloodied scarf was strewn across the floor, reunited with its owner.

THIRTY-ONE

KOE

Embers fluttered in the soft breeze, finding their way into the cracks of wood, settling down in the splints and igniting a small flame that ate away until the wood turned into ash. The fires continued throughout the city of Oarlon, in every district, in every home. The news of the Queen's death and thus the last hope to clean the air died with her.

With everyone at their breaking point, the city descended into madness. Screams echoed throughout the darkness of the night, breaking through the smoke-filled sky and acting as a blanket suffocating the city. Now all the monsters were coming out. Every hidden darkness that people had repressed for so long erupted, and those around them suffered the consequences.

In the Leaf District, glass shards and doors ripped from their hinges lay in front of homes, often with bodies scattered about inside. In one particular house, three bodies wearing all black clothes and masks lay in pools of their own blood next to the brick they'd thrown through the window. Just a few feet away, a couple with shotguns in hand lay wide-eyed, facing toward one another, their throats having been slit by Koe as the smoke from the barrels still rose.

In the Iron District, a man, chiseled and strong in stature, broke a scrawny man's neck for killing his lover in a drunken hover crash a decade ago. Koe moved behind the muscular man as he sat on his knees, crying over the dead body, staring at his hands and realizing what he'd done. He didn't have long as Koe pressed his blade against the man's throat and drew it back. The man fell onto the scrawny one, their bodies atop one another and their cheeks touching.

In the Crown District, what was left of the Queen's soldiers tried to fend off the bloodthirsty citizens who were trying to kill any advisor or associate of the Queen left alive. But since the war with the Knightmares, few soldiers were left to defend the city. They blew the heads off even the most innocent, who were just standing around shouting or even those staying silent, watching. One soldier, sweaty and trembling, threw his gun away and bolted, only to be sniped by a fellow solider.

As the mass killings continued, the citizens pushed against the soldiers' shields, using rocks and blunt instruments to smash their skulls in. The lines of soldiers broke, and the disorganized mob squeezed through the hole they'd made into the houses of the nobles. Screams and gunfire added to the rest of the chaos. Anyone who walked out of the house, no matter on which side, ended up on the ground, motionless and spewing blood as Koe moved past.

Koe took a hoverer abandoned in the street and left the city burning behind him, returning to the now black, charred temple that he'd spent so much time in. A small whisper had been in his ear ever since Rus died. It led him to the bank of the lake — and there the Knightmare crown sat.

The whispers grew louder, pulling him closer. Koe snatched the crown and returned to his hoverer, leaving the ruined temple for the last time.

The trees dwindled. The snow on the ground was now just little pockets here and there. Rolling hills filled his view until the sun faded, and even in the dead of night, with the moon and his hoverer's headlights as the only glow that lit the world, he kept on full speed into the darkness.

The dawn of the morning sun peeked from the horizon. He must've traveled for hours. Clouds still darkened the sky overhead. Koe brought the hoverer to a stop at the side of the road and climbed out on weary legs. Before him, the sun's rays touched a flower pushing its head out from the snow. The black petals overlapped each other beautifully in stunning symmetry. The white stem almost blended in with the muddy snow next to it.

But it wasn't just one flower — no, almost like they were summoned, all the flowers poked their heads out, blooming instantly like they'd been waiting for someone to come. The flowers turned the field into a meadow, and that's when the crown Koe hadn't realized he was still holding shook so violently he almost dropped it.

The whispers, while still hisses, grew louder.

Koe removed his hat and let it fall to the wayside as he placed the crown on his head. A shadow drifted like smoke from the crown, shifting into a vaporous human figure, constantly reforming itself as the vapors dissipated into the air.

"My champion," said the Shadows in a voice like thunder. The earth shook. "At long last, we meet."

"I thought it was time we spoke," said Koe.

The Shadows hovered around Koe, leaning in close. "Yes, you've had my eye for a long time, Koe. You are my new Seer. My savior."

"Savior?"

"The Light... was my love. We were destined to be together, but the Light did not see it that way. They could not love what they saw to be evil, and I cannot help my nature," said the Shadows without a trace of remorse.

"After so many years of fighting, we were both weak. The Light's followers defeated mine in a final battle, so with the remaining survivors, what could I do but curse the land? Even my love, the Light, could not break it. So they created a cure and a prophecy, putting their foolish faith in a single human to break the curse, knowing that only one whose heart was full of light—and willing to sacrifice it all—could break it."

The Shadows' hand touched the top of a flower petal as it fluttered by. The smoky fingertip turned to light, sizzling like a burn. It drew back, the Shadow holding the hand closer as if stung.

"The Light chose Sera. She did find the cure," said Koe, grabbing one of the flowers and ripping it from its stem. He held it up to the few rays of sunlight that broke through the gloomy clouds.

"Not exactly," said the Shadows, chuckling and standing tall. "The Light chose someone, but it did not choose Sera."

Now it was Koe's turn to chuckle. "The inscription on her back. You deny that was the Light's prophecy?" he asked.

"No, it was. You see, I never knew what the prophecy said. I never knew what or where the cure was. Until you."

But why? Koe wondered if this was the reason the Shadows had protected him, healed his broken spine, but he wouldn't give the satisfaction of asking.

"Yes, the boy, pure of heart, full of light. The Light chose the boy who held no power, no desire but love. When the boy sacrificed himself for his friend, the shapeshifter — another being of the Light — the inscription appeared on his back. But no one bothered to save the boy. The guard's eyes were weak and he saw nothing, and the lashes covered the boy's back and the prophecy from any hopeful eyes for all these years." The Shadows drifted around Koe, touching his back.

Koe slipped his jacket off and removed his shirt. The shadows that covered his body were all too familiar, the tingling on his back ran down every square inch. He looked over his shoulder, and now that he was holding the flower, the cure in his hand, he could see the light pierce through the shadow, trying to break free. But it was clear, the lines where he'd been whipped glowed from beneath.

He always thought it was just his lashes every time he felt his back sting, but it was really the Light calling out to him.

"The Light…" began Koe.

"Yes, the Light did not choose Sera," said the Shadows, chuckling once more. "I did." The Shadows grew a little taller and bigger, looming over Koe.

"Once the shadows covered the boy, I saw the Light's prophecy, but the Light made it a riddle, a task for the Chosen One to prove themselves. I still could not see the cure, and I could not take the chance that the Light would find another way." The Shadows were more animated now, clearly thrilled to finally reveal themselves to Koe.

"So I placed the prophecy in an ancient book with hints of magic that would draw in whoever found it and give them the inscription on their back. But I did not want just anyone — I wanted someone in power. An agent of the Light, willing to do anything. Sera was perfect. Over those fifteen years as Queen, her desperation grew and her mind weakened. The book called to her, just like the whispers you hear from the crown you wear or the daggers you summon to your hand. After much persistence, it finally broke through her defenses, and she became the Chosen One to the people."

"You gave her the visions?" said Koe.

"No, that was the Light's blessings. But you see, the Light is selfish. They want all their agents to serve them for the greater good, above all else, even the ones they love. Once you were lost, the Light turned to Sera, hoping she could take your place. Sera was willing to sacrifice herself just like the Light wanted, but she also was willing to sacrifice everyone else, and as the Queen, she had the power to do it."

"You took a big risk, giving her the prophecy," said Koe. "The world only has a few more years before the curse kills everyone. Why not just wait?"

The Shadows formed a huge throne from the mist behind them, sitting down and resting their arms on the armrests. "As long as people have hope, the Light lives. And as long as the Light lives, while weak, they are still plotting against me. They would find a way. I had to make sure the cure would be destroyed."

"You could've just killed me, and the Chosen One would be dead," said Koe.

"Yes, I could have. But I saw my pain in you, Koe. The Light chose you because you would sacrifice yourself to save the world. I would not sacrifice you like the Light did."

Koe touched the flower petal with his finger, the shadow that covered his skin burning away and the tip of his finger, skin and nail showing for the first time since he was a boy. The shadow hissed like it had before, and a burning sensation ran up and down his arm, but Koe didn't flinch.

"Sera tossed you aside because to her, you weren't important. Aiva saw you as a monster. Everyone else in your life, even your fellow Knightmares, hated you," said the Shadows. "But I have always cared about you." Koe dropped the flower onto the ground. His boot crushed the petals.

"Good," said the Shadows. "Together, we will rid this world of the cure, and after, everyone still alive will turn to the shadows to save themselves from the poisoned air. You will be my will. You will lead my followers, and once and for all, we will extinguish the Light forever."

Koe threw his shirt and coat back on, grabbing his hat to dust the dirt off the brim. "The Light is naïve to put their faith in humans. Now they tear themselves apart because that's what we are at our core—rotten and selfish," said Koe, pausing.

"Exactly," said the Shadows, beyond gleeful.

"But you're just like the Light," said Koe.

The Shadows leaned forward, and while there was no expression to be seen, Koe knew the Shadows had been caught off guard.

"You've used me. As long as people follow you, you don't care about their names or what their faces look like. You want everyone to sacrifice who they are to serve you. Just like the Light does."

"You do not know what you're—"

Koe held his hand up to stop the Shadows as they pushed themselves off their chair. The throne disappeared into the mist.

"You'll get your wish; the cure will be destroyed and afterwards, I'll take this crown and bury it, never to be found. I will watch as humanity kills itself and the survivors choke on their last breaths. Once it's my time, the Light will die and you'll be left all alone on this void of a planet, with no one to serve you, no one to talk to, so you can wander eternity all alone."

The Shadows charged, but Koe took off the crown and the

Shadows disappeared. Only their whispers of hate and fury lingered in the air.

Koe fitted his hat to his head again and returned to his hoverer. He opened the fuel tank lid and powered up the bike. He swerved the hoverer around the field, letting the fuel pour out of the tank and rain down on the flowers. Once he'd completed a thorough sweep of the field, he drew his gun and aimed.

The wind blew the flowers toward him, and the sunlight broke through the clouds, shining down upon him brighter than ever. It didn't matter that the Light was trying to call to him. This all had to end.

A single gunshot erupted a flame that spread across the whole meadow. He pushed his hoverer into the flames. The resulting explosion sent a cloud of black smoke billowing into the air.

The flowers cried out as they withered and burned. Koe watched the flames dance and tear into the meadow, the flower petals disintegrating, the stems blackening.

Koe turned his back to the flames, walking away from the world as it burned behind him.

Nikai is the author of *To Kill the Chosen One*. He also wrote *Spirits of Sarana*. He grew up in Seattle, Washington, where he began creating and writing his own stories from an early age. Inspired by various Chosen One characters throughout fiction, he started writing *To Kill the Chosen One* as a twist on the genre and an excuse to tell a darker tale. He currently lives in Los Angeles, California working in entertainment and learning how to dance.

For more information, please visit Nikai at:

Wordsofafeatherpress.com

And follow on Instagram @ Nikaij

Made in the USA
Middletown, DE
22 August 2024

59606983R00213